The Devil's Due

Steven F. Freeman

This is a work of fiction. Names, characters, places, and incidents are products of the author's imagination or are used fictitiously and are not to be construed as real. Any resemblance to actual events, locales, organizations, or persons, living or dead, is entirely coincidental.

Cover design by www.LLPix.com

Copyright © 2015 Steven F. Freeman

All rights reserved.

ISBN: 1505666414
ISBN-13: 978-1505666410

DEDICATION

To the members of my critique group, whose feedback has inestimably improved this work.

ACKNOWLEDGMENTS

Many thanks to Ruth Gresh, Cheryl Snapperman, Myron Kaufman, Lynn Hesse, Chris Daniel, Priscilla Gould, Sarah Redmond, Elaine Rivers, Sarah Neau, Willow Humphrey, Sharron Grodzinsky, and Kathy Golden for their invaluable feedback and assistance.

CHAPTER 1

As Divband led his followers into the chamber, the girl inside the room looked up, her obsidian eyes wide with fright. Her arms encircled a column engraved with bas-reliefs of mythic creatures and fierce warriors. A thick knot of ropes around her wrists on the opposite side of the column kept her bound to the spot. The flicker of candles conferred a ghoulish appearance to the images carved on each of the circular chamber's twenty-one columns.

"Hello, my dear," said Divband. "What is your name?"

"Giti," replied the girl in a trembling voice as she turned her head to look at him.

"I apologize for your restraints."

"What have I done?" wailed the prisoner, who looked to be about fifteen. "Why am I being punished?"

"You are not being punished. You are being honored. Only you—a person pure in spirit and body—can fulfill the essential role in our ceremony."

"What role? What do you want with me?"

Divband approached Giti. Her flawless complexion shone through a face distorted with terror. Divband couldn't blame her. He saw how Ghoyee, his right-hand man, eyed her. A man of Ghoyee's physical enormity and lustful glances would strike fear into the heart of any living creature. But Divband had no intention of letting Ghoyee have his way with Giti. She was destined for a more important role.

"The ancient charms can be invoked only through one who has not been defiled by the world," said Divband. "You will serve as the conduit through which we call forth the black *jinnd* to aid our cause—and theirs."

"How?" asked the girl. "I know nothing of the ancient spirits or their ways."

"You role is simplicity itself. You must allow us to proceed with the sacred anointments."

"What kind of anointments?" She screwed her face into a mask of skepticism.

"Just ink. I use it to draw a pattern on your body."

The teen remained silent for a moment. "And if I refuse?"

Divband sighed. "Then I would be forced to administer medicines that will ensure your compliance. But the black *jinnd* respond most readily to a mind that is unaltered, so I would really rather not resort to those measures. Be a good girl, and don't resist."

Giti's eyes darted from face to face but seemed to find no answer in the serious expressions she found there. Really, what choice did she have? She lowered her head in apparent acquiescence.

Divband motioned to Ghoyee and Meskin, another follower. The two unbound the girl's wrists and led her to an ancient, rectangular altar standing in the center of the chamber.

"Lie down," said Ghoyee, gesturing to the thick, stone slab.

Giti complied, her hands shaking as she moved her body onto the flat surface.

"Bind her hands and feet," said Divband.

"But I am not struggling!" she said, fear spreading anew in her eyes. "Why must my limbs be bound?"

"After the anointing is complete, we must leave you in here for some time—long enough for the black *jinnd* to sense your presence and respond. During this interval, we wouldn't want you to have second thoughts and leave."

"I won't go," said the girl. "I promise. You can't—"

"Bind her mouth, too," cut in Divband. "The sanctity of Iblis' temple must not be defiled with such noise."

Ghoyee grinned. He drew a band of black cloth from a satchel at his side, wrapped it twice through the teen's mouth, and cinched it with a knot, rendering her mute. Then he and Meskin fastened new strips of cloth around her wrists and ankles and secured them to ancient stone rings affixed to the floor underneath the altar. The girl seemed too stunned to offer much resistance.

Divband stepped forward. He peeled back Giti's shirt to expose a perfect abdomen. Reciting an ancient creed, he picked up a silver bowl from an adjacent table. After dipping a wooden brush into the bowl's dark contents and wiping away excess fluid, he began to apply strokes to the girl's stomach. He replenished the supply of ink several times before completing a dark circle. Inside the circle, he painted a series of intersecting lines, eventually forming a pentagram, the points of which ended on the arc of the circle. Only upon finishing the anointing did he discontinue his chant.

"Light the incense," said Divband.

Four more followers set small, richly-patterned urns on the four corners of the table, then lit the sticky gum within the bowls. Tendrils of smoke began to rise, and a sweet, sickly smell permeated the room.

Divband turned to the group of roughly forty believers. "Now, my friends, we must pray to the black *jinnd* to look favorably upon our request," he said, glancing at the bound figure on the table. "The ways of the black *jinnd* are beyond man's understanding."

"Powerful are the black *jinnd*," came a uniform response from the assembled crowd.

In observance of the ritual's requirements, the group began a low chant as they filed out. Before exiting the stone arch that served as the room's primary entrance, Divband looked back over his shoulder.

The girl's eyes, wide with fear, seemed to beg for mercy. If only she knew what the coming hours would bring.

CHAPTER 2

In the dusty haze of Kabul, a young Afghani exited her dwelling and glided down the street. She hoped Uncle Dani had not heard her leave. This might be her only chance to send a message.

"Mastana!" boomed a voice from behind her. "Where are you going?"

"To the market, Uncle," she replied. "I would like to prepare Qabili Palao for dinner, but we do not have all the ingredients."

"Don't worry about that now," said Uncle Dani. "Besides, what do you think you're doing, going out by yourself? You know I have to escort you."

Although Afghanistan had officially relaxed its enforcement of sharia—Islamic law—over the last decade or so, Uncle Dani adhered to the strict interpretation that prohibited single females from venturing outside without a male relative acting as escort. Uncle Dani adhered to other, more extreme notions of Islam as well.

"Can you take me to the market, Uncle?"

"No. You need to take care of your mother. Her pain grows worse."

Last month, the oncologist responsible for treating Mother's pancreatic cancer had made a somber announcement: the disease had metastasized throughout her body. Mother was expected to live only a few more weeks, perhaps as long as a month.

"Yes, Uncle." Hanging her head, Mastana returned to the house. She traversed the hall and entered her mother's bedroom.

"Mastana, is that you?" came a weak voice.

"Yes, Mother," replied Mastana as she reached her mother's bedside. "How are you feeling?"

"Ah—the pain! Where are my pills? Bring them to me, my dear."

"Yes, Mother."

Mastana removed two large orange pills and a tiny white one from a pair of bottles on the nightstand. She passed them to Mother, who swallowed them with a splash of water and a look of agony. The pain in Mother's abdomen seemed to grow worse every day.

The painkillers and anti-nausea tablets rendered Mother more comfortable but held out no hope of curing her. Mastana hated the pills. They took Mother off to another place, a pain-free world to which Mastana couldn't follow. The teen knew she was being selfish. She couldn't deprive Mother of medicine just to have a conversation with her. Besides, such an approach wouldn't work. The old Mother—the one with the lively mind, who would stay up talking on all manner of subjects until three in the morning—existed no more. The mind of the mother before her now drifted in and out of focus as it battled pain and the stupefying effects of powerful narcotics. Each day, the flame of Mother's intellect dimmed, like a candle deprived of oxygen.

Soon, Mastana would be alone with Uncle Dani. The thought made her shudder. For years, Mother had shielded Mastana from her Al-Qaeda uncle. With Mother gone, Uncle Dani would waste no time recruiting Mastana into his nefarious plans. He had already hinted as much during the last week.

Mastana knew the Americans weren't perfect, but as a group, she liked them. Her family had sold clothing to them for years. And the Americans at Camp Eggers had nursed her back to health after she had been injured by a marketplace bomb outside their gates. She had no intention of helping her uncle plot against them.

Desperate for help, Mastana longed to send a message to the American she most trusted—the injured soldier who had personally pulled her from the bazaar's flaming wreckage the day of the bombing and carried her to safety. She and the soldier had become friends while she recovered in the camp hospital. She didn't know exactly how he could help but felt sure he would think of something.

But first, she had to find a way to send a message to

him. She had hoped to visit the internet café next to the marketplace, but Uncle had foiled that plan. If he prohibited her from traveling alone, how would she ever send for help?

After watching Mother drift into a fitful slumber, Mastana returned to her own bedroom to hide the tumult of emotions battling inside her chest. Tears of frustration soon gave way to raw fear. She had to find a way to contact her soldier friend before her life was forfeited in Uncle's unrelenting jihad against the Americans, but how?

CHAPTER 3

Alton Blackwell knotted his tie and turned to Mallory Wilson. "You about ready?"

"Yeah, just give me a minute to finish my makeup."

After more than two years of friendship followed by sixteen months of dating, the two had become engaged five months ago. Tomorrow, they would tie a knot of a different sort with an early-spring wedding.

Mallory dabbed at her left eye, then turned around to face Alton. "How do I look?"

He shook his head and smiled. "Honestly, I don't think you realize how ridiculously beautiful you are."

She returned the smile. "I'm glad you think so, Sweetie, but I meant am I ready for the rehearsal dinner? Everything look okay?"

Alton studied his fiancée. Mallory's sable locks flowed

in delicate cascades down her shoulders. The olive hue of her skin complemented the pale yellow dress hugging her petite, athletic frame. "You look amazing, as always."

"So do you, Sweetie. Your stylist did an especially good job on your haircut," she replied, hooking her arm through his.

Alton ran his free hand through his closely-cropped, chestnut hair. He kept himself in good shape with a consistent regimen of swimming and strength training. But between his height, which ran only slightly above average, and his disabled leg, an injury he had sustained while serving as an Army communications captain in Afghanistan, he still marveled that he had scored such a prize as his fiancée.

"Okay, let's do this," he said.

The couple emerged from the dressing room and walked down an empty hallway replete with richly-framed oil paintings and a thick, Persian carpet. The entire building had been reserved courtesy of Mallory's mother, who had maintained her membership in the elite club after retiring several years earlier.

The couple pushed open the thick, oak doors of the country club's banquet room to reveal a picture of Old South money. Plush, velvet drapes with gold ties covered enormous windows, and years of cigar smoke had deepened the hue of the Brazilian cherry floors. A mahogany bar adorned with gold leaf spanned most of the room's rear wall, while a set of four sparkling chandeliers running the length of the rectangular room completed the scene.

Alton nudged Mallory and pointed to the back wall, where David Dunlow gestured in an animated fashion to a bar employee while Fahima, his wife, looked on.

When Alton and Mallory had served in the Army in Afghanistan, David had been their closest comrade. He had married the lovely Fahima, a barmaid at Gandamak's Lodge, the Kabul restaurant in which the three soldiers had often met during their off-shift hours. A year ago, Fahima had immigrated to the US to marry David, and the four of them remained close friends.

Alton and Mallory joined their best man and maid of honor along the wall.

"Congratulations, Mallory…Al," said David. Early in their friendship, David had unilaterally assigned Alton the nickname of "Al," and despite lodging many protests over the years, Alton had never persuaded David to drop the moniker.

"Thanks, I think," said Alton. "You're not inflicting your humor on this poor guy, are you?"

"Hey, he loves my jokes."

"Or he's hoping for a tip," whispered Mallory in Alton's ear.

"If he's been listening to David's jokes for long, he's earned one," whispered Alton in return. Turning to the others, Alton raised his voice. "It looks like everyone's here. I guess we should take our seats so we can get this show started."

As Alton approached the guests-of-honor table, he

saw Kayla and Ruth, his younger sisters, seated next to Gail, his mother. Beverly Wilson, Mallory's mother, occupied a seat on the other side of the two empty chairs reserved for Alton and Mallory themselves. Scott, Mallory's older brother, sat beside his mother.

The couple took their appointed seats, and Alton cast his gaze around the banquet hall. One of the room's other tables was occupied by colleagues from Mallory's FBI white-collar crime division. Another was filled by Alton's closest friends from the Washington branch of Kruptos, arguably the world's most advanced data encryption and security firm. As manager of the branch, Alton had supposed few colleagues, if any, would be willing to make the long trip to his Charlotte, North Carolina wedding, so he had been pleasantly surprised that eight had decided to make the journey.

The evening proceeded as rehearsal dinners usually do, with copious tears shed throughout the room and numerous toasts offered up to the happy couple. To Alton's ears, the speeches echoed many he had heard in the past, but they now took on an entirely new meaning. His friends had done a fine job crafting thoughtful remarks, yet—in a way—they still fell short. How could any turn of phrase ever articulate the magnitude of the joy he would experience the next day? The words sufficient to impart such powerful emotions had yet to be created.

As the evening wound down and the guests trailed out, Alton found himself alone with Mallory at their table. He loosened his tie and rested his hand atop hers.

Mallory studied him for a moment. "You look thoughtful, Honey. What's on your mind?"

"I'm almost afraid to tell you."

"Why?"

"Honestly? 'Cause I don't want to lower your opinion of me."

"Nothing you say can do that," said Mallory.

"I hope you're right."

"So what's this big secret?"

Alton stretched out his damaged leg in front of him, easing the dull throb that had grown progressively worse during the long evening. "Do you remember the day I first met Scott, when he came to visit you in the hospital after the Rabinil case?"

"Of course. How could either of us forget that day? It was the first time we found out we had secretly loved each other for months."

"Well, *before* we made that discovery, and I first saw you and Scott together, I hated him."

Mallory wore a shocked expression.

"But then," continued Alton, "when I learned he's your brother, well…I thought he might be a decent sort of guy after all."

Mallory punched his arm and laughed. "So Alton Blackwell was jealous."

"Yeah, I was. From your point of view, he seemed like the perfect guy: someone you'd clearly known for a long time, tall, muscular…and not disabled."

Mallory shook her head and put her free hand on his. "Well, now you know better. *You're* the perfect guy for me."

And for the first time, Alton did know it—completely, with all of his heart and intellect. The knowledge conferred a peace of mind he had never experienced, especially as he considered the better chapter of his life opening before him the next day.

"And you're the perfect girl—for me or anyone. I'm just the guy that won the lottery and gets to marry you."

CHAPTER 4

After two hours, Divband and his followers made their way back to the chamber where Giti remained bound to the stone altar. As he approached the chamber door, Divband could see the girl struggling against her restraints. She quieted as they entered the room.

The group assembled in a broad circle around the altar. Standing behind the girl's head, Divband placed his hands on her shoulders and closed his eyes. After intoning an incantation for half a minute, he opened his eyes. "The ancient spirits are here. They accept the offering we make to the great Iblis and the other black *jinnd* and have agreed to enter into the usual covenant."

Giti struggled to turn her head to look at Divband, but the gag and arm restraints limited her range of motion.

"And now," said Divband, "let us affirm the covenant as we have been taught."

The assemblage began to chant, beginning with a low murmur that steadily grew in volume.

As his followers repeated the ancient verse, Divband withdrew from the folds of his robe a necklace from which dangled a silver pentagram in a circle. The charm's design mirrored the one he had created in ink on Giti's torso.

Divband placed the talisman on Giti's abdomen. "Iblis and the rest of the black *jinnd*, hear our prayer. We consign this young one to your fold as a new wife of Iblis, and we entreat you to provide the power to defeat our enemies. Give us the might to deliver the full wrath of your anger to those who deny your supremacy, to those who try to take the land as their own."

Divband reached over to a small table on which rested a black cloth and an Athame, a double-edged blade with a black handle. After placing the cloth over Giti's face, he lifted the ceremonial knife from the table and held it above his head. "Let the ancient ritual be fulfilled."

He removed the charm from Giti's abdomen, leaving undisturbed the symbol displayed in ink. "Blood for power," he chanted.

"Power for blood," replied the throng in unison.

The girl's muffled screams echoed through the chamber as Divband plunged the knife into a portion of the circle's arc on her torso. He began carving the outline of the circle with the knife's blade still buried in her body. Within seconds, the girl fell silent. Divband continued until he had finished carving the entire arc of the grisly circle.

With a wave of Divband's hand, the chanting stopped, reducing the room to silence. The slow drip of blood from the table onto the stone floor produced the only discernable noise. Crimson droplets filled in cracks between crowded bas-reliefs covering the floor in a circle about the altar. As the blood continued to flow, the winged creatures and scowling faces depicted in the carvings appeared themselves to have suffered fatal injuries.

Divband turned to Ghoyee.

"Transport the knife. Wash it in the waters of the Cophes, that Iblis' power may be released into our land," he said, using the ancient name of the body of water now known by most as simply the Kabul River.

Turning to the other followers, he continued. "Move the body and incense into the Sanctuary of Death. They must remain undisturbed for the requisite eleven hours. You know what to do after that."

The followers nodded and began their grim task in silence. Loosening the cloth restraints from Giti's still form, four of the zealots carried her lifeless body from the room, while four more carried the incense urns.

Divband watched the procession. Once the chamber emptied, he retreated to a windowless room on the opposite end of the central building. He had converted the small antechamber into a makeshift office.

After washing his hands in a silver basin and drying them with a threadbare towel, he dropped into a black wicker chair and steepled his fingers in front of his face, lost in thought.

Noticing a lingering drop of blood on the side of his hand, Divband smeared the residue onto the towel and smiled. The ceremony had gone off without a hitch, but today's sacrifice, as well as the preceding seven, were just the beginning. He had bigger plans, secrets known only to his most trusted follower. His group of zealots might be small now, but it was growing, and the uninterrupted string of successes he had enjoyed thus far filled him with optimism for the future. With enough supporters, no one would be able to stop the newly-resurgent Brotherhood of Stones.

CHAPTER 5

On a bright Saturday in late March, Alton Blackwell married Mallory Wilson.

The ceremony was performed at Fellowship United Church, one of Charlotte's oldest and most celebrated structures. White hydrangeas and splashes of ribbon adorned the ends of the pews, while white orchids, greenery, and candles framed the wedding party at the front of the church.

Standing with Mallory at the altar, Alton gazed upon his bride with the joy and disbelief many feel on such an occasion. Mallory's dazzling smile conveyed a similar state of mind.

The couple had decided to write a portion of their vows, supplementing biblical enjoinders to pure, fervent love with their own promises of support and fidelity.

Mallory gazed into Alton's eyes. "Those who know me understand how unbelievably happy I am. I have loved you almost since we met, although you didn't know that for a while." Several attendees chuckled, but a welling of tears threatened to render Mallory incapable of further speech. "With other men, I always wondered how long they would stay. With you, I don't have to wonder about that. I know you are committed to me and our relationship. I pledge my love to you, my husband, the father of our future children, the love of my life."

Alton admired Mallory's capacity to recite the speech unaided. On such an important occasion, he hadn't trusted himself to remember everything he wanted to say. Mallory smiled as Alton withdrew a slip of paper from his pocket, straightened it in his hand, and cleared his throat. "Mallory befriended me at a time when I wasn't a friend to myself. Those bonds of friendship have grown under the tender care of our heavenly Maker into something infinitely superior, a relationship without description or equal. Beyond hope, beyond despair, beyond reason, beyond madness, beyond trust, beyond fear, beyond death, beyond the transitory emotions of a day or a week or a lifetime, the unchanging flame of my love will burn steady and strong, a beacon illuminating the truth and fidelity of my undying love for you—always."

The pastor declared them man and wife, eliciting cheers from the congregation. After exchanging their first married kiss, Mallory leaned over and whispered to her husband. "I love you…so much."

Mallory shielded her face as tears tracked down her cheeks. By this time, the conclusion of the thirty-minute ceremony, the family and friends in attendance had likewise met their quota of joyful tears.

After posing for a round of photographs both inside and outside the church, the wedding party traveled to the reception at Carolina Manor, Beverly's Wilson's exclusive country club.

Alton and Mallory were hailed by a chorus of greetings as they entered the banquet hall, which retained all the finery of the previous evening but was now festooned with a dazzling array of floral arrangements and formal dinner tables surrounding a champagne fountain.

"Okay, you two," said Cherie, their wedding planner. "Let's get the reception line going. Why don't you stand over there near the gift table?"

The couple moved to the indicated spot.

"Ladies and gentlemen," announced Cherie to the assemblage, "I present Mr. and Mrs. Alton Blackwell!"

Her announcement produced the expected cheer.

As friends and family members queued up, Alton leaned over to Mallory. "Did I tell you how fantastic you look in that dress?"

"Only three times."

"Sorry. I guess I was distracted…by you in that dress."

"Not any more distracted than I was seeing you wearing that tux. Now that I know how good you look in it, I'll have to find more occasions for you to wear one."

The Devil's Due

The festivities lingered into the evening. By eight o'clock, however, only family members remained, seated around the principal table.

"Are you ever going to open your presents?" asked Ruth, Alton's youngest sister.

"Yeah, I guess we should," replied Alton. "Otherwise, we'll be here all night."

"Why don't I keep track of who gave what gift?" said Beverly Wilson. "That is, if Gail is agreeable."

"Of course," said Gail, who hadn't stopped smiling all day except to cry. "I'll handle the distribution honors."

The company settled into the task, and before long the gift table sat empty. After exchanging heartfelt words of tenderness with their family members, Alton and Mallory drove to Charlotte's impeccable Ritz-Carlton Hotel for the first night of their honeymoon.

As they entered the luxurious Uptown Suite, Alton took Mallory's hand. He led her to the window and drew aside the curtains, revealing the city's twinkling skyline. "It's not quite as nice as the view from Imàgo," he said, referring to the Roman restaurant in which he had proposed to Mallory last autumn, "but it'll do."

"Maybe not, but it's pretty in its own way," replied Mallory. "Anyway, I'm not here for the view. I'm more interested in the company."

Alton gazed into his bride's eyes, his heart overflowing in ways language could never capture. "I've been trying to figure out ways to tell you how much today means to me, but words are so deficient to the task."

"You did a pretty good job at the wedding, Sweetie. Good thing I wore waterproof mascara. But I know what you mean. I struggle myself. I love you so much, but I don't know how to tell you."

Alton paused to gather his thoughts. "When I was wounded in Afghanistan, I couldn't have imagined my life would take the road leading up to this moment. Even in my wildest, most optimistic moments, I never dreamed of finding anyone like you. I feel so blessed just to know you, but now to have you as my wife…" He stopped, not trusting his trembling voice to continue.

Mallory brushed his cheek, then her own. "Most girls dream about finding a knight in shining armor, but how many really do? You were a hero in Afghanistan the day I met you, and you're still my hero—my knight."

Alton recalled the day he met Mallory. They had both pulled wounded civilians from flaming wreckage following the detonation of an insurgent bomb in a bazaar across the main gate from Camp Eggers, the military compound in which they had worked. "That was quite a day for both of us, wasn't it? You know it wasn't too long after that day that my feelings for you deepened.

"And once I began loving you," continued Alton, "I knew I'd never be the same man again—whether you loved me or not, whether you married me or not. I knew some essence of you had mixed into my soul and become part of me, changing me for the better. And until I close my eyes to this earth for the last time, that will always be true."

The Devil's Due

"I know," said Mallory. "That's why you're my knight. And why I'll be yours—forever."

CHAPTER 6

The sun dipped behind a pair of buildings standing across the narrow street. Long shadows darkened the bedroom, causing Mastana to snap out of her reverie and look up.

Mother had finally drifted into a restless sleep. She required ever-increasing doses of narcotics to overcome the pain brought on by the cancer's relentless advance. Mastana knew her mother couldn't hold on much longer.

Uncle Dani had spent much of the day on the phone. Mastana hadn't been able to make out all of his words, but the ones she had understood, as well as Uncle's impassioned tone, had told her enough. He was planning another attack against the Americans. The thought sent a shudder of repulsion through her frame.

Mother's breathing eventually slowed, indicating a deeper slumber. Mastana made her way out of the room and tiptoed to her own bedroom down the hall. To avoid making any noise that might alert Uncle Dani, she held the doorknob twisted until it was fully in place in the doorframe, then slowly released it. She crept into bed fully clothed and pulled the thin, woven blanket up to her chin.

Mastana hadn't heard Uncle Dani's voice for a while. She hoped he had left the house. Although he occasionally stared at her maturing body with a lascivious expression, it was not his advances she feared. Uncle might entertain lustful thoughts, but his true passion lay in the jihad.

"Mastana!" called Uncle from the front of the house. Mastana didn't answer. She could always pretend to be asleep if he found her.

Footsteps in the hallway grew loud and faded again as Uncle passed Mastana's room and entered Mother's. A moment later, a loud click from a distant doorknob and nearing footsteps heralded Uncle's approach. Mastana closed her eyes and prayed Uncle would continue past her room. Perhaps he had only wanted to tell her something that could wait until morning.

She heard the door to her room swing open, and footsteps approached her bed.

"Niece. Are you asleep?"

Mastana made a show of issuing a small yawn and squinting as she opened her eyes. "I am awake now, Uncle." She swung her feet around and raised herself to a sitting position on the side of the bed.

Uncle Dani raised an eyebrow at her clothes. "How is your mother?"

"She was in much pain earlier. I had to give her an extra pill to help her sleep."

"She will not awaken for a while, then," he said. "That is good. I need to talk to you about a great mission, and I do not want you to be distracted by your mother."

Mastana said nothing, but her heart accelerated. She prayed Uncle's conversation would flow in an unexpected direction.

"Saturday is the day the soldiers in the American military base allow our citizens inside their courtyard to sell goods. As you know, they only allow approved vendors inside, and even then they often search the goods and people for weapons. You and your mother have been selling clothing to them for a long time. They recognize you now, right?"

Mastana could scarcely form a response. "Yes, Uncle."

"And do they often search you for weapons?"

Mastana shook her head.

"Excellent. They trust you. You are young, female, and well-known. You were even a patient at their hospital for several weeks after the bazaar bombing outside its gates a few years ago. They think you are their good friend. You are the last person they will suspect of delivering Allah's jihad."

"Jihad, Uncle?"

"Yes, my niece. They might decide to search the

goods you are selling, but they will not search your body. My leaders have developed a smaller vest for you to wear. It will fit under your clothes and will not draw suspicion."

"Am I to wear this vest on Saturday, Uncle?"

"Yes, Mastana. This is a great honor. You will be assured of meeting Allah in the next life."

The teen nodded and cast her gaze to the floor, afraid her eyes would betray the terror and abhorrence that must surely be flowing from them.

Uncle Dani took a step closer to her bed, bringing himself to within a foot of her trembling frame. "We will talk more of this tomorrow. I must ensure you understand all instructions, especially how to detonate the bomb."

"Yes, Uncle," whispered Mastana.

Uncle Dani left the room, and Mastana lay in bed, far too agitated to sleep. Several hours later, she heard her mother begin to moan. She scurried to Mother's room and helped her swallow more of the small, white pills.

After thirty minutes or so, Mother's moans subsided, and she drifted back to sleep.

Mastana grasped her mother's hand as silent tears fell onto the coarse blanket. "Oh, Mother, if only you could awake and advise me! I don't want to leave you in your final days, but I am so afraid of Uncle Dani. What would you have me do?"

CHAPTER 7

As rays of morning sunlight pierced through cracks between the hotel room's plush curtains, Alton rolled over and faced his bride. "Good morning, Mrs. Blackwell."

Mallory broke into a huge grin. "Morning, Sweetie."

Alton kissed his beloved, letting the contact linger. "Okay, I know intellectually that I'm a married man, but it really hasn't sunk in yet."

"I know. Me, neither. You're not going to be mad if I forget and say Mallory *Wilson* a few times, are you?"

"No, of course not. As long as we're married, you can take all the time you need. Speaking of that, still no regrets changing your name?"

"No," replied Mallory. "It's funny. I always thought I'd keep Wilson if I ever got married. But once I met you...I don't know, it just felt right making the change."

"Hey, I'm cool with it either way, as long as we're married."

The couple dressed and descended to the hotel's restaurant for breakfast.

Alton stirred the coffee in his mug with a teaspoon and let a wave of contentment wash over him. "Well, yesterday was a big day, of course, but considering that we're leaving for our honeymoon in a few hours, I'd say today is, too."

"Tell me about it. I can't wait for the cruise. I've never been to Antigua before."

"Um…about that. There's been a small change in our itinerary."

Mallory fixed Alton in a penetrating stare. "Alton Blackwell, not again," she said, referring to the previous autumn's Italian vacation Alton had initially disguised as a trip to Myrtle Beach, South Carolina.

Alton couldn't suppress a grin. "It's not my fault this time. Your mom wanted to surprise us with a kick-ass honeymoon. She had to tell one of us, and I ended up being the one she drew into her confidence."

"So she could surprise me. That sounds like her. But wait—I thought the rehearsal dinner and the reception were Mom's wedding gifts. That's what she told us."

"That was part of the plan. Otherwise, you wouldn't be as surprised about the honeymoon trip."

"Well, it worked. I'm shocked. So, if we're not going to the Caribbean, where *are* we going?"

"How do you feel about Tahiti?"

"Sweetie, it's not nice to tease me. Where are we really going?"

"Bora Bora, Tahiti—seriously."

"No way. I've always wanted to go there!"

"I know. I remember all the Pinterest searches you ran on it last year."

Mallory studied Alton again. "Seriously? You're not tricking me again? We're really going to Tahiti?"

"I promise."

Mallory gave a whoop of elation. "Yes!"

After a moment, the restaurant's other patrons turned back to their meals.

"I don't suppose we have one of those huts over the water," said Mallory, "the ones with glass panels in the floor?"

"Of course. They were in half the Pinterest pictures you saved, so I knew that'd be your dream honeymoon."

"Okay, I'm officially in heaven. But wait, darn it…"

"What's wrong?" asked Alton.

"I told everyone at the reception yesterday we'll be cruising in the Caribbean. I even put it in our wedding announcement in the paper. No one besides Mom knows where we're really going."

"They'll find out soon enough," said Alton with a chuckle. "Now, our flight leaves in three hours, so we should probably wrap up breakfast pretty soon."

"So…is our whole married life going to be like this—me not knowing what's really going to happen until the last minute?"

"Only as far as pleasant surprises are concerned—unless you want me to stop."

"You have my permission to surprise me whenever you want, Mr. Blackwell."

CHAPTER 8

Divband motioned to Ghoyee. "Come into my chamber."

Once his subordinate entered, Divband glanced down the narrow, stone hallway to ensure their privacy, then pulled shut the full-length curtain that served as a makeshift door.

"How many recruits are attending tonight's gathering?"

"Eighty-two."

The leader rubbed his hands. "Excellent. To date, we've converted just over half the recruits into followers. If forty convert tonight, our ranks will exceed two hundred."

"With all due respect, Master, that still doesn't seem like many."

"Give it time, Ghoyee. We just started recruiting last month, and already our numbers have more than doubled. Plus, consider the nature of our membership. Yes, we've recruited some field laborers, but our followers also include politicians, doctors, attorneys, bureaucrats...those who stand to be disenfranchised by our country's political turmoil and the Taliban's resurgence."

"But do these professionals join us simply because they're unhappy or worried about losing their position in society? If so, perhaps they don't believe in the power of Iblis."

"Maybe some of them don't at first, but I think they all will eventually. Didn't you grow up hearing of the power of Iblis and the white and black *jinnd*?"

"Of course—everyone did."

"That's my point. We all know the old ways, the ancient rituals the Taliban and Al-Qaeda sought to suppress. Even the doctors and attorneys know of this. They may be skeptical at first, but they will understand the wisdom of our beliefs soon enough."

"But what if one of those doctors decides to tell the government about our...activities?"

"It's a necessary risk. They provide most of the funding for our organization, much more than the peasants can give. Plus, think of the advantage of having members of the Brotherhood of Stones inside the government and other professional ranks. If the government begins to plot against us, we will know from the moment it happens."

"And if a member decides to betray us?"

"Then he will be the next to join Iblis, maybe as a servant instead of a wife. I think in that case, he would be our last traitor."

A hint of malice showed through Ghoyee's smile.

"Go," said Divband. "Have our members prepare the satellite temple for tonight's gathering."

That evening, a crowd of recruits filed into a smaller temple located roughly twenty kilometers from the Brotherhood's central temple. There was no reason to give away the secret of their primary location to those who might not join their ranks. The satellite temple consisted of a large, circular chamber with two back rooms the size of walk-in closets. Cushions had been laid out around the perimeter of the room, and eventually most were filled by the recruits as well as a few current members of the Brotherhood. A circle of several dozen candles in the room's center cast ominous shadows in the enclosed space.

Divband surveyed the room. The attendees formed an eclectic group—farm laborers sat next to men wearing business suits, who in turn were joined by others in hospital scrubs and civil service uniforms. The cult leader knew he had a tough sell, but desperate people often turn to leaders who offer the right kind of promises.

Divband stepped into the center of the chamber. "My friends, thank you for attending tonight's gathering." He began to circle the room, pausing frequently to look each man in the eye. "Let me ask you…how many of you are happy with the current state of our country and our government?"

Only two or three hands raised in response.

"We have endured years under the Taliban and their Al-Qaeda cronies, followed by another decade under the rule of foreign occupiers. And what has all this brought our country? Nothing but chaos, despair, and ruin. Our government is riddled with corruption and incompetence. Our factories lie empty, yet there is not enough work for the people, so they turn to producing illegal drugs. Our police forces are understaffed, underequipped, and undertrained to protect us. And our courts are dictated by bribes rather than the rule of law.

"So what can we do? I'll tell you. We begin by undoing the damage wrought by those who have attempted to rule our country these last twenty years. My friends, I know that, like me, you long for the old ways… not the blasphemy taught by the Taliban and Al-Qaeda, but the whispering of ancient charms…and curses."

"Curses?" exclaimed an attendee to Divband's left. "My grandfather always told me to avoid the evil ways of the black *jinnd*."

"That is what my grandfather said, too," replied Divband. "'Beware the evil spirits.' But why do you think our forefathers tendered such a warning? Because there is great power in the black ways—a power feared by both our ancestors and the Taliban."

"But why not use the white *jinnd*, as our ancestors taught?" pressed the attendee, a young man wearing hospital scrubs.

"Did the white *jinnd* protect us from the Taliban and their perverse notions of Islam? No, they did not. Why do you think the Taliban prohibited our ancient charms? Like us, they fear the power of the black *jinnd*. Only Iblis and the black *jinnd* possess the power to expel the vile forces that continue to occupy our country."

Murmurs broke out throughout the room, and several attendees drew in their collective breaths. "You want us to align with Iblis, the evil one?" asked the hospital worker.

"I want us to cultivate a relationship with the only entity capable of ridding our country of the corroding influence of the Taliban and coalition invaders. Iblis possesses this power, and I intend to form a partnership with Iblis that will restore the old ways. Maybe you do not remember the old days, young man, but in those times, the sacred *ziarats* and local shrines were places of worship, not idols to be torn down by the Taliban. The use of charms and ancient healing was respected, not banned. Singing and dancing to sacred music was encouraged, not prohibited. And the poetry of our Sufi mystics was revered, not forbidden."

Many of the attendees nodded to these words, seemingly mesmerized.

Divband continued. "Like you, I have watched my family suffer under the Taliban and coalition forces. Who can look at the past two decades and see anything but a disaster? It's time to force a return to the old ways. Iblis and the black *jinnd* possess the power to make such a change."

"How can they help us?" asked a grizzled-faced, elderly man wrapped in a thin sweater.

"I'm glad you asked that, my friend. As we've all been taught since childhood, Iblis longs for brides to join him in the afterlife. In exchange for these brides, he provides special gifts: healing, insight, strength, wisdom, wealth, and countless more. How many of you would like to receive these gifts, and in doing so, rid our country of the yoke of oppression we have endured so long?"

While some of the attendees remained clearly skeptical, others grew more animated and broke into nods and smiles.

"To those who would join our fight, I invite you to sign your name to this record of Brotherhood. As a token of our mutual loyalty, I will present you with a sacred charm, a talisman possessed only by our members. If you do not join, I feel sorry for you—that you do not care enough about your family and your country to rise up. But unlike the Taliban, we will not punish you for refusing our offer. We desire only those who come of their own free will and accept the gifts Iblis and the black *jinnd* are ready to bestow."

Divband's concluding statement, drawing a stark contrast between his organization and the Taliban, seemed to generate even more enthusiasm. Roughly half the attendees queued up to sign their names, while the rest wandered out of the temple into the chilly evening.

Before stepping to the front of the line to greet his new followers, Divband leaned over to Ghoyee. "Follow the hospital worker and discover the location of his home. We may have to take extra measures to ensure his silence."

Divband stepped back to the front of the line and produced a radiant smile. "Welcome, son of Iblis. I present this talisman as a token of your initiation into the Brotherhood of Stones."

He handed across a necklace made of tightly-woven cord. On the end of the necklace lay an all-silver pendent depicting a pentagram inside a circle.

CHAPTER 9

The next afternoon, Mastana tucked the blanket around her mother's sleeping form and kissed her forehead. An extra dose of the small, white pills had been necessary to lull Mother back into a drugged slumber. Her parent no longer experienced periods of lucidity, instead alternating between sleep and incoherent pain. Mastana gazed upon the unconscious figure and wiped the tears that had tracked down her cheeks.

"Goodbye, my mother. I will see you again—in the life to come."

Kissing her parent one last time, Mastana left the room. She crept down the hallway and peeked into Uncle Dani's quarters. Just as she hoped, he lay asleep in his traditional mid-afternoon nap, enjoying a warm respite from the chilly afternoon.

Mastana tiptoed up the hallway and exited the dwelling, taking extra care to close the door in absolute silence. Uncle had forbidden Mastana to leave the house, but what of that? Saturday—five days hence—was market day at Camp Eggers, the day Uncle had commanded her to wear an explosive vest into the midst of the soldiers and initiate her own transition to the next life. At this point, her uncle's commands hardly mattered.

Dust swirled around Mastana's ankles as she strode down the street. She turned into a dimly-lit store with an "Internet Club" sign fastened at an awkward angle above the door.

"How much to use a computer?" she asked.

"Twenty-five Afghani for the first hour," replied the teller, who chewed a wad of gum as she fiddled with the dial on an antiquated radio.

Mastana slid a pair of banknotes through the narrow slot in the teller's cage.

"Number eighteen," said the worker, handing Mastana a piece of plastic in the shape of a credit card. "Insert this into the slot when you get there."

The teen made her way between two long tables on which rows of computers rested. Other customers occupied most of the spaces, and the monitors' artificial radiance lit their faces with an eerie glow.

Mastana reached her assigned seat and used her card to activate an internet connection. Upon seeing a "VoIP" icon on the computer screen, she breathed a sigh of relief. This was the functionality she had been counting on, the ability to place a telephone call via the computer.

After double-clicking the icon, she withdrew a scrap

of paper from the folds of her clothing and carefully entered a series of numbers. She pressed the "dial" button and held her breath.

"This is Alton Blackwell."

"Alton, it is me, Mastana! I need—"

"I'll be out of the office until April third," continued the recording. "If you need assistance before my return, please contact—"

Mastana clicked the "disconnect" button and fought back tears of despair. April third—nine days from now!

She couldn't return home. Uncle Dani must have already sensed her reluctance to execute his devious plan. Surely he wouldn't let her out of his sight before the hour of her mission arrived.

Mastana had considered wearing the vest into the American base but leaving it undetonated, instead telling the soldiers of her uncle's plan. But would they believe her? They may suspect her of complicity in the plot, only turning to them when she couldn't figure out how to set off the explosives. That path carried even greater risk.

Where could she go for help? Who should she call? She had no other family in all the country. Overcome with despair, Mastana rested her head in her hands and wept.

CHAPTER 10

Alton and Mallory's plane touched down in Bora Bora's Motu Mute Airport, a landing strip constructed on an island located in the middle of a pristine lagoon.

Upon disembarking from the plane, the couple stood on the tarmac and gawked at their surroundings. Alton swept his gaze from the lighter, aqua shades of the lagoon to the rich, blue waters of the Pacific Ocean. "For the second time in as many days, words are letting me down."

"Tell me about it," said Mallory, "This is…gorgeous."

"We should send a picture to your mom. After all, we wouldn't be here if not for her."

"That's a good idea. And if you talk to her, you can tell her I'm still in a state of shock."

"Ha! I think I'll just text her. If she and I get into an actual conversation, I might not escape until dinnertime."

"True."

Alton pulled his cellphone from his pocket and snapped a few pictures of the airport's tiny yet beautiful island location. He turned to Mallory. "I think I'll wait and e-mail the pic when we have Wi-Fi in the hotel. I'd like to send it to the guys at Kruptos, too."

"Can't you just text them?"

"Normally I would, but Redmond told me his cellphone was stolen the day before our wedding, so I don't know if he'd get it. I know with e-mail I'm good to go."

Mallory looked skeptical. "I hope this isn't a ploy to check your work e-mail while we're here."

"It's not. I promise. You think they expect a guy on his honeymoon to check e-mail? I don't think so."

The couple joined the rest of the airplane's passengers and crew on a ferry headed for the mainland. They boarded a shuttle sent by their resort, the Four Seasons Bora Bora, and within minutes found themselves inhabiting a slice of tropical paradise. Standing in the lobby of the reception building, the couple engaged in a new round of rapt examination while studying the stunning hotel and its grounds.

"Maybe you should send Mom a bunch of pictures," said Mallory. "She'll definitely want to see this."

"Thanks for reminding me," said Alton. "Let me send the photos from the airport now, before I forget. And I promise—I won't read any work messages."

A hotel employee offered a fruit tray while Alton connected to the hotel's Wi-Fi and sent several photos to Mallory's mother, thanking her for the extraordinary honeymoon trip. He then sent the same set of pictures to his work colleagues with a brief salutation.

Just before shutting down his e-mail app, an unusual message caught Alton's eye. He tapped the message and frowned as he read the brief sentence.

"Honey, they're going to take us to our bungalow in a golf cart," said Mallory. "Isn't that cool?"

"Really? Wow. I wonder how many other surprises are in store."

The couple arrived at their over-the-water bungalow, and the driver deposited their luggage in the room.

Reia, a hotel employee who had accompanied them, checked them into the resort using the desktop terminal in their bungalow. "Would you like a tour of the grounds?" she asked. "We can take you around in the golf cart again."

Mallory started to answer in the affirmative, but Alton cut in. "We'd love that, but can we ring for you to come back a little later? I'd like to settle into the room first."

"Of course, sir. Just let us know when you're ready."

As soon as Reia left, Mallory turned to Alton. "I know that expression. What's up?"

"When I sent the photos to your mom and my Kruptos friends, I saw an incoming message I definitely wasn't expecting."

"Alton…"

He held up an interposing palm. "It wasn't work. It arrived just a few hours ago. Take a look at this."

The message header indicated the sender was Mastana, the young Afghani Alton had befriended several years ago after rescuing her from a terrorist blast in a Kabul marketplace. The terseness of Mastana's message matched its desperation: "Alton, help me."

CHAPTER 11

Divband leaned his head into the cramped nook assigned to Ghoyee, his right-hand man. "Follow me."

Ghoyee obeyed, joining his master in the dimly-lit hallway. He cocked his head but left the question unspoken.

"I would like to inspect the security points," said Divband, who had recently ordered his followers to transform a circle of ancient, stack-stone guard huts into modern, fortified defensive positions. "We must verify their effectiveness against intruders."

"All of them? That will take a while."

"So be it. Ensuring the security and secrecy of our movement must continue to be a top priority. We can't afford to let our guard down."

The two strolled into the darkness, heading for the site's perimeter. Twelve guard huts surrounded a circular compound of ancient buildings, ranging from small, mud-brick shacks to the central building, a sprawling edifice of imposing granite walls, arched windows, and a huge ceremonial chamber. For illumination, the interior of all the buildings had been strung with hundreds of yards of florescent lights, a modern contrivance oddly out of place in the archeological site. Although the compound's desert location lay only an hour's drive from Kabul, ranges of mountains to both the north and south provided an effective measure of concealment.

"How many future brides of Iblis reside in the cells?" asked Divband, his hands clasped behind his back.

"After yesterday, we are down to four."

"In that case, it's time to collect another. Giving the girls a few days in the cells has made them more compliant when the time for their marriage ceremony arrives. It's good to take the fight out of them ahead of time."

Ghoyee grinned as he always did when contemplating this subject. "As you wish, Master. Shall Meskin accompany me?"

"Take as many as you need to get the job done. I wouldn't think you'd need more than one other person."

Ghoyee puffed out his chest. "No, me and Meskin are enough."

"How soon can you collect one?"

"I don't want to rush. Remember when we almost collected the prefect's daughter? I would like to pick the new bride from a different neighborhood, one we haven't harvested in before."

"Good idea. Pick out two possibilities from your new neighborhood, then bring a description of them to me before harvesting."

"I'll begin looking tomorrow. It shouldn't take more than a few days."

"Perfect."

After finishing the inspection of the first guard hut and recommending the repositioning of a mounted machine-gun tripod, they continued their trek.

Ghoyee turned to Divband. "Master, do you believe in the power of Iblis and the black *jinnd*?"

"What a question! I bring a message of hope to the hopeless…of power to the powerless. It is the idea of this message, not my personal beliefs, that carry our movement forward. And when people believe in Iblis and our cause, and act on those beliefs, Iblis' power will become a force in our land."

CHAPTER 12

After showing Mastana's plea for help to his wife, Alton switched off his phone. "Now what? How the heck do we respond to something like that? And realistically, how much help can we provide from here?"

"Given our vast distance from Afghanistan," said Mallory, "not much."

Alton drummed his fingers. "Why don't we go grab some dinner and give the question some thought? We need to be sure we give her good advice."

They traveled from their bungalow back to the reception building. The sounds of gentle surf and laughing children drifted into the "Polynesian Breeze" open-air restaurant as the host led them to a table.

Alton leaned back into his chair, allowing the gentle wind to wash over him. The tangy air and vibrant colors of hibiscus and other tropical flowers created an atmosphere conducive to contemplative thought. "I was thinking about Mastana's message on the way over here."

"Yes?"

"Do you remember Kamaal, the interpreter back in Camp Eggers' hospital? He helped us translate for Mastana, back before she eventually admitted she knew how to speak English."

"Yeah, I remember him. Nice guy with big eyes, right?"

"Yes, that's him. Why don't I call and see if he can help Mastana with whatever problem she's having? At least he's in the same city, not ten thousand miles away in the middle of the Pacific."

"Sounds like a good idea to me," said Mallory.

Alton checked his watch. "I'll call now."

He dialed Kamaal's number and waited. He began to fear he would reach the man's voice mail, but the interpreter picked up after the fifth ring.

"Hello?"

"Kamaal, it's Alton Blackwell. Do you remember me?"

"Of course!" said Kamaal. "How are you, my friend?"

"I'm fine. Mallory sends her regards, too."

"You are together?"

"Yes, indeed."

"That is wonderful! And are you still just friends, or a little bit more?"

Alton couldn't help but smile. "A little bit more. In fact, we're on our honeymoon."

"Ahh…you are a sly devil," replied Kamaal with a laugh. "And how is your young friend, Mastana?"

Alton shifted in his seat. "That's actually why I'm calling you, Kamaal. Mastana sent me an e-mail message a few hours ago. All it says is 'Alton, help me.'"

"Poor girl!" said Kamaal.

"Indeed. I figured she must not have your e-mail or phone number, or she would have called you."

"That is correct," said Kamaal. "She doesn't have any way to contact me. Once she left Camp Eggers, I never spoke with her again."

"So here's my problem. I only have her e-mail address, not her phone number. I don't know what's wrong, but even if I did, I'm thousands of miles away. So, I have a request. Can I reply to her message with your phone number and e-mail address? That way, she'll have someone she can contact locally."

"Certainly. She was a nice girl. I will help her."

"I appreciate it. I hope I don't ask too much, but would you mind calling me if you hear from her? I'd like to know what's going on."

"Yes, I will call you. Don't worry."

"Thanks, Buddy," said Alton, ending the call.

After composing and sending a brief message to Mastana, Alton leaned back in his chair. "Well, now we wait."

"Do you have any idea what might be going on with her?" asked Mallory.

"Just speculation. We still e-mail each other, but I haven't heard from her recently. Her mom has been sick for a while. Perhaps she's taken a turn for the worse."

"But doesn't her uncle live with them? Why wouldn't he help?"

"Maybe her uncle *is* the problem," said Alton. "Remember how he was in Al Qaeda? Mastana always seemed afraid of him."

"Could be. We'll just have to wait and see what she says, I suppose. Even if we took the next flight out, we wouldn't get there for a day. It's better to let Kamaal look into it first."

"Yes." Alton experienced a curious mix of emotions, happy to be honeymooning with Mallory yet worried over Mastana's safety. "Mallory, do you feel a little guilty about…uh…resuming the honeymoon spirit?"

"Yes. I know what you mean. We're both worried, but we've done all we can do for the moment. Let's see what Kamaal says, then we can figure out our next steps."

"Yeah, you're right," said Alton.

They dined on sea bass and two glasses of Chablis in

the breezy, open-air restaurant. The crash of distant waves mingled with soft strains of music from a ukulele player and guitarist who demonstrated an impressive repertoire of Polynesian music.

Alton watched Mallory polish off the last bite of a dessert concoction made of caramelized bananas and ice cream. "How'd you like to check out the view from our bungalow, Mrs. Blackwell?"

"I thought you'd never ask."

Hand in hand, the couple strolled along a sidewalk bordering the beach. Frigate birds dove towards the water, and sandpipers scurried across the wet sand. A sailing crew pulled a large outrigger canoe onto the shore and helped a couple of tourists step out. To the right, a steep volcanic mountain covered with palm trees and other lush, tropical foliage shot into the sky. In contrast to the soothing touch of his wife's hand, the late-afternoon sun felt hot on Alton's skin.

They arrived at their over-the-water quarters, a tasteful affair accented with teakwood and white linens.

Mallory slipped under the covers of the four-post canopy bed. "Join me." Her eyes held a bewitching look.

Alton felt his heartbeat accelerate. He lowered himself onto the bed and leaned into a kiss, tasting her. Within moments, their bodies entwined, and Alton could think of nothing but the ineffable beauty before him.

Later, they lingered in bed, the afterglow of passion matched by the last beams of light cast by the fading sun.

"I love you," said Alton. "You've made my life better than I would have ever thought possible."

"I love you, Sweetie." She laid her head on his chest. "I'm looking forward to growing old together."

The sound of gentle waves washing against pilings drifted into their bungalow. Alton laid his arm on Mallory's back and pulled her close. For a quarter hour, they remained bound together in peaceful, fervent love.

An indigo-blue sky soon gave way to nightfall. Stepping onto the wooden porch, the couple gazed in rapt silence at the swath of southern-hemisphere stars filling the night sky. Lacking civilization's omnipresent glow, swirls and constellations blazed across an obsidian sky, a dazzling display unlike Washington's washed-out nightscape.

Alton's heart overflowed with silent gratitude, yet his concern for Mastana's plight lingered. As he gazed into nature's starry patterns, he couldn't imagine a more stark contrast than that between the tranquility of this island paradise and the dangerous, militant environment of Kabul, the city in which black clouds of despair had nearly overwhelmed him.

Mallory slid her arm through his. "It's beautiful," she said.

"Absolutely, but still not as beautiful as you." Alton pulled his bride close and lifted a silent prayer of thanks to heaven for having guided him to this place of joy in his life.

CHAPTER 13

In the morning, Alton awoke and gazed at his sleeping wife, grateful for the privilege of repeating this ritual for the rest of his days.

Remembering yesterday's many conversations concerning Mastana, he checked his phone.

"Good morning, Sweetie," said Mallory, rolling towards him. "Any word from Kamaal?"

"Morning, Honey," he replied. "Not yet. Hopefully, he'll call us soon. In the meantime, want to take Reia up on her offer to take a guided tour of the property?"

"Sure." Mallory smiled and ran a hand down his arm as she leaned in for a kiss.

Reia picked up the couple in a golf cart. She drove inland a hundred yards, then turned onto a trail bordered by intermittent palm trees. Through the foliage, they could detect the sights and sounds of the Pacific Ocean on the right, while on the left, a series of lagoons shimmered in the bright morning sun. An egret sailed overhead in silent flight, landing near the cart path. In the distance, the verdant peaks of extinct volcanos, the center of Bora Bora, rose from the ocean.

"Sometimes there are albatross here," said their guide, "but I don't see any today."

She motored down the trail until it ended at the thatched-roof main lodge, where a blend of exotic aromas from a nearby restaurant wafted by. They returned down a parallel trail, this one running closer to the ocean.

After the tour, Alton and Mallory found a couple of lounge chairs on a nearby beach. The bright noon sun stung Alton's eyes with its intensity yet felt pleasantly warm on his bare skin. And the cool waters of the Pacific Ocean provided a refreshing respite from the tropical heat.

They remained in their spot most of the day, watching the sun sink lower in the sky and enjoying a late dinner brought directly to their chairs by an accommodating staff member.

Alton finished off a mango chicken sandwich and glanced at his wife. The sea breeze pushed a few stray tendrils of Mallory's dark locks in front of her face. How could a woman look so beautiful while doing so mundane an act as brushing aside an escaped strand of hair?

While Alton contemplated this question as well as the piña colada he had nursed for the last twenty minutes, his cellphone rang.

"Hello?"

"Alton, I am Kamaal."

"Hey, Buddy! How are you?"

"I am well. You said you would like to know if I heard from Mastana, correct?"

"That's right," said Alton. "Does this mean you've heard from her?"

"More than that," replied the Afghani interpreter. "She is with me now—here in my house."

"Really? Awesome! I'm so relieved. Can I…would you mind if I spoke with her?" said Alton, putting his cellphone on speaker so Mallory could participate in the conversation. He placed the phone on the small cocktail table between them. Mallory moved closer and slipped her hand into Alton's.

Kamaal laughed. "She is taking the phone from my hands as we speak. Here you go…"

"Alton! Is it you?" came an excited voice.

"Yes, it's me. How are you, Mastana?"

"I am so happy to hear your voice! I didn't know what to…" A sudden, sharp intake of breath was followed by gentle sobbing.

The teen's vulnerability touched a tender chord in Alton's breast. He promised himself to do all he could to help his young friend, whatever her problems may be.

"Take your time," he said. "I can wait until you're ready to talk. I hope that whatever is wrong, you can tell me about it."

His statement evoked another, louder round of weeping. At last, after a long sniff, Mastana spoke. "I did not know what to do or who will help me."

"Let's start at the beginning. What kind of trouble are you having?"

"My Uncle Dani wants me to do terrible things to the American soldiers."

"What kind of things?" asked Alton, stealing a glance at Mallory.

"Saturday is market day at Camp Eggers. Uncle Dani made a bomb for me to wear under my clothes. He said I was to explode it when I am inside the camp."

Mallory tightened her grip on Alton's hand.

"My uncle says the soldiers will not expect an attack from a girl," continued Mastana, "especially one who was in the hospital there for a long time. I do not want to do this, so I ran away last night. I tried to call you, but I got the recording of your voice."

"That's when you sent me the e-mail message?"

"Yes," replied Mastana. "For the last few days, I didn't know what to do, but I knew you would be able to help me. And I was right. When I got your message with Kamaal's phone number, I was so happy."

"What about your mother?" asked Alton. "What does

she think about your uncle's plan?"

Mastana broke down again. Alton could make out Kamaal speaking to her. Although the interpreter spoke in his native Pashto tongue, his intonation suggested words of encouragement and kindness.

Eventually, the girl cleared her voice and resumed the conversation. "My mother cannot help. Her cancer is much worse. She is…dying. I think she will live for only a few more days. Yesterday, I tell her goodbye, but she is too sick to understand me."

"I'm so sorry, Mastana," said Alton, noticing Mallory's eyes welling up with tears.

"Thank you. I know you mean it. I did not want to leave my mother, but I think she will not want me to die for my uncle, even if that means I must leave her during her last days. After Saturday, I would not be with her anyway. I would already be dead."

"Mastana," said Mallory, "I'm sure your mother wants more than anything for you to live. If she could speak, she would tell you how happy she is that you're alive and away from your uncle."

"I think you are right," said Mastana, "but already I miss her. My heart is crying."

"So your uncle didn't even wait for your mother to die before he roped you into his Al-Qaeda plans," observed Alton. "One thing I don't understand—how has he not been caught by now?"

"My mother and I are afraid of him. If we told the

American soldiers about Uncle Dani and they came looking for him, he would know we had betrayed him. He would kill us."

"I'm surprised Afghani Security Forces or Coalition troops haven't collected him on their own, though," said Alton. "We have a Military Intelligence unit in Kabul for that reason—to discover and address terrorist threats. I've given his name to them twice, for Pete's sake. They should have captured him by now."

"Uncle Dani is careful to hide his intelligence when he is around the soldiers. He acts like he is not smart, so they will not suspect him. But he is clever—and evil."

"I see," said Alton. "Maybe MI lost his name in the paperwork shuffle. Say, you're not going back home, are you?"

"No, never," said Mastana. "As I said, Uncle Dani would kill me for betraying him."

"I'm glad you realize that."

"Alton," said Mastana, "What am I to do now? Where am I to go?"

Alton pondered in silence for a moment. "If I could arrange for you to leave the country, would you be willing to go?"

"Yes, I think so. I do not have any other relatives here in Afghanistan. I have no one who will take me in."

"Based on your circumstances, I think I could apply for your immigration to the US as a political refugee.

How old are you now?"

"I have sixteen years."

"Okay," said Alton. "You'd be considered a minor. I can apply to the US Embassy in Kabul on your behalf. I believe they'll require you to have a sponsor, and I can fulfill that role. I can move forward with the application if that's what you want to do."

"So I would move to the United States?"

"Yes, if it's approved," said Alton as Mallory nodded in agreement.

"I would like that, but where would I live when I get there?"

"That's a good question. Honestly, I don't know right now, but I can work on that at the same time we're waiting for your immigration application to be approved. But don't worry. We'd have an answer by the time you'd actually arrive in the US."

"I like that—is good plan," said Mastana. "But Alton, where should I go now, until we know if I can go to the United States?"

"Hmm…you probably won't have to wait too long for an answer, especially since you're a minor. Maybe I can find a hotel out of the city, away from your uncle—"

"Wait," said Mastana. "Kamaal wants to talk to you. I will put his phone on the speaker so we can both talk."

"Alton," said Kamaal, "Mastana can stay with me until she goes to the United States. We can't put her in a hotel by herself—not a girl with only sixteen years and a terrorist uncle looking for her. It's too dangerous."

"That would put my mind at ease, Kamaal," said Alton. "Are you sure you don't mind?"

"Not at all. You are not the only person who can help someone," he said with a chuckle.

"Thank you," said Mallory, "from both of us. Mastana, would that work for you?"

"Yes. I would feel better being here than staying by myself," said Mastana, her voice reflecting palpable relief.

"Kamaal," said Alton. "I want to be as prepared as possible for the political-refugee application. I won't know exactly what documents of hers we'll need until I speak with the Embassy staff, but it wouldn't hurt to collect the obvious stuff. Can you work with Mastana to gather any identification paperwork she has, especially her birth certificate?"

"Yes, I will help her. But what if her birth certificate is in her house? She can't go back there."

"That's true," said Alton. "I'll ask the embassy to e-mail a request to Kabul's Central Records Bureau to authorize a release of the document to you."

"Okay. That will be better, I think."

"Thanks. So, I think that's it for now. Why don't I call you back in the next day or two, as soon as we have some news from the Embassy?"

"That will be wonderful!" sang Mastana. "I knew you

would help me, Alton."

Alton looked at Mallory with a smile. "We'll have you safe in no time. You take care, and I'll speak with you soon."

"Okay. Bye-bye!" said Mastana as she disconnected the call.

"Well, that was an interesting turn of events," said Alton, turning to his wife.

"Especially during our honeymoon."

"Sorry, I didn't mean to volunteer you for all…this," he said, gesturing at his now-silent phone.

"I didn't mean that the way it sounded," said Mallory. She leaned over and rested a hand on his arm. "Sweetie, I don't mind. I think it's cool that you're helping her out. Not everyone would do that."

"Well, I've had people help me out—you more than anyone. I'm just paying it forward."

"I still think you're a sweetheart," said Mallory. "So, assuming Mastana is approved to immigrate, where will she stay? Do you have any ideas about that?"

"Yes. What about David and Fahima?"

"Do you think they'd be up for that?"

"We won't know for sure until we ask," said Alton. "But you know, after I left Kabul, Fahima agreed to keep an eye on Mastana, which she did quite faithfully. Ever since she's come to the US, Fahima has told me how much she worries about Mastana. I think Fahima would be glad to help, at least until we can line up some place more permanent."

"And if she and David don't agree?"

"That seems unlikely, but in that case, I can ask the Embassy what they recommend. If all else fails, she could stay with us for a little while, if that's okay with you."

"Of course."

Alton placed a call to the US Embassy in Kabul. Upon completing the conversation, he turned to Mallory. "We have a teleconference scheduled at ten o'clock tomorrow morning. They normally prefer an in-person interview, but when I explained our circumstances, they said a phone call would be sufficient."

"Well, that's good news. Want me to text Kamaal to let him and Mastana know?"

"Sure."

"Anything else you want to tell them?"

"Just that I'll call with an update after the appointment."

Mallory began thumbing the text message, shading the phone's screen from the tropical island's fading sunshine. She finished and looked up. "Well, that's that."

Alton glanced at his watch. "Okay, it's eight o'clock in Washington. I'd better call David and Fahima before it gets much later."

"Do you know if David is working today?" asked Mallory.

"No idea. If he is, he won't be able to take a call from me. But if I can't reach him, I can always try Fahima."

Alton hit a number on his "favorites" list and listened to a series of rings that led to a voice-mail recording. "David's not picking up. Let me try the missus."

Alton enjoyed greater success this time as Fahima answered right away.

"Hello?"

"Fahima. It's me, Alton."

"Alton—what a surprise! How are you and Mallory? Are you having a good time on your honeymoon?"

"It's been wonderful," replied Alton, "but I did get a bit of unexpected news. And now I have a big favor to ask."

"What is that?"

"I received an e-mail from Mastana yesterday, and I was able to talk with her just a few minutes ago. Her mom's cancer has gotten worse. She's only expected to live a few more days."

"Oh! I am so sorry for Mastana and her mother," exclaimed Fahima.

"There's more. Do you remember how her uncle was a member of Al Qaeda?"

"Yes."

"Well, he was trying to recruit Mastana to carry out a suicide mission against US forces at Camp Eggers."

"Oh, my goodness! Poor Mastana! What should we do?"

"Don't worry. We've got it covered. Mastana's uncle wanted her to go on the suicide mission this coming Saturday, but she ran away from home a couple of nights ago. For now, she's staying with one of the interpreters from Camp Eggers, but she needs a permanent residence. I suggested that she apply for political-refugee immigration status in the US, and she's on board with that plan. I have a teleconference with the US Embassy in Kabul tomorrow morning to apply on her behalf."

"It is wonderful you are doing all these things, Alton."

"Yes, well, here's where I could use your help. If Mastana is approved to immigrate to the US, she'll need a place to live. Is there any chance she could stay with you and David until we line up something more permanent?"

"I will speak with David when he returns from work, but I'm sure he will say yes. He tells me what a sweet girl Mastana is for helping me escape from the Al-Qaeda kidnappers in Kabul."

"Good point. This is his chance to return the favor. Hopefully, she won't be with you all for too long."

"She can stay with us as long as she needs to. I might not be alive if she did not help me."

"Thanks, Fahima. You know Mastana will be thrilled to hear she'll be staying with you all—assuming her immigration application is approved."

They chatted for a few more minutes and ended the call.

"Well, that's settled," said Alton. "Now we wait for tomorrow's appointment."

"Good," said Mallory. "That means I have you all to myself between now and then."

"And I have you." He tipped back the last sip of piña colada from his glass. "I have to admit I'm relieved in a selfish way."

"What do you mean?"

"I'm happy our honeymoon won't be interrupted—at least not much as last fall's Italian vacation. I'd leave if we had to, but I'm glad the need isn't there."

"I hear you. I feel the same way. Now that we know she'll be safe, we can focus on the two of us."

Alton stretched his bad leg. "I think I could focus better with a walk on the beach. What do you say?"

Mallory flashed her dazzling smile. "You don't really need me to answer that, do you?"

The couple returned to the bungalow to deposit their beach bag, then left for their walk. A pale moon rose over the lagoon. Further out to sea, the placid surface of the water appeared silver in the moonlight.

His hand in Mallory's, Alton strolled beside his wife down the beach. A flawless conch shell washed ashore at their feet. He picked it up and handed it to her. They continued their walk and spotted tiny crabs darting along the shore, poking and prodding the sand for food.

The waves crashed in a rhythmic fashion. They seemed louder now than during the day, but Alton couldn't be sure whether their volume had truly increased or, with the absence of daytime distractions, he was simply more cognizant of the waves' presence.

"How's your leg, Sweetie?" asked Mallory.

"Fine. The best it's been in a long time, actually."

"That's great. So we don't need to head back yet?"

"Nope," replied Alton. He walked a few more paces and glanced at his wife. "You look thoughtful—anything on your mind?"

Mallory stopped and faced her husband, reaching out to take both his hands in hers. "Yeah. I was just thinking about us. I never thought I'd be this happy in a relationship."

Alton couldn't help but smile at the affirmation.

"We were both in the Army," continued Mallory, "so I don't need to tell you what most guys there are like. They're not exactly committed for the long term. Their timeframe is more like a few hours, maybe a few weeks if you're lucky. But with you, it's so different. I've finally found the man I've been waiting for, someone who loves me, someone I know will be with me, always. For a long time, I wondered if I'd ever find someone like that. I don't have to wonder anymore. And it feels so much better than I thought it would. I can give you all of my heart and know that it's safe with you."

"If I could think of some way to tell you just how happy I am to hear that, I would."

"I know, Sweetie. That's why I love you." She squeezed his hands.

"It's funny…some people play the lottery, hoping to change their life for the better. I don't need to do that. Any money or prize I can imagine would shrink to insignificance beside you."

"So says my knight in shining armor," she replied with a smile while looping her arms around his neck.

The smell of her perfume, a gardenia scent she had purchased at the gift shop yesterday, mingled with the fresh sea breeze, producing an intoxicating blend of aromas. Grasping her face in his hands, Alton leaned into a deep kiss. Mallory dropped her arms to his back, pressing herself against him.

She drew back. "God, Alton, how do you make me feel like that?"

"Like what?"

"Like a flight of butterflies are playing volleyball in my stomach."

Alton drew a deep breath and exhaled. "I'm glad you like it as much as I."

"I do. And I don't care how good your leg feels," she whispered into his ear. "I think it's time to head back to the bungalow. We're not finished yet."

CHAPTER 14

After ending the call with her American friend, Mastana allowed the first rush of relief to wash over her. Her confidence in Alton had not been misplaced. He had indeed devised a brilliant plan, one that would permanently remove her from the grasp of her scheming uncle.

Mastana turned to face Kamaal. The interpreter looked much as she remembered him from four years ago, except that now the stubble on his head was slightly longer than that on his face. Kamaal's body still formed a slightly rounded shape, like an egg, and his oversized eyes gave him the appearance of perpetual surprise. Most importantly, though, he seemed to have retained his cheerful, kindly demeanor. Mastana couldn't have imagined an Afghani she would have been happier to see at that moment.

"I have not properly thanked you for all you have done for me, honorable Kamaal," said Mastana, tearing up.

"Come, come," replied her host, looking a little flustered. "It is nothing. You have helped others, no? We all take our turn. It is pleasing to our Maker that we should do so."

"It is certainly pleasing to me that *you* do so," replied Mastana. "You are very kind."

"Thank you. I hope you will be comfortable here."

Until now, Mastana had been running for her life and, earlier today, had been ecstatic to accept the offer of sanctuary from Camp Egger's jovial interpreter. For the first time, though, she considered the awkwardness of their arrangement—a young woman cohabitating with an older, unmarried man. She trusted Kamaal. His eyes held no ulterior motive. But what about his neighbors? How would she be viewed by members of Afghanistan's tradetional society?

"Honorable Kamaal, you know that I am grateful for your help. Because of this, I am anxious that your kindness does not bring any hardship upon you. What will your neighbors think of my presence in your home?"

"I don't know if you saw when we drove in, but I don't have any neighbors close by. An unfinished building lies between me and my closest neighbor, Mr. Busri, and he is half blind and half deaf. I don't think anyone will see you here. And if they do, they might frown a little, but that's all."

"I am relieved to hear this. I would be sad if your kindness injures your reputation."

"I think it will be fine. No one ever comes down

here." He seemed anxious to turn the subject. "Since you will be a guest here for a few days, would you like a little tour of the house?"

"That would be nice."

Kamaal led his young charge from the kitchen and family room in the front of the abode down a hallway to two small bedrooms in the back. The house contained few decorations, but a collection of homemade tapestries and aging photographs on the walls lent it a cozy ambience.

"This bedroom on the left is mine," he said, "and this one on the right will be yours. I will need to move these clothes off your bed, though. Ay, what a mess! I am sorry—"

"Honorable Kamaal," interjected Mastana, "you do not really think I am concerned about clothes on the bed, do you? You and Alton have saved me. You have given me a new hope."

"You are a good girl. And I'm glad you think I am honorable, but you may address me as simply 'Kamaal.' Now, let me introduce you to the other members of my household."

"There are others?"

"Yes—here they are now," he replied, pointing to a pair of cats wandering in from his bedroom. "Boosah and Lala, there you are, my rascals. Sleeping again, no? That is all you ever do." He rubbed them behind their ears, eliciting a steady drone of purrs.

The one named Boosah rubbed against Mastana's leg. She leaned down to pet him. "You have no dogs?"

"I am often at Camp Eggers, so I am not at home enough to take care of dogs. But cats—they can take care of themselves. And they are happy to see me." As if in confirmation, Lala approached and rubbed herself against his leg. "You see?"

A growling stomach intruded upon Mastana's smile. During the events of the last two days, anxiety had eradicated her appetite. Now that she was safe, though, she seemed to have found it again.

"Would you like me to prepare dinner?" she asked, eager to express gratitude to her benefactor in some tangible way.

"You know how to…? I mean, that would be nice. I am not so famous for my cooking. If you eat too many of my dinners, you might not live long enough to make your journey to America!" He laughed at his own joke.

"I will be happy to make it."

"But seriously, are you not hungry and tired yourself? Would you like to rest while I prepare a simple meal?"

"I am not too tired to make us a dinner. Do you like Qabili Palao?"

"I love it, but I don't think I have all the ingredients you would need for that."

"If you tell me where your market is, I will buy whatever you're missing."

"I don't think that's a good idea. What if your uncle is looking for you?"

"He doesn't know you or where you live, and we are far from his house. To be safe, though, I will wrap this burka around me," she replied, removing one of the few articles of clothing from the duffle bag she had carried from her home.

"Okay," said the interpreter. "In that case, here is some money."

"Wonderful," said Mastana. "I will see what you already have and then go buy the rest."

As Mastana set about assessing the rather bare pantry, another round of elation swept through her mind. The impending death of Mother still saddened her, deeply. But after weeks of fear and uncertainty regarding the evil designs of Uncle Dani, the path now opening before her—one of safety and security and maybe, one day, a new family—seemed almost too good to be true.

CHAPTER 15

"Master, can I speak with you for a moment?" asked Ghoyee, staring into the gloom of Divband's small office, a cramped space located in the compound's central building on the opposite end of the ceremonial chamber.

"Certainly," replied Divband. "Come in, and draw the curtain. Now, what have you come to see me about?"

"Yesterday, you asked me to begin searching for new brides of Iblis. I have found two excellent candidates."

"Good work. That was quicker than you thought, no?"

"It was. I intended to search for several days, but earlier today, I canvassed a large neighborhood and saw two suitable brides."

"Tell me about them."

"The first seems to have about thirteen years. It is hard to be sure because she is a little skinny."

"Do her neighbors live close by?" asked Divband.

"Yes. There are houses on both sides."

"Hmm…she hardly sounds suitable."

"For her age, she is quite pretty, and her cleanliness is more certain, don't you think?"

"Perhaps," said Divband. "Tell me about the other girl."

"She is a rose ready for the picking," said Ghoyee, his eyes lighting up. "A little older, perhaps fifteen or sixteen years…jet-black hair…dark, supple skin…a woman's body yet an air of purity suggesting that she, too, is undefiled by the world. Plus, her house lies on the end of a street, sixty or seventy meters from the closest neighbor."

Divband licked his lips. "It sounds like you already have a favorite, no? The second one?"

"Yes, Master. If the choice was up to me, I would select her. Honestly, I was lucky to find her."

"What do you mean?"

"I was turning my car around at the end of a street when I saw her walking along the road," said Ghoyee. "She was wearing a burka, so I decided to wait a moment and observe. When she entered her house, I could see through the window. She took off the burka, and that's when I saw what a prize she would be for us."

"Very good. Study the routine of the girl and her family. Identify the times when she is alone. Once you have done this, report back to me."

CHAPTER 16

The next day, Alton and Mallory conducted their teleconference with the US embassy in Kabul, then spent the rest of the day exploring more of their temporary tropical home, venturing beyond the borders of their resort into the unspoiled land beyond. They hiked along a trail at the foot of the island's central volcano, snaking around its base on a path lined with palm trees, ferns, and bamboo.

During their hike, Alton received a text from Fahima, stating David had embraced her proposal to let Mastana stay with them until her permanent place of residence could be established.

"Well, that's a load off my mind," he told Mallory.

"Definitely. I'd have been surprised if they had said no, though."

"Me, too. But it's still nice to have their actual answer."

Back in the bungalow, at an hour he judged to be dinner time in Kabul, Alton sat on the side of his bed and phoned Kamaal.

After trading small talk for a minute, Alton broached the reason for his call. "Remember how Mallory and I had our teleconference with the US Embassy this morning? I wanted to follow up with you on the outcome."

"Just a minute," said Kamaal. "Let me get Mastana."

Alton waited for a moment, then Kamaal said, "Okay—we are both here."

"Hello, Alton," said Mastana. "I am happy to hear your voice."

"And I'm happy to hear yours. Did Kamaal tell you why I'm calling?"

"Yes, and now I am so wondering what you will tell me."

"Don't worry. I have good news. Based on the suicide mission your uncle wanted you to perform, and your status as a minor with no other relatives to care for you, the Embassy staff has already started processing your application to immigrate to the US as a political refugee. They've already gotten the green light from Homeland Security. Your visa isn't official yet since your application still has to be approved by the ambassador. But the staffer we spoke with said it's virtually certain you'll be approved."

"Oh, that is wonderful!" said Mastana. "So I will

really go to the United States?"

"Yep—that's the plan. I'll be your sponsor, and part of my role is lining up a temporary place for you to stay until we've identified a permanent guardian."

Mastana's voice became a little more subdued. "Do you know where I will stay? Will it be near you and Mallory?"

"I have some good news to share on that topic, too. How would you like to stay with David and Fahima Dunlow?"

"With Fahima? The same Fahima who talks to me all the time after you leave Kabul?"

"That's right."

"You are not joking, Alton? I will be sad if you are teasing me."

Alton suppressed a laugh. "I would never tease about something this important. I asked Fahima and David, and they said they'd be happy to take you in."

Mastana said nothing in reply.

"You may need to wait a minute," said Kamaal in a kindly voice. "She is too happy with this news to speak."

"No worries," said Alton. "Mastana, to answer your other question, Mallory and I live just a few minutes from David and Fahima, so you'll be able to see us all the time."

"Thank you. I am so happy!" The teen paused for a

moment. "Wait, you said 'Mallory and I.' Are you finally married?"

"We sure are. In fact, we're on our honeymoon right now."

"I'm sorry to bother you at such a time, but I am happy that I will see all of you—all of my friends from Camp Eggers! And Fahima!"

"Yes, it's worked out pretty well."

"Alton," said Kamaal, "what are the next steps?"

"The embassy will work on her application. Once it's officially approved, they'll start scheduling flights and will work out the details of Mastana's travel to David and Fahima's house in the US. They said it would take about a week. Are you okay with Mastana staying with you until then?"

"Of course."

"It is like a dream," said Mastana. "A few days ago, my uncle was trying to kill me, and I had no one to help me. Now, I will be in a new, safe country with my friends. I will miss Afghanistan, but I have nowhere to go here."

"I'm glad it's worked out," said Mallory. "I think you'll enjoy living with Fahima and David. They talk about you regularly."

After wrapping up the call, Alton turned to Mallory in satisfaction. "That went well. Mastana is happy, and we can get back to our honeymoon."

"Sounds good to me," said Mallory, snuggling next to

The Devil's Due

her husband. "I'm all about happy endings."

CHAPTER 17

Divband addressed a gathering of recent Brotherhood converts seated in a circle inside the main ceremonial chamber. The flickering of several dozen smoky candles cast erratic shadows on the stone walls and encircling stone pillars.

"And so it is written that we enter into a covenant with Iblis. We give him that which he desires—brides in the afterlife—and in turn he shares his powers with the faithful. As we have been taught since childhood, Iblis guards his power jealously. He provides it only to those who agree to meet his needs. So while the sacrifice of young lives may at first seem tragic, we know that it serves a greater good, for ourselves and our country."

The group members nodded in mute agreement.

Divband wrapped up the meeting, and the zealots filed out. Ghoyee waited in the chamber until only he and his master remained.

"Yes?" asked Divband.

"I have spent the last week tracking the movements of the new bride."

"And do you perceive a pattern to her movements?"

"Yes. She remains in the home almost all the time. When she leaves the house, she always wears a burka. But once inside, she removes it."

"She is not in school?"

"No—not this week, at least."

"I wonder if her father is Taliban. That would explain her absence from school."

"I don't know."

"Is she often alone?"

"Yes," said Ghoyee, warming to the subject. "Her father is gone every day until seven o'clock. She is alone until then."

"No other family members?"

"Not that I have seen."

Divband considered the matter. "The time for the next wedding ceremony grows near, which means the number of brides will decline. Take Meskin and collect the girl. We mustn't interrupt the flow of Iblis' power to his believers."

CHAPTER 18

Alton and Mallory relaxed on the wooden patio of their bungalow, enjoying the late-afternoon breeze. A flock of ring-billed gulls drifted overhead, and bright sunshine sparkled off the aqua waters of the lagoon. Somewhere down the beach, a couple played in the surf. Alton rested his hand atop Mallory's, enjoying the beauty of both his wife and the tropical location.

He took a sip of a fruity tropical drink—what was it called again? A Lavaflow?—and set it back on the small table at his side. As he did so, his cellphone rang. He answered it and spent most of the next fifteen minutes listening, only occasionally asking a question or two.

"That was the US Embassy. They approved Mastana's application."

"Thank goodness! She'll be relieved to hear that."

"Tell me about it. They apologized for the delay and said they'll start making arrangements for Mastana to fly to the States next week. They also said that since she's a minor, we'll have to do another round of paperwork once she arrives in Washington to register me as her guardian."

"That seems easy enough. I was beginning to wonder if we'd hear from the Embassy before we left here."

"Me, too. But I've been e-mailing Mastana all week. She seems to be happy, so I wasn't too worried about the delay. After all, we are talking about the government. 'Hurry up and wait,' right?"

"Ha—true! I wish I could be there when Mastana finds out the news."

"Me, too. We'll see her soon enough, though."

He fell into silence, and Mallory studied him for a moment.

"What 'cha thinking about?" she asked.

"Just really pleased how this has worked out—for Mastana's sake. I was also thinking about how history sometimes repeats itself."

"How so?"

"Mastana and I seem to be following the same kind of path—from barely escaping death in an Afghanistan bomb blast to experiencing a better life back in the US. I just hope the US portion of her journey turns out to be as good as mine has been."

Mallory squeezed his hand. "I hope so, too."

"I imagine changing countries and cultures might be

difficult, but Mastana's already proven how resilient she is. Plus, she'll be with Fahima. I have a feeling she'll be all right." Alton broke out of his reverie and glanced at his watch. "It's pretty late in Kabul now. I'll send Kamaal a text to let him know the latest."

Alton thumbed the message, asking the interpreter to share the news with Mastana.

"Well, that's settled. One more week, and Mastana will start her new life in the US."

CHAPTER 19

In the seven days since coming under Kamaal's protection, Mastana had settled into something of a routine. Once Kamaal left for work at Camp Eggers, she would use his laptop to check her e-mail for any messages from Alton. Most days, she would send him a brief update as well. That finished, she would set about deep-cleaning a different room in the house. Following that activity, she would write in her journal any thoughts that entered her mind—the day's events, her feelings of gratitude, her wonder and trepidation at starting life again in a new country.

As dinnertime approached, she would begin preparing the evening meal, aiming to have it ready by the time Kamaal returned from work around seven o'clock.

As she prepared the meal this day, the one-week anniversary of escaping Uncle's clutches, she heard the side door open as always.

"Hello, Kamaal," she sang out. "You are a little early

today. I don't have dinner ready quite yet."

She stepped around the corner to greet her benefactor but stopped dead in her tracks. A strange man with a grimy turban and malevolent grin stood just inside the door.

"Who are you?" asked Mastana.

"It doesn't matter who I am. My master would very much like to meet you."

Mastana turned and bolted towards the home's front entrance. Rounding the corner, she pulled up as the door trembled under a terrific blow. As she stepped backwards, the door crashed inwards, and a giant of a man entered. "Hello, little one."

Mastana turned and fled down the hallway, toward the bedrooms at the back of the house.

The first man gave chase, cackling as he went.

Mastana grabbed a rectangular picture frame off the wall and snapped it like a Frisbee towards her pursuer. The man instinctively turned his head, but the frame caught him on the corner of his eye, whipping his head backwards.

"Bitch!" he snarled as he put a hand to the wound.

"Come now," said the hulking man to his companion. "That's no way to talk to a future bride of Iblis."

"Easy for you to say. She didn't peg your eye." Blood dripped down the man's cheek. He charged again, his earlier lascivious look transformed into one of fury.

Mastana noticed the man kept his wounded eye closed. She leaned to his blind side and launched a punishing kick to his groin, sending her attacker to the floor, gasping for breath.

The giant's smile faded. He cracked his knuckles as he advanced down the hallway towards her.

Mastana scrambled into her bedroom, slamming the door shut and turning the lock on the knob. She prayed the door would delay the attacker long enough to afford her escape through the bedroom window.

She raced to the window and tugged it with all her strength. Years of rust had sealed it as tight as a prison door. She grabbed the blanket off the bed and wound it around her hand. With her fist protected, she punched through the window's glass and knocked off a few lingering shards. As she removed the blanket and threw it on the bed, the door flew inwards with a resounding crash.

Mastana jumped towards the window's opening. She made it halfway through the gap before an iron fist closed around her ankle. She kicked with her free leg, eliciting a curse from the man as she connected with one of his limbs.

The enormous man grabbed her other leg and pulled her backwards with seemingly no effort. He caught her before she could fall on the floor and twisted an arm behind her back. "I can't damage you. Divband wouldn't be pleased. But keep struggling, and I promise I'll hurt you in ways he'll never see."

The man removed a soaked rag from his rear pants

pocket and held it over Mastana's mouth and nose. Within seconds, the room began to spin, and the world tipped to the left at an impossible angle. She dropped to one knee, unable to stand, while the light began to fade. With the sound of her abductor's cruel laughter providing a diabolical soundtrack, Mastana slipped into unconsciousness.

CHAPTER 20

Alton and Mallory stepped off the Jetway into Washington's Dulles Airport.

"Now back to reality," said Alton.

"Don't remind me," said Mallory. "But it's okay. That was the perfect honeymoon." She squeezed her husband's arm.

"We'll have to send your mom some 'thank-you' flowers," said Alton.

"Yeah, we should. She'd appreciate that."

As they drove home from the airport, Alton checked his voice mail, his first opportunity since leaving Los Angeles International Airport six hours earlier. "I got a message from the Embassy in Kabul. They want to set up some time for an in-person meeting with Mastana and

Kamaal to cover the next steps and travel logistics."

"Wonderful! You'll have to let them know."

He continued listening. "I also got a call from Kamaal."

"What'd he say?"

"Just for me to call him. I hope everything's all right. He sounded stressed." Alton checked his watch. "It's a little late there, but not too bad. I'll call him now."

After dialing, he switched the call over to his Explorer's Bluetooth system.

"Hello?"

"Kamaal, it's Alton. I got your voice mail message."

"Alton, I have…some bad news."

Alton glanced at Mallory. "What's up?"

"I came home from work a few hours ago. Mastana is not here."

"What? Where is she?"

"I do not know. There was a great struggle here. The front door and a bedroom door were kicked in. There is a picture frame smashed in the hall and blood on the floor near it. And in the back bedroom, Mastana's bedroom, all the glass is broken out of the window."

"Dammit! So someone came for her."

"Yes—all the signs suggest this."

"Alton!" Mallory gripped Alton's closest arm, wide-eyed.

Alton fought to clear his mind of a surge of alarm, knowing he would need to stay calm if he was to help his young friend. "Was Mastana's bedroom door the one broken in?"

"Yes."

"Could she have escaped through her bedroom window while the assailant was breaking down her door?"

"It is possible. But if this is so, why has she not called me? Or you?"

"True. It doesn't look good, does it?"

"I am afraid not. Oh, and here is something else. I looked in my backyard outside the broken window. The glass is all over the place, but none of it is pressed down into the soil as if someone had stood on it. So, I do not think anyone went through that window."

"Kamaal," said Mallory, "do you think Al-Qaeda was involved?"

"It must be. Perhaps Mastana's uncle was able to track her down."

"That's what I was thinking, too," said Alton. "But how?"

"I don't know, but I am worried for Mastana if she is his prisoner."

"Have you contacted the police?" asked Mallory.

"Yes," said Kamaal with a sigh. "There is little they will do."

"What!" said Alton. "Did you tell them about all the evidence of a struggle?"

"Yes, they think perhaps she got into a fight with a boyfriend. They said maybe she was upset after the fight and went off to be alone for a while."

"We know that's not what happened," said Mallory. "How long will she have to be gone before they take it seriously?"

"I do not know. The police say there is no verified crime. Plus, you know how they are in my country. They don't worry about women as much as men. If a man is a victim of a crime, the police will look into it. But if it's a woman, they don't do so much…even when they do know a crime happened."

From his experience serving in Afghanistan, Alton knew the interpreter's words to be true. "So now what? We just wait for the police to decide to do something at some point—if ever?"

"I do not know." Kamaal sounded discouraged. "I am hoping you will have a good idea."

Alton felt the burden of responsibility descend upon his shoulders. After all, he had guided Mastana to Kamaal's house, the location from which she had been kidnapped. More importantly, he owed a debt of gratitude to the resilient teen, back from his days in Afghanistan. "Let me tell David and Fahima what's happened. We'll put our heads together, and I'll get back with you in your morning. Will that work?"

"Yes, thank you. In the meantime, I will ask my neighbors down the street if they saw or heard anything."

"Thanks, Buddy," said Alton. "We'll check in with you soon."

David and Fahima met the Blackwells in their apartment an hour later. Alton shared the grim news, recapping the conversation he and Mallory had conducted with Kamaal.

David smacked the end table in frustration. "So the police won't do anything? How stupid can they be?"

"You know how it is there," said Alton. "This is the same culture that lets a man kill his wife if she 'dishonors' him. They're just not anxious to rush to a woman's aid."

David looked grim. "Then maybe *we* rush to Mastana's aid."

The same idea had been brewing in Alton's mind. "You mean we go there ourselves?"

"Exactly. Fahima might not be alive if Mastana hadn't intervened with her Al-Qaeda kidnappers. I say we return the favor."

In a way, Alton felt Mastana may have also saved his own life, albeit in an indirect manner. Shortly after sustaining his leg injury, a time when the oppressive clouds of depression had threatened to push him to commit an unspeakable act, Mastana's need for friendship while hospitalized had helped pull him back from the brink. Without her presence, would he have had sufficient reason to push forward with his own recovery?

"Honey," said Alton, turning to his wife. "Mastana and Kamaal acted on the advice I gave them. That means I bear some responsibility for what's happening now. I hate leaving you so suddenly, especially after we just got home from our honeymoon, but I think I should go with David—"

"Not without me, you're not," cut in Mallory. "I can take care of myself in a tight spot. You know that."

After serving with Mallory in Afghanistan and working three cases together since then, Alton did know it. "I'm well aware of your capabilities. I'm just not crazy about your being in such a potentially dangerous situation."

"We're a team. I'm not leaving you."

Alton nodded and grasped her hand. "Okay. Honestly, I'll be glad to have you there."

"And I can help," said Fahima. "I know the streets of Kabul since my childhood. And I speak Pashto."

"We'll already have one interpreter: Kamaal," said David. "And you're not a former soldier."

"Maybe I don't go into all the dangerous situations," said Fahima, "but I can help you discover the information you seek. You will need to find out where Al-Qaeda takes Mastana, right? I have many friends on the streets of Kabul. Do you think they will give information about

Mastana to you, an American? No, they will only give it to me, someone they trust."

"She's got a point," said Mallory. "Plus, four heads are better than one—or three."

"Okay," said Alton, "I'll call Kamaal and let him know we'll be coming. We'll go there as soon as possible—before Mastana's uncle has a chance to send her on a suicide mission after all."

CHAPTER 21

The first trace of consciousness seeped back into Mastana's mind. She opened her eyes. A feeble beam of light shining between vertical bars on the room's wooden door provided the only illumination. In the foreboding darkness, she couldn't be sure she had regained full consciousness.

Mastana realized her head lay against a hard wall at an awkward angle. She moved her hands up to raise herself off the wall, only to discover a rattling chain affixed to her right wrist. The other end of the chain led to a modern-looking steel plate bolted to the floor.

So she was a prisoner.

She pushed herself up to a sitting position and examined the shackle. She tested it with a series of yanks and wiggles, but it was sealed with a heavy lock and held fast. She tried inserting one of the bobby pins from her hair into the shackle's keyhole, but the sliver of metal merely twisted into a useless shape without impacting the lock in the slightest.

Mastana studied her surroundings. The moldering stones from which the floor and walls were constructed seemed ageless, and a musty smell permeated the air. In the ancient, windowless cell, torches would have seemed a more appropriate source of light rather than the steady electrical beam that stabbed from the hallway into the space's gloom.

Mastana heard distant voices but did not recognize any of them. The voices were so muffled, she wasn't sure she would recognize them regardless.

How had Uncle Dani discovered Kamaal's house? Surely, her abductors had to be part of her uncle's horrible Al-Qaeda band. And Uncle certainly had a compelling reason to seek her out.

Mastana shuddered. She remembered the grisly fate met by other unfortunates Uncle and his Al-Qaeda comrades had captured. It was only via the ingenious machinations of Alton Blackwell that Fahima had escaped Al-Qaeda's clutches several years ago.

Mastana knew she, too, had to escape, but how? She considered what Alton would do in this situation. He would probably look for anything that could be employed as a concealed weapon or used to pick the locks. Using her sense of touch more than vision, Mastana methodically canvassed the surface of the small room in which she was held prisoner. The cell's tiny dimensions allowed her to cover virtually the entire floor, despite her restraint. She found a small pot, presumably for excrement, but no food or water or other potentially-helpful objects.

She removed the three remaining bobby pins from her hair and attached them to her undergarments. They hadn't helped with the locks, but who knew how they might prove helpful later?

The hopelessness of her situation began to set in, almost overwhelming her. Ingenious as they were, Alton and Mallory lived on the other side of the planet. Even if they had lived in Kabul, what could they do? How could they, or anyone, find her?

As she sat against the wall in the darkness, Mastana felt warm tears trickle down her face. These would be the last, she decided. If she were to have any hope of escaping, she would have to keep her wits about her every moment. Uncle might be evil, but she would fight for life until her last breath.

CHAPTER 22

Divband sat in the stone alcove that served as his office, reviewing the background records of recent converts to the Brotherhood. At the sound of a tap on a plate mounted in front of his office, he looked up.

"Can you talk?" asked Ghoyee.

"Yes, come in."

"You wanted an update on the latest bride. I wanted to let you know we brought her in."

"Where is she?"

"Chained in cell number three. We got her in there before she woke up, just like the others."

"Good…good. How does she look?"

"Delicious."

Divband frowned and locked Ghoyee in a stare.

"You're not…tampering with the brides, are you?"

"No, of course not."

"That's good, because as much as I value your assistance, I would have to put an immediate stop to such activities. And you know how I put a stop to things."

"I know, Master. I would never touch the brides. Now, *looking*, on the other hand—"

"Don't let me—or anyone else—catch you looking… or making that kind of comment," interrupted Divband. "You represent me. Your conduct must be beyond reproach. Nothing you do or say must conflict with my teachings. If my followers see such inconsistencies, you'll shake their faith."

"I'm sorry. I—"

Divband help up an interposing hand. "We have an understanding, right?"

Ghoyee swallowed. "Yes."

"Good. Now, about the new bride…were you able to collect her without damage?"

"Yes, no damage to her, at least" said Ghoyee, snickering, "but Meskin ended up with a nasty gash on the side of his face."

"He was careless?"

"Somewhat. Plus, the new bride…she put up a fight. She has more spirit than the others. It might take a little more time to break that spirit."

"All the better that you didn't wait any longer to collect her."

"True, Master."

"Good work, Ghoyee. I knew I could count on you." He looked down at the ledgers on his desk. "Unless you have other business, you may leave me now. I have much to do."

As his subordinate exited the room, Divband returned to his task, updating the ever-increasing rolls of the Brotherhood with another group of recruits.

CHAPTER 23

The following day, the band of Americans arrived in Kabul. They filed off their Emirates flight and entered the airport terminal.

Alton had never expected to return to Afghanistan, the land where he had sustained his IED wounds and suffered the most profound depression following that injury. As he examined the Kabul cityscape and the mountains beyond, he experienced a tightening in his chest—not horrible, but not expected, either. Coming back to this place was proving to be a little harder than anticipated.

Taking a deep breath, Alton led the rest of his group to the luggage carousels, then to the airport exit, where he spotted Kamaal pacing to and fro.

"Kamaal!" said Alton, embracing his old comrade.

"My friends!" said Kamaal as the others circled around and peppered him with handshakes and hugs.

"The joy it gives me to see you, I cannot tell. I have been so worried."

"We've all been worried," said Mallory.

"I already feel better knowing you are here," said Kamaal. "Now we can make some real progress."

After walking along the airport sidewalk in silence for a minute, Kamaal turned to the others. "How long will you be able to stay here in Kabul?"

"As long as we need to, to find Mastana," said David.

"I know you came here as soon as you heard the news, so I was thinking you did not have much time to make arrangements at your jobs. I was worried that you might have to return soon."

"We told our bosses what was up," said Alton.

"And they did not worry about your work responsibilities? And former soldiers coming back to Afghanistan as civilians?"

"They were a little worried, yes, but we reassured them that our intent was to help the local police in their investigation—you know, devote more time and energy to it than the police might have available on their own. And we all have contingency plans in our jobs—people lined up to step in if we're out unexpectedly—just in case of emergencies like this."

"I see."

"Speaking of the police, do you think that would be a good place to start—the police station?"

Kamaal looked doubtful. "I have already been there."

"True," said Mallory, "but perhaps our coming with you will lend support to your assertion that Mastana truly was kidnapped. As you said, they won't devote any resources to tracking her down until they're convinced a crime was committed."

Fahima spoke up. "I think Mallory is right. If all five of us go to the police, they will listen, especially since we have three men."

"Kamaal, would you mind if we swung by your place first?" asked Alton. "I'd like to see the spot of the abduction in person, if you don't mind."

"Yes, is good idea. I will take you."

Kamaal moved over to walk beside David and Fahima. "Alton and Mallory spoke of you, but I don't believe we have met. You are married?"

"That's right," said David.

Kamaal peered around David to study Fahima. "You are from Kabul, no?"

"Yes," replied Fahima in a rather timid fashion.

Kamaal turned back to David. "How did you meet your lovely bride?"

"At a bar—can you believe that?"

"Really?"

"Yeah—she worked at this place called Gandamak's

Lodge. When I was stationed at Camp Eggers, I used to go there after work."

"So that is when you became fond of each other?"

David grinned. "Yeah. So when I eventually went back stateside, we worked to get her a visa. It took some time, but eventually she got it and came to the US. We got married a few months later."

"What a wonderful story—even though, my friend, you have stolen Kabul's prettiest rose and taken her off to America."

David looked with pride at his wife's jet-black hair, almond skin, and pleasing curves. She truly was a vision. "I can't argue with you on that."

They reached Kamaal's Corolla in the airport parking lot. After loading their rolling suitcases into the trunk, they headed for the interpreter's home.

"I will show you the evidence that points to a crime," said Kamaal as soon as they entered his house. He began their tour of the pertinent spots by walking down the hall.

"Is this the picture frame you found on the floor?" asked David.

"Yes. I found it here in the hallway. And see the blood spots just down the hall? I did not clean them, in case the police wanted to come here and check."

"Good thinking," said Mallory.

They entered Mastana's bedroom, the door of which remained splintered.

"I did not touch anything in here, either," said Kamaal.

Fahima fingered a shard of glass that had fallen inside the room. "She tried to escape," she murmured, more to herself than the others. "She did not want the bad man to catch her."

After examining Mastana's bedroom, Alton returned to the front of the house. "The kidnapper kicked in this door?"

"Yes."

"Both the door and the frame are pretty solid. That must have been a pretty strong guy."

"I think so."

"What about your neighbors? Did they hear or see anything?"

"They say they did not. My neighbors live pretty far away, so this is probably true. But the people…many are afraid of Al-Qaeda. Even if they did see something, they might not tell me."

"I understand," replied Alton. He wondered at the strange expression that overtook Kamaal's face for a moment. Guilt? Fear? Something else? Whatever it was, Alton couldn't blame him. Surely the man must be experiencing a tumult of emotions, much as Alton himself was.

"Okay, if we're done here," said Mallory, "let's head to the police station."

"So, who exactly will we be talking to?" asked Alton as Kamaal maneuvered his Corolla through mid-day traffic.

"Before, I talked with a guy named Captain Poya. I guess we will talk with him again."

"Captain, huh? Is he military or civilian police?"

"He is ANP—the civilian police."

"And how high up is he in the food chain?"

Kamaal looked puzzled. "The 'food chain'?"

"Sorry, I meant is he a top official, or are there higher-level people we can speak with if he doesn't want to help us?"

"Ah, I see. I think in the ANP, a captain reports directly to his provincial chief of police. The chief is pretty high up in the food chain, so I don't think he will care about a small crime like this."

"Small to them, maybe," said Mallory.

Kamaal shrugged. "When you are investigating a new terrorist attack every week, the disappearance of a girl is not such a big deal."

They arrived at the police station and entered a small lobby. Kamaal and Fahima approached the front desk, while the others stood behind them. As the Pashto conversation dragged on, Alton wondered how their request could require so much conversation. Surely, the police were already familiar with the case.

At last, the desk sergeant picked up his phone and conducted a brief call. He buzzed a security door and waved them through.

"We are seeing the same man as before, Captain Poya," said Kamaal as they walked down two short corridors.

They reached the largest office Alton had seen in the building. The man behind the desk rose as he saw them approach. "Come in, come in."

"You speak English?" asked David.

"Yes, I studied it in the college."

"Thanks for seeing us. I'm Alton Blackwell."

"I am Captain Hadi Poya. Let us sit over there."

They piled into chairs surrounding a stained, oval table on the opposite side of the room from the captain's desk.

Kamaal introduced the other members of the party.

"So," said Poya, "you are here about the missing girl again, right?"

"Mastana, yes," said Mallory. "We just came from the scene of her abduction."

"Abduction, you say? And how do you know this?"

"I'm a United States FBI agent. I'm trained to assess a crime scene, and there's an abundance of evidence at Kamaal's house. I guarantee you an abduction occurred there."

"Okay, Agent Wilson, I believe that you saw evidence of a scuffle, but we don't even know for sure that a *crime* occurred there, right? For all we know, she ran away with her boyfriend after a fight. This happens a lot."

"She didn't have a boyfriend," said Mallory. "She just escaped her Al-Qaeda uncle a few days ago. No one from her old neighborhood knew where she was—at least we didn't think they knew until she disappeared. There are signs of a struggle, and now Mastana hasn't contacted anyone for two days, despite the fact she's scheduled to depart for the US in a week—a trip that was the answer to her prayers. Surely you'd consider this an abduction."

Poya sighed. He tapped his fingers on his desk while staring far off into space. "Did you hear about the murder of the two Red Cross workers in a taxi a few days ago?"

They shook their heads.

"I'd like to help you," he continued, "but I already have to investigate that crime as well as two other terrorist attacks from earlier this week. I don't have the resources to investigate anything but the most serious civilian crimes. I certainly don't have the manpower to look into a missing girl."

"Abducted girl," insisted Mallory.

"Captain," said Alton, "if there's someone you could assign to the case, even part-time, we'd be more than happy to do some groundwork to assist them. Frankly, that's why we're here. We appreciate your resource constraints and would like to help the investigation any way we can."

"Is nice you want to help me, but that still doesn't give me any more manpower in my department to work on this." More to himself, he continued, "If Nur Hanif was still here, I'm sure he would help you. He always had a soft spot for the children's cases."

"Nur Hanif?" asked Alton.

"He is man who used to work for me, but he turned his back on us."

"What do you mean? He quit the police force?"

"That's right. Now he works with his father at the electric utility. You can talk with him if you like."

Alton checked his growing impatience. "But surely you have a policeman who can spare just a few hours—"

"No," cut in Poya, "not with a man like Bina…how you say…breathing down my neck."

"Bina?"

"Yes, Jaweed Bina is governor of Kabul Province. My boss, the chief of police, reports to him. And Bina wants us to put all our resources on finding the terrorists."

"I understand the need to do that," said Mallory, "but what about crimes of the non-terrorist variety? You just let them go?"

"For the bad stuff—murders, rapes, things like that—we investigate. But not for something like this. Bina knows that his job depends on keeping the terrorists contained. If Al-Qaeda and the Taliban come back, Bina is out of a job…and maybe his life. So that's where he keeps his policemen focused."

"So there's no one on your force who can help, even for a few hours?" asked Alton.

"I am sorry, but no. But if you get a ransom note or find something on your own—stronger evidence of a crime, for example—call me. I will assign a man to investigate. I just…I can't risk my job based on such questionable evidence."

"I understand," said Alton while shooting a quieting look in the direction of David, who looked to be on the verge of protesting. "We'll let you know as soon as we dig anything up."

As they exited the station, David leaned over to Alton. "How could you let him brush us off like that?"

"He's the only person in authority we can work with here. Like it or not, we have to stay on his good side. Otherwise, what do we do if we find the kind of evidence he needs? If we piss him off bad enough, he could just continue to ignore us."

David nodded. "I see what you're saying, but it still seems like bullshit to me."

"Agreed. But we can't do any more good here. Let's

focus our energy where we can make some progress."

CHAPTER 24

Mastana awoke to oppressive darkness. How long had she been asleep? For that matter, how long had she been awake before falling into her latest slumber? She guessed she had been held prisoner here a day in total, but really, how could she know? The light in her cell never varied. A perpetual dusk reigned.

Before exhaustion had overtaken her, Mastana had witnessed a robed figured open the door to her cell and place a tray on the floor. After the man had left and locked the door, Mastana had approached the tray. It had contained only a basin of water and four pieces of *naan*, a type of Afghani flatbread. She had made short work of the rations, but upon awaking now, the minimal nutrition of the last day or so had caught up with her. Her limbs felt heavy, and her mental acuity seemed…fuzzy. She knew she must somehow acquire more food if she hoped to survive.

Mastana turned her head toward a noisy clanking

down the hallway from her cell. Was someone coming? Hopefully, the sound heralded person bearing more food.

Footsteps approached her door. The rattling of a heavy key in a lock was followed by a surge of bright light as the door swung open.

Mastana shielded her eyes at first. Once they had adjusted to the radiance, she recognized the man filling the doorway. It was he who had abducted her from Kamaal's house. She knew many of Uncle's Al-Qaeda associates but did not recognize this man.

The abductor squeezed through the door and looked at her. Not knowing what to say, Mastana remained silent.

The man took two strides and stood beside her. "Stand up."

Mastana did as commanded. What would resistance gain her now, except a retaliatory beating or starvation that would render her even less capable of escaping later?

"You are not damaged from our encounter yesterday, are you?" asked the man.

"I do not know. I do not think so. I am very sore, but I think it is from sleeping on the hard floor."

"Let me see your face."

Mastana turned but did not meet his eyes. Now was not the time for defiance.

The man stroked her ebony hair and caressed her cheek. "You look…perfect. Divband will be pleased."

The man let his hand drop. "There is one rule above all others here. You do not speak until you are spoken to. When you *are* addressed, your responses must be in a subdued voice. Do you understand?"

Mastana nodded.

Turning on his heel, the giant man exited her cell without uttering another word and locked the door behind him.

Who were her captors? And why did they keep her here in limbo? Surely they must be members of Al-Qaeda, but Mastana had yet to encounter Uncle or any of his associates known to her. She knew Uncle's wrath with her would be terrible, but the enormous man who had just visited frightened her just as much, only in a different way.

Why was Uncle waiting so long to admonish her in person? He certainly hadn't shrunk from confrontation in the past. After seeing the hulking man's lustful glances, though, Mastana didn't prefer his presence any more than Uncle's.

Mastana sat down on the cold, stone floor and listened to shuffling footsteps file past her door. She speculated on her eventual fate, uncertain whether to pray for knowledge or ignorance. Still undecided, she drew up her knees and laid her head on them. She waited for the next bout of fatigue to pull her back into sleep, allowing her to escape into the freedom of her dreams.

CHAPTER 25

During the drive back to Kamaal's house, Alton stared out the window. He had left Kabul three years ago, retiring from the Army after nine months of post-injury rehab had failed to requalify him for field duty. Since his discharge, he had pushed the memories of his time in Afghanistan into a secluded corner of his consciousness—still there, but a mere shadow of its former intensity. He hadn't been prepared for the resurgence of powerful memories brought on by the onslaught of Kabul's sights, sounds, and, in particular, smells. He hadn't realized the extent to which Kabul possessed its own unique blend of aromas, but upon disembarking from today's flight, the mixed scents of spices, oils, asphalt, exhaust fumes, and who knows what other substances had elicited a collage of memories—some pleasant, but most not.

Mallory placed her hand on his arm. "You okay?"

"Yeah—it just feels weird to be back. How about

you? You feeling all right?"

"Yes, I'm fine."

"You all can be seated, and I will bring the food," said Kamaal as they entered his house.

"Wait, I just realized…you have a table?" asked Alton. While deployed in Afghanistan, he had never seen a dining table in a local's home, since Afghanistan custom dictated eating from a tablecloth laid directly on the floor.

"Yes," replied Kamaal. "In my role as an interpreter, I sometimes have guests from Camp Eggers come for a meal. Is better if I have a table for them."

"I see."

As he approached the small table, Alton glanced down the hallway. Droplets of dried blood on the floor served as a grim reminder of the task at hand.

Kamaal placed bowls in the center of the table for them to share. As he returned with a pitcher of water, an imam's call to prayer could be heard in the cool breeze blowing through the open window. David walked over and pushed the window shut.

"The police won't help us, not until we basically do their job for them," said David as he resumed his seat. "So, what do we do now?"

"Let's focus on the obvious first," said Alton. "We're pretty certain Mastana is a captive of Al-Qaeda. More specifically, her Uncle Dani is the key. She is either with him, or he at least knows where she's being held. So, our goal should be tracking down Dani's house, the same house Mastana was in until a week ago. Kabul's city records don't show anything. I checked into that before I left the States. Kamaal, did Mastana ever mention to you where her uncle lives?"

"No. She only said he lives far from here. She was quite glad about that. I never thought to ask her exactly where that was. I mean…why would I need to know?"

"Quite true," reassured Mallory. "None of us knew that would be important information."

"Okay," said Alton, "so let's keep noodling on other ways to find Dani's house. What other approaches can we take?"

"I can ask my friends if they heard about any Al-Qaeda activity last week," said Fahima.

"Realistically, what are the odds of one of your friends possessing useful information?"

"Realistically? Not much. Al-Qaeda is a closed society. Nobody hears much. But every now and then, my friends and I would hear information—rumors, really—about recent attacks. Maybe we will get lucky, and a rumor will lead us back to Dani."

"So Fahima will follow up with her friends," said Mallory, "but we can't count on that approach producing results. What other avenues can we pursue?"

"What about the guy Captain Poya mentioned…what was his name?" said David.

"Nur Hanif," said Fahima.

"Right. We could ask him to help."

Alton pondered the option. "I'm not sure how much help an ex-cop can give, but I don't see what harm it can do. I suppose even though he's not a cop anymore, he still might have friends on the force who can supply key intel."

"Okay—so how do we find him?" asked David.

"Poya said Hanif is working for the electric utility," said Mallory. "Why don't we go there tomorrow morning? It'd probably be the quickest way to see him."

The next morning, the group assembled inside the main lobby of Kabul Electric Co, LTD. After speaking with the security guard seated behind the main desk, Kamaal returned to the others. "He will take us to Hanif's office."

They followed the guard down a narrow, cinderblock corridor that vibrated with the soft hum of the adjacent power plant.

With a comment in Pashto, the guard waved them through a door.

They entered a cramped office with a small, square table and chairs pushed up against the wall. Above the table appeared a white board covered with hand-drawn electrical schematics. The mild breeze produced by a lazy ceiling fan did little to alleviate the room's stuffy atmosphere.

"I am Nur Hanif," said the occupant in excellent English. "The guard said you wanted to see me, but he did not say why."

"Thanks for seeing us. Let me explain," said Alton. He recapped the events of the last eleven days, from Mastana's escape from her uncle to her subsequent recapture two days earlier.

"I am sorry to hear your young friend is missing," said Hanif, "but I don't see what that has to do with me."

"You used to work for Captain Poya in the ANP, correct?"

Hanif's mouth straightened into a grimace. "Yes."

"Poya told us you might be able to help us locate Mastana."

"Didn't he tell you I am not a policeman anymore?"

"Yes, but he also said you have an affinity for cases involving children."

Hanif sighed. "I did, but I have an even greater affinity for my own children. I have a baby boy and a girl of six years. I would like to live long enough to see them grow up.

"I did well as a policeman. I was more educated than most, so I became a lieutenant faster than usual. But after two of my friends in the police force died from terrorist attacks, I started to wonder when it would be my turn. When you're a policeman in Afghanistan, you don't know how much time you have.

"My father had always wanted me to join him here at KE. I had planned on that career when I was young, even got my electrical engineering degree. But after the fall of the Taliban, I wanted to help make my country strong again, so I joined the police. Once I decided being a policeman was too dangerous, I came here. Captain Poya was not happy. The Taliban killed his father, so he wants as many people as he can find to fight them. But my father is happy, my wife is happy, and my kids are happy. This job here at KE…it's not so dangerous."

"I understand," said Alton, "and I don't blame you. I'd probably do the same thing. But this is a special case. Poya refuses to help us—says Governor Bina wants him to ignore all but the most extreme civilian crimes in order to stay focused on rooting out terrorists. It's a race to recover Mastana before Al-Qaeda does something… terrible to her. You know that better than we do. What are our odds of finding Mastana alive without the help of someone with your unique qualifications?"

Hanif stood and paced the room. "How would I explain this to my wife?"

"Based on the events we've told you, do you consider Mastana's life at stake?" asked Mallory.

"Yes, I think so."

"That might be a place to start explaining to your wife, then," said Mallory.

Alton studied the man. "Hanif, if your heart is telling you not to do this, then I don't think you should. Like you said, you have a family to care for. But if your heart is telling you to help, all of us—including Mastana—would be grateful."

Hanif pondered in silence for a moment. "I hate Al-Qaeda. I would love to see their plans ruined, and this girl recovered." He fell into silence again. "Okay, I will help you."

"Wonderful," said Alton, while Kamaal produced a jubilant-sounding exclamation in his native Pashto tongue. "So, what next steps do you recommend?"

"I know you are in a hurry," said Hanif, "but I will need a little time to verify you are who you say you are."

"How are you gonna do that?" asked David.

"If I can't track down such a simple piece of information as your identities, what use would I be trying to track down your young friend?"

"Point taken," said Alton. "What do you need from us?"

"Copies of passports from the Americans, copies of identity cards from my fellow Afghanis. The photocopier is in the break room next door."

"Great. Any idea how long you'll need?"

"Not long. I call you tonight, okay?"

"Perfect—and thanks again for your help," said Alton.

CHAPTER 26

Alton received a call from Nur Hanif at three o'clock that day.

"Done already?" asked Alton.

"Yes, as I said, this kind of background check is not so hard."

"Great, so what's next?"

"Why don't we meet after I get off work?"

"Sounds good. Can you come to Kamaal's house?"

"Yes. Give me directions, and I will be there as soon as possible. I leave KE at five-thirty."

Several hours later, Hanif joined the group around Kamaal's table. "I am sorry, but I cannot stay long tonight. I have to get home to explain to my wife about…this," he said with a sweep of his hand.

"We understand," said Alton.

"Anyway, let me tell you…I did some checking before coming here. The only report of Al-Qaeda activity in Kabul from two days ago involves the bombing of a mosque in the southwestern sector, far away from this place. I don't think it is connected with Mastana's abduction."

"Agreed," said David.

"I will try to do more checking tomorrow. I have a couple of friends in the Afghani Army's MI. I would like to see if they have heard of any Al-Qaeda activity, especially involving a kidnapping."

"Okay, so we'll meet back here after you get off work tomorrow?" asked David.

The dismay Alton felt in the delay must have shown.

"I will take the afternoon off," said Hanif. "We cannot wait too long to get started."

"That'd be great."

"One thing we know for sure," said Hanif. "Al-Qaeda terrorists are always well armed. Did you bring any weapons with you?"

"No. How could we?" said Alton. "You know how tight the restrictions are when you fly in here."

"True. Well, it won't do us any good to find Mastana if we're outgunned. Our first stop tomorrow should be acquiring weapons."

"How are we going to do that?" asked Mallory.

"I know some black-market people a little ways outside of town. They should be able to sell you just about anything you want. Did you bring money?"

"Yes," said Alton, whose experience in Afghanistan had led him to expect this turn of events. "And gold."

"Gold is even better—will get you more stuff."

"Okay, so we'll plan on seeing your…um, associates tomorrow afternoon. Anything else we can do tonight?"

"I don't think so. I will call you tomorrow when I'm getting ready to leave work."

The former policeman departed, and Alton turned to David. "Hanif mentioned contacting Afghanistan Military Intelligence. Do you have any US Army MI contacts at Camp Eggers you could ring up?"

"I don't know. I haven't been stationed there for over three years. I doubt any of the guys I worked with are still there."

"I know it's a long shot, but could you poke around? Maybe someone will at least recognize your name and be willing to give us some intel on recent Al-Qaeda activity. Anything they can tell us will help."

"Sure, Al." He glanced at his watch. "In fact, shift change is coming up in about thirty minutes. Why don't I call now, before day shift leaves? They're usually more up-to-speed than the night-shift guys."

Alton nodded. "We'll wait on the group discussion until you're done with the call."

David returned a quarter-hour later. "No surprises—I couldn't find anyone I worked with back in my service days. But I did connect with the current MI officer, Colonel Rand."

"I don't recognize the name," said Alton. "Was he in-country when we were there?"

"Yes, but he didn't work for MI back then," replied David.

"I remember hearing the name," said Mallory, "but I never worked with him. I think he was a major back then."

"Kamaal, do you work with Colonel Rand?" asked David.

"No," replied the interpreter. "I know of him, but I don't work with him. He speaks Pashto, so he has no need for my services."

David leaned back in his chair. "I'll tell you what, Rand seems perfect for the MI role. His mom is Afghani, so he has dual citizenship in both Afghanistan and the US. He said the same thing Hanif did. He hasn't heard of any Al-Qaeda activity over the last two days except the mosque bombing. He said he'll let me know if he hears anything more. I told him about Dani's plot to send in a teenage girl on market day wearing a bomb vest under her clothes. Rand was grateful for the intel, of course, but still didn't offer up any more information."

"Too bad he doesn't know anything," said Alton, who was beginning to wonder if they were setting a record for dead ends. "Kamaal and Fahima, what about media reports? Do you think it would do any good to scan the newspapers for any articles that might tip us off?"

"It might," said Fahima. "The newspapers here are like the US. They know people like to read about crime stories."

"Okay. Do you have online access to the news?"

"Yes. The 'Kabul Press' is online."

"Maybe you can search it using keywords," said David. "'Kidnap,' for example."

"Yes, we will try this," said Fahima as Kamaal nodded.

"While you're doing that, we'll scan the articles in Kabul's English-language papers," said Alton. "Maybe something will pop out."

A few hours later, the group reconvened.

"Any luck?" asked Alton.

"Not really," said Fahima. "We saw older articles about kidnappings, but nothing from the last few days."

"Same here." Alton glanced at his watch. It would be midnight in ten minutes. "Well, let's call it a night. We'll need rest for tomorrow. And maybe one of us will have a good idea or two after we've slept on it overnight."

As the group spread blankets on the floor of Kamaal's front parlor, Alton fell into contemplation. He hoped to find Mastana and leave Kabul as soon as possible, mostly for her sake but also for his own. He settled into his makeshift bed with the memory of the imam's recent evening call to prayer lingering in his mind. Like a sinister metronome, the call seemed to mark off the loss of another block of hours to find Mastana. He had to track her down…before time ran out.

CHAPTER 27

At noon the next day, Hanif called Alton. "I will meet you at Kamaal's house, then we will go see about the purchase we discussed yesterday."

"Good. Let me know when we should be ready to leave."

Several hours later, the group motored out of the city limits and headed into the surrounding villages. Hanif drove the lead vehicle, while Kamaal brought up the rear.

During their drive, Mallory glanced down at the floorboards for the third time. "Hanif, are those embroidered cheeseburgers on your socks?"

The man smiled. "Yes. It is a little hobby of mine, collecting unusual socks."

"I'm guessing those must be your most unusual pair."

"It depends on what you think is most unusual. I also have pictures of…let me see…dinosaurs, basketballs, goblins, and fried chicken."

"What does your wife think about all that?"

Hanif snickered. "She is quite forgiving. She knows it is my interest, so she does not object. Speaking of spouses, did I hear you say you and Alton met here in my country?"

"That's right," said Mallory. "We both served at Camp Eggers. Alton was Signal Corps, and I was Quartermasters. So, how did you meet your wife, if you don't mind my asking?"

Hanif laughed again, harder this time. "You know in Afghanistan, arranged marriages are still pretty common. My parents and Ara's—my wife's—decided that we should marry. I called Ara and found she felt the same as I, that we were both much too modern to go along with this plan. Our views were so similar in this matter that we talked about it for quite some time. I thought, 'This is a nice girl,' so I asked her to a restaurant, and we talked about many things until it closed. We went out again the next night. A few months later, we called our parents and had to explain that we were getting married, not because they told us to, but because we decided on our own."

Alton chuckled. "That's a cool story—not something you'd hear at home."

After driving for nearly an hour, they turned onto a dusty road intersecting acres of farmlands.

"What do you know?" said Alton, who rode in the passenger seat of Hanif's aging Mercedes Benz C240 wagon. "A farm that *isn't* growing opium poppies."

"They don't want to draw attention to themselves," said Hanif. "They grow poppies on a different farm."

Five minutes later, Hanif and Kamaal pulled into a farmyard framed by a series of dilapidated buildings. It hardly seemed a likely place to buy weapons, but Alton supposed that was the point.

"I will text them to let them know we are here," said Hanif. Two minutes later, the doors of the ramshackle barn swung open.

"Here we go," said Hanif as he pulled his car inside. Alton swiveled his head to ensure the others followed in Kamaal's Corolla. Once inside the barn, they dismounted from their cars and waited for Hanif's contacts to appear.

A short, stocky man with unusually-long hair trudged toward the waiting customers. A motley assortment of flunkies filed behind him. Most of them carried rifles.

"I'm not crazy about this, Al," said David.

"Me, neither, but let's see how it unfolds. We have to trust that Hanif knows what he's doing."

Hanif spoke with the leader, who identified himself as Jahandar, then turned to Alton. "He wants to scan all of you for electronic bugs."

"Fine," said Alton. It wasn't like this transaction was constructed on a foundation of trust.

Two of Jahandar's subordinates brought out hand-held spectrum analyzers. The high-tech devices seemed oddly out of place among the barn's piles of grain and rusting farm implements. The men finished their scans and nodded to Jahandar, who once again struck up a conversation with Hanif.

"Now he wants to see the money," said the former policeman.

"I have it, but I want to see evidence of goods first."

Jahandar seemed unhappy. He grumbled, then barked a command to a lackey. The man scurried off and reappeared a minute later with a late-model A4 Carbine, the US soldier's standard rifle.

"Do I even want to know where this weapon came from?" asked Alton.

"You don't," said Hanif.

Alton turned to Mallory. "Welcome to Afghanistan, where anything can be bought, as long as the price is right." He removed a handkerchief from his pocket and unfolded it, revealing three Canadian one-ounce, maple-leaf gold coins. He removed one and passed it to the arms dealer, returning the rest to his pocket.

"Ask him what I can get with eleven of these," said Alton, turning to Hanif.

"Eleven!" said Hanif. "Okay, I will ask."

Jahandar tested the coin in his teeth. Apparently satisfied, he cracked the barest trace of a smile, but his features remained tense. He spoke again to Hanif.

"He asks what kind of weapons you are looking for."

"Let's see...If I had my druthers, I'd want knives, pistols, rifles, grenades and hopefully a grenade launcher. And plenty of rounds for all of them."

"Don't forget phosphorous grenades and body armor," chimed in David.

"Right. Those, too."

After a lively conversation, Jahandar gestured them to follow him to another part of the barn. His men swept a few inches of grain off the floor, exposing a trap door. They raised the door and switched on a light. A flight of stairs led into an underground bunker.

"He says what you want is down there," said Hanif.

"Hanif, how much do you trust these guys?" asked Alton. "This feels a lot like a trap."

"I worked with them for almost four years. They were good informants. Of course, I'm not a policeman now."

"I guess it's either go down the hole or leave empty-handed," said Alton. "Okay, I'll go only if some of us can stay in our cars while the others are down there."

"Okay, I will tell Jahandar."

Alton leaned over to his friends. "Kamaal, Fahima, and Mallory, why don't you all stay in Kamaal's car? If this is a trap, you can escape and bring back help."

"By then, it would be too late," said Mallory.

"Maybe, but there's no point in all of us bearing the risk."

Mallory looked stricken. For her sake, Alton added, "I'll be okay. This guy isn't going to win Miss Congeniality, but Hanif says he's trustworthy. If some of us are going to go down there, I'd rather have the rest of you all up here watching our backs."

"Okay," said Mallory, still plainly unhappy.

Alton turned to Hanif. "Tell Jahandar the three of us will go."

With the arms dealer leading the way, David and Hanif joined Alton in a descent into the underground chamber's shadowy depths.

CHAPTER 28

As the trio descended into the subterranean room, Alton glanced around. With stair-mounted lights providing the only illumination, the dark space felt like a tomb. Alton hoped it wouldn't serve as one.

They reached the bottom of the stairs, and Jahandar flipped a switch.

Bright, florescent lights blinked on, revealing a cache of weapons that could have equipped a small army. Shelves and tables lined the earthen walls. Every horizontal surface bristled with arms of every conceivable sort. The armaments were organized by category, beginning with small arms at the room's entrance and working up to M240 machine guns and several varieties of mortars in the last section. Ammunition of all sorts, electronic gear, knives, helmets, and other types of protective clothing occupied a second chamber branching off the rear of the room.

"Holy shit!" said David, glancing around. "It looks

like the center spread for Mercenaries Illustrated."

"No kidding," said Alton. "I didn't think they'd have half the stuff I mentioned up top, but now I'm thinking we'll be good."

Keeping an eye on his hosts, Alton made his way to the first table and began a methodical tour around the perimeter of both rooms, handing desired items to one of Jahandar's men as he progressed.

When finished, Alton examined the pile. "Ask him how much all this will be."

Jahandar spent the next twenty minutes taking a careful inventory on a faded ledger. He retired to a corner with a calculator and spent another ten minutes totaling the bill. He brought the calculator over to Alton and showed him the total on it.

Alton turned to Hanif. "I don't have nearly that much. Is he expecting me to haggle?"

"In this business, yes."

"In that case, tell him I appreciate his hospitality, but I don't have that kind of money. Tell him I offer half."

Jahandar snorted upon hearing Alton's offer.

"He offers a ten percent reduction," said Hanif, "and he will include an extra case of ammo for the A-fours."

"How about a forty-percent cut without the extra rounds? I've already picked out all the ammo I need."

The negotiations continued until Alton and Jahandar

reached an agreement. They shook hands, and for the first time, Jahandar smiled.

Hanif listened to Jahandar. "He invites us inside his house for tea."

Alton didn't want to linger, but he knew ignoring the invitation would represent a serious breach of Afghani etiquette. He needed to stay on good terms with the man in case he needed to resupply later. "Tell him we'd love that." He could always make it quick.

Alton removed the two remaining gold coins from his pocket and passed them directly to the arms dealer. Turning to Hanif, he said, "Tell him I'll provide the rest of the payment once we've loaded our purchases into the cars."

Alton and the others climbed up from the underground chamber, back into the natural light of the barn. He wasn't sure if his relief at that moment derived from finding such an incredible stash of weapons or simply emerging from the cellar alive—perhaps both. The others' relief, especially Mallory's, seemed to mirror his own.

Jahandar barked orders to his men, who began carrying the goods upstairs.

Ten more minutes were needed before the complete set of supplies lay in a pile on the barn floor. Four A4 rifles, all including under-the-barrel M203 grenade launchers, nestled against six Berettas, the pistol of choice in the Afghanistan streets. A case of frag grenades straddled cases of smoke grenades and incendiaries. Also resting nearby were flak vests, helmets, binoculars, face paint, Rucksacks, web gear, six sets of night-vision goggles, and multiple cases of ammo. Knowing that some combat situations called for silent weapons, Alton had also purchased three SIG Sauer P226 handguns with suppressors and six M9s with the intention of using them as knives rather than rifle-mounted bayonets. For stealthy communication, six sets of sub-vocalization microphones and earpieces lay in a neat stack.

"Good grief," said Mallory. "They must have a department store down there."

"You have no idea," replied Alton. "I'll tell you about it on the drive back. Okay, let's load this stuff in our cars, then I'll give Jahandar the final payment. He invited us in for tea, so we'll need to do that before we leave."

They all set about packing the smaller items into the rucksacks. As they handled the weapons, David leaned over to Alton. "Just like being back in the service, huh?"

"A little too much." What was it about being back in Kabul that bothered Alton so much? It wasn't like he hadn't been involved in combat over the past year.

"You all right, Al?" asked David.

"Yeah. Why?"

"You kinda went off to some other place for a second there."

"I'm fine—just feeling a little déjà vu seeing all this stuff, I guess." He continued packing in silence.

Once the smaller items had been stuffed into

Rucksacks, the group loaded all the gear into their cars.

Alton surveyed the portion of the stockpile packed into Hanif's Mercedes. "I'm glad you own a wagon. We needed it."

After sharing the obligatory tea with the arms dealer, the band set out on their return journey to Kabul, hopeful they were one step closer to securing Mastana's release.

CHAPTER 29

The chains that bound Mastana to the floor seemed brand new. Had they not, she might have tried to work them free from the floor anchor. As it stood, she realized struggling against her restraints would only weaken her, rendering her less prepared for any future opportunity for escape that might present itself.

Hearing the now-familiar rattle of a door opening down the hallway, Mastana steeled herself for potential action. Sure enough, the door to her cell swung open, and a man stood silhouetted in the light. Mastana had not seen this captor before.

"Step into the light," he said.

Mastana did as commanded.

"Ghoyee was right. You are pretty."

Not knowing how else to respond, Mastana bowed her head. Better to let her captors perceive her as a subservient, compliant female, an impression that would leave them less prepared for a potential jailbreak in the future.

"You will play an important role in an upcoming ceremony."

The statement sounded foreboding, but Mastana couldn't exactly say why. "What am I to do in the ceremony?"

"You don't need to know that yet."

Mastana's mind raced. To have any chance of escape, she had to learn more about her captor's plans. "How am I to do my best in the ceremony if I don't know how to prepare?"

"My dear, no preparation is necessary," replied the man as he canvassed her body with a single sweep of his eyes. His lips curled in a cruel smile. "You are already…perfect for the role."

CHAPTER 30

Alton and the others regrouped at Kamaal's house.

As they climbed out of the cars and filed inside, Mallory pulled Alton aside. "Is your leg bothering you? It seems like you've been favoring it a little more than usual."

"Yeah, it's weird. Ever since we arrived, it's gotten a little worse. Maybe it's just psychosomatic," he added with his best attempt at a smile, but Mallory's worried look persisted.

"I'm sorry, Sweetie. We can always try the massage later. That usually helps."

"That'd be great." This time Alton's smile was genuine. His wife really had perfected the technique and could be counted on to ease away the worst of the pain in his thigh.

They gathered around Kamaal's table once again.

"Okay," said Alton, "we have plenty of gear to rescue Mastana, but we still don't know where she is. I suggest we keep working on locating her uncle's house."

Everyone nodded.

"If we can discover Dani's cellphone number," continued Alton, "we might be able to track him that way."

Kamaal shook his head. "The Al-Qaeda types have learned their lesson. They use burner phones now—untraceable. Use it once, then throw it away. But that makes me think. What about a computer? If Dani has one, can we use its IP address to track him down?"

"It's a good idea, but I don't think it'll work," said Alton. "Mastana said she sent me her e-mail message from an internet café. Why would she go to the trouble of going there if she had a computer in her house? She could just wait for her uncle to go to sleep or leave, then send the message.

"That does give me an idea, though. Maybe I could use the IP address associated with her e-mail message to track down the internet café itself. It can't be too far from her house, assuming she walked."

"That might work," said Kamaal, "but if you discover the location of the business, then what?"

"I don't know. But we'll be a lot closer to finding her uncle's house than we are now."

CHAPTER 31

That evening, Divband donned his ceremonial black robe. The crimson sash he used to cinch it delineated him from his followers, who wore their robes without embellishments.

He entered the ceremonial chamber. The atmosphere was redolent with incense, and the light from a hundred candles cast grotesque shadows on the walls.

Like a bride before the wedding, Divband never entered the chamber until the ceremony began. As such, he had to hide a thrill of excitement as he passed through the door and took slow, deliberate steps toward the altar. Look at the turnout! Every sacrificial ceremony had seen an increase in the number of attendees. These people represented his most dedicated followers, the ones who would obey orders without question.

He forced himself to maintain the solemn demeanor the grim ritual demanded. There would be plenty of time later to reflect on the rapid growth of the Brotherhood.

Divband executed the ritual as before, beginning with the creation of a circle-and-pentagram pattern on the girl's abdomen, followed by the waiting period, then concluding with the consummation of the girl's marriage to Iblis—a consummation in blood.

Passing through the chamber's doorway, he leaned over to Ghoyee. "Remind the followers of the meal in the Gathering Sanctuary. And once they're seated, give each person one of these." He passed a canvas bag knotted at the top.

Ghoyee loosened the knot and peered inside. "Silver coins, Master?"

"Yes. Our followers must reap a reward from the ceremony. It gives them reason to believe in Iblis' power and generosity."

"Where did you get—?"

"I can't answer too many questions, Ghoyee, but remember how I told you it would be to our advantage to admit professionals to our ranks?

"Yes."

"One of our members is a treasury director."

Ghoyee hoisted the bag to eye level. "So this comes from our government?"

Divband smiled. "Let's just say it started in America and made a brief stop in our national coffers before ending up in this bag."

"I'll do as you say, Master."

"Don't forget one for yourself."

Following the post-ceremonial banquet, Divband returned to his antechamber-turned-office. During times like this, a mixture of thoughts flickered through his mind. Reviving the Brotherhood of Stones had been his brainchild. Would he have garnered so many followers had the fabric of Afghanistan society not been slowly unraveling? He didn't know, but in any case, the point was moot. Desperate people needed a message of empowerment, a message he delivered in spades.

Most of the time, the uninterrupted success of his project helped Divband forget the anger for a while, but in quiet moments like this, the rage returned. The painful memory of his life's inflection point, the day everything changed, materialized unbidden in his mind. On a June day in his eighteenth year, he had sneaked to the house of Veeda, his girlfriend, while her parents were away. He had begun the encounter filled with anticipation and desire, but everything had gone horribly wrong. After finding himself unable to satisfy her, Divband had retreated that night in blinding shame and humiliation, frustrated with his body's insubordination. Worst of all had been his girlfriend's laughter, a mocking sound he still heard in the wind on cold nights.

Perhaps he would never experience the pleasure of carnal knowledge, but then again, neither would the brides of Iblis. Like him, they would retain their purity against their will, carrying it with them to their graves. But unlike him, they would never know the thrill of power he experienced in his role as leader of the Brotherhood of

Stones. People lived and died by his command. Such power might not be quite as satisfying as possessing a fully-functioning body, but it provided a measure of compensation for his sexual deficit, as did the inevitable arousal Divband experienced during the sacrificial ceremonies.

Would the roll call of brides ever cease? Divband doubted it. There could never be too many girls dying for Iblis—or himself.

CHAPTER 32

A few hours ago, Mastana had heard the shuffling of many feet outside her cell door. She believed she had also heard the whimpering of a female voice, followed by gruff recriminations from several men. If true, that implied she wasn't the only prisoner here. Was that why her captor had commanded her on the first day to remain quiet? So the prisoners would remain unaware of each other?

After hearing the other girl, Mastana had maintained a vigil, hoping to learn the location of the girl's cell by listening for her return. As the hours dragged on, though, a sick dread filled Mastana's heart. The prisoner never returned. While Mastana wanted to believe the girl had been freed, every experience during her captivity refuted this conclusion. She promised herself to do everything she could to avoid making that walk herself.

Hours later, the large man, her abductor, opened her cell door once again.

"Don't worry," he said. "I'm just here for the view."

"May I speak?" asked Mastana.

"Depends on what you have to say."

"I was only going to comment that the view from here is also quite pleasing."

The man snorted. "So you think I look good?"

"Indeed. A burly man such as yourself would catch any girl's eye. May I ask your name?"

"I am called Ghoyee."

"Ah—a fitting name. Ghoyee, can you tell me what your master wants with me?"

He dropped his gaze to the floor. "You'll find out soon enough."

"Very well. But can you at least tell me how I was selected? I mean…why me?" asked Mastana, desperate to gather more information about her abductors.

"He only goes for the young, pretty ones—like you," replied Ghoyee with a malevolent grin.

Mastana grabbed onto that fact. "So no older ones, or young ones whose bodies are broken?"

"Absolutely not—Divband knows what he wants."

"And do you, Ghoyee, know what *you* want?"

Ghoyee snapped his head up and fixed her in a penetrating gaze. Mastana produced what she hoped was an alluring smile.

"I think this conversation has ended," he mumbled.

"I hope I will see you again, Ghoyee."

Her captor left, locking the door behind him.

Mastana shuddered at the false attraction she forced herself to show the abhorrent man. But she hadn't been dealt too many favorable cards in this game, and she intended to make the most of any potential opportunities to escape.

CHAPTER 33

The following morning, Fahima busied herself on the phone, reaching out to her Kabul friends for information on recent Al-Qaeda activity. Meanwhile, Alton booted up his laptop and activated its encryption program. He then opened an e-mail tracking program he had personally helped develop as a manager for Kruptos.

"Okay, here's the e-mail message Mastana sent to me during my honeymoon," he said, opening the file. "Let's see what it can tell us."

For a few minutes, the chattering of laptop keys merged with the muted sounds of traffic and pedestrians from the street outside, producing an air of quiet anticipation.

"I think I have it," said Alton. "Yep, here's the IP address of the node that Mastana used to send the message to me. Let me activate a trace back to the source location. Okay…yes, there it is. It's registered to 'Internet Café of Taimany.'"

"That is a Kabul neighborhood," said Kamaal.

"Can you find this particular internet café?" asked Alton.

"I think so," said Kamaal, as he broke out his smartphone. "Let's see…yes, here it is. I have an address. Shall we go there now?"

"Yes," said Alton. "We can give Hanif a call on the way, but I don't see any reason to wait for him even if he can't make it."

They left Kamaal's house and proceeded directly to the internet café. Given the late-morning hour, Hanif could not yet join them, but he promised to do so when his workday ended.

Alton led the group through the doors of the business. The dim lighting and background hum of clattering keyboards gave the room an otherworldly feel.

They approached the cashier's cage. A young girl chewed a wad of gum and gazed at them with a bored expression.

After verifying the date/time stamp on Mastana's message, Alton turned to Kamaal. "Ask her who was working here at three-seventeen in the afternoon on March twenty-fifth."

Kamaal did as instructed, carrying out a conversation in Pashto. At first, the girl seemed unable—or at least unwilling—to supply the information. Kamaal continued to press his case, and at last, with a resigned sigh, the worker opened a week-at-a-glance calendar and folded it back a page. She uttered a short sentence.

"She says she was working here at that time."

"Good," said Alton. "Do you have a photo of Mastana from this week?"

"Yes," replied Kamaal with an embarrassed laugh. "She insisted on taking photos of the two of us every evening during our dinner."

"Awesome. Bring up one of her pictures and show it to the worker. Ask her if she recognizes Mastana."

The cashier studied the picture and nodded.

Kamaal and the worker exchanged a few sentences in Pashto. "She says she does not know Mastana well, but they go to the same school."

"Ask her if she knows where Mastana lives," said Mallory.

After another exchange, Kamaal nodded to the girl and stepped away from the cage. "She says to take a right out of here, then turn right at the fourth intersection. She does not know which house Mastana lives in, but the bus drops her off at the end of that street every school day—until last week."

"Now we're getting somewhere," said Alton. "Let's take the car for a recon trip. We don't want to be spotted, so let's drive past Mastana's road on the first run to see what we're dealing with."

They arrived at the indicated street and glided by. Kamaal turned into a gas station several blocks down the road.

"We're in luck," said Mallory. "Mastana's street is only a block long, then it ends in a T-intersection."

"Let's drive down the street itself and see if we spot anything that suggests Mastana's house," said David.

"Kamaal," said Mallory, "Did Mastana ever describe her house? What it looked like?"

"No, not that I remember."

"What about her neighbors? Did she ever talk about them?"

Kamaal squinted his eyes in concentration, reducing them for the moment to a more normal size. "You know, she didn't mention any *human* neighbors, but she did tell me about a yellow dog that lived next door. She said she'd look over the wall and call to it."

"Fantastic," said Mallory. "We find that yard, and we've narrowed Mastana's house down to two possibilities: one of the houses on either side of it."

David rubbed his chin. "If we're driving, we're not going to have much time to look. I'm a little worried about missing something."

"That's a good point," said Alton. "When we go up Mastana's street, do you think we can use our phones to take photos without being spotted?"

"Yeah," replied David. "The sun is still pretty bright. With its reflection off the window glass, people looking at us won't be able to see inside the car very well."

"Good," said Alton. "I'll take pictures from the right side. Mallory, why don't you take the left?"

Mallory nodded.

"I will write down the street name and house numbers," said Fahima. "We might need that information, too."

"Okay, let's go find that dog," said Alton. "We do that, and we're one step closer to finding Mastana's uncle."

Pulling onto the block, Kamaal motored along slowly, allowing his passengers time to snap pictures and take notes. Doubling back, he travelled up the street and turned onto the main thoroughfare.

"Did anyone see the dog or anything else important?" asked Alton.

A chorus of negatives formed the answer.

"Okay," said Mallory. "Let's head back to Kamaal's place. If we stay here too long, we could be spotted. The last thing we want to do is raise any suspicions."

As they left the area, Alton spoke up. "I counted twelve houses. Even though we don't know where the dog lives, maybe we can use the process of elimination to help us figure out which house belongs to Mastana's Uncle Dani."

"Sounds good," said David, "but exactly what do you mean?"

"Well, any house that *does* have internet access

probably isn't Dani's. We've already established the fact that Mastana's family didn't have a computer at home, so why would they pay for an internet service they didn't need?"

"I don't think many houses in that neighborhood will have internet," said Kamaal, "but is worth checking."

Back in the interpreter's house, Alton worked to crack the security of the internet service provider for Mastana's former neighborhood. As he did so, the others scanned the photos of Mastana's neighborhood for signs of the yellow dog but could find none.

At the end of nearly two hours, Alton stood and stretched his back. "Okay, got it. Kamaal, I'll need your help again. KI, the ISP for that neighborhood, uses security software written in English, so I was able to crack their firewall. However, the company's databases themselves are in Pashto. Do you think you can look up the addresses Fahima wrote down and see which ones have internet?"

Kamaal looked a little worried. "I will try."

While Kamaal worked, Alton studied the photos they had taken earlier, noting the identifying characteristics of each house.

After another two-hour interval, Kamaal looked up with a twinkle in his eye. "I am done. Five of the houses have internet. Is a little more than I would have guessed."

Everyone gathered around the laptop computer. Alton removed a spiral notebook from his backpack and turned it to a blank page. He sketched a bird's-eye picture of Dani's neighborhood. "Each of these twelve squares represents a house, six on each side of the street. Fahima, can you label the houses using the addresses you recorded earlier?"

Referring to her notes, Fahima finished the task in the space of a minute.

"Kamaal, can you put an X through each house that has internet service?"

Swiveling his head between the computer monitor and Alton's notebook, the interpreter eliminated five houses.

"Okay, that narrows the list down to these seven," said Alton.

"But now what?" asked David. "We still don't know which one is the right one."

Alton glanced at his watch. "It's getting close to five o'clock. Why don't I call Hanif and see if he has any ideas?"

Alton rang the ex-policeman and brought him up to speed.

"I have to admit," said Hanif, "I am a little surprised you were able to find out this much information already. But is good. We are close to finding Dani's house. It is too bad you didn't spot the dog, but I have a suggestion to make regarding that."

"Yes?"

"Why don't I drive down there myself when I leave

work? You have already been on that street once today, and we don't want to raise any alarm if someone notices the same strange car driving through their neighborhood again."

"Okay—that's a good idea. I'll put Fahima on the phone to guide you to the street. It's a little out of the way. Will you be able to come over here to Kamaal's house after your recon?"

"Yes, I will be there as soon as I can, probably in an hour or two."

Later, Alton looked up as he heard the squeal of tired brakes outside the window. He stood up and met Hanif at the door. "So, did you find the dog?"

"Yes, I saw a big, yellow one."

Alton produced the map he had constructed earlier. "Which house has it?"

Hanif studied the map. "Is here—the fourth house on the right."

"Dang."

"What's wrong?" asked Mallory. "Oh, wait. I see it."

"Want to enlighten the rest of us?" asked David.

"The house with the dog has internet, but neither of the houses on either side do. That means Dani's place could be either one of the adjacent houses." He brought up the photos from their earlier reconnaissance trip. "It could be either this one, the house with the hammock out front, or this other one, the house with the junker in the driveway."

"So the 'dang' was about the fact that we still haven't narrowed it down to just one house?"

"Exactly," said Alton, "but it doesn't have to stay two houses for long."

"What do you have in mind?" asked Mallory.

"We still have a few hours of daylight. Let's stake out both houses. We have enough people to do that."

"I like the idea," said David, "but how would we know Dani if we saw him?"

"I was just getting to that," said Alton. "Not long after Mastana went home from Camp Eggers' hospital, she sent me a picture of her family in an e-mail, including her uncle. Let me blow up that photo and crop it to show just Dani's face. It's a little old—four years, more or less—but we'll just have to hope it's good enough."

"And if we see him, then what?" pressed David.

"We adjust to the tactical requirements of the situation."

"What does that mean?" asked Fahima.

David grinned. "It means we improvise, based on what we see when we get there."

"It also means we bring some of the equipment we bought this morning," said Mallory. "If we do find a nest of Al-Qaeda insurgents, we'll want to be ready for anything."

CHAPTER 34

The clang of the cell door jarred Mastana awake. She rubbed a hand across bleary eyes, then opened them to the perpetual twilight of her cell.

Between the anxiety attendant with her captivity and the discomfort of the rough stone floor, getting a restful sleep had proved to be impossible. Instead, she alternated between bouts of restless slumber and groggy consciousness.

She looked to see who had opened the door.

"Hello, young one," said Divband.

"Hello, my Lord," she replied, opting for the title she judged least likely to provoke anger. She prayed he would not send for the guards to take her down the hall. For some reason, she feared that outcome most of all.

Divband produced a menacing smile. "Indeed you are correct. I am master of this place…and you."

He approached Mastana. Grabbing her chin with his hand, he turned her from side to side as if inspecting livestock.

"Good," he muttered, nodding.

"You are pleased, my Lord?"

"Yes, so far. You have not…been with a man, have you?"

"No." Mastana dared not lie about a fact so easy to confirm.

"Good. You are flawless in body and spirit. Perfect for the upcoming ceremony."

An alarm sounded in Mastana's mind. Was this ceremony the same one to which the other prisoner had been led? The prisoner who had not returned? Had Mastana passed a test that marked her for an ominous fate?

"My Lord, I do not want to upset you, but I think I should tell you about an…imperfection."

"What do you mean?"

"Four years ago, I was in a marketplace in Kabul when Al-Qaeda exploded a bomb. I was injured—badly. I still bear many scars on my left side. I am afraid I may not possess the perfection you seek."

"You lie."

"I would never lie to you, especially about something so easily verified. Would you like me to show you the scars?" She moved a hand to her shirt but awaited his command before proceeding. The scars had healed over time and were now quite minor, but at least she had something to show if necessary.

"Yes…wait, no. I can see you are telling the truth." Divband scowled at the revelation and mumbled to himself.

Mastana read conflicted emotions on the man's countenance. Had she bought herself more time or condemned herself?

"But your face is untouched?" asked Divband.

"That is correct, my Lord."

"I think that will be sufficient. My followers will not know about the imperfections."

Mastana bowed her head.

Muttering again, Divband exited the room and slammed the door shut.

"Lock this!" he commanded a guard.

Mastana listened to the receding footsteps. She still could not decide if revealing the presence of her scars had helped her odds of survival. Perhaps she had made things worse. All her instincts, though, told her that letting events play out by themselves would lead to disaster. Better to die fighting for her life than passively await her fate.

CHAPTER 35

"Okay," said Alton, addressing the group gathered around Kamaal's table. "Let's divide into two teams, one for each target house. Alpha Team will cover the house with the hammock out front. Bravo Team will cover the house with the junker in the driveway. In case someone outside either house starts talking, we'll need to have at least one Pashto speaker on each team to translate. Fahima, why don't you and David form Alpha Team? Hanif and Kamaal, you can form Bravo Team. I'll go to Alpha and Mallory can go to Bravo."

Fahima glanced at Mallory's worried expression. "Alton, I think Mallory would like to be on the same team as you."

"But then we'd have an unequal number—"

"Is okay," interjected Hanif. "We will all be near each other, right?"

"That's true," replied Alton. "In that case, Mallory

and I will both be on Alpha Team. I'd prefer that, to be honest.

"Let's talk about our tactical objective. Our primary goal tonight is identifying Dani's house. Once we've done that, we'll scout the layout of the yard and house, if we have an opportunity. We'll want to collect that information and take at least a little time to plan next steps before we try a raid on the house. We'll only have one chance to use the element of surprise, and if we blow it, they could kill Mastana before we reach her—if she's actually in the house. Are we all cool with that approach?"

Everyone nodded.

"Good. Does everyone remember the side street we saw yesterday, the one west of the T-intersection?"

Again, everyone nodded.

"Let's park both cars behind the old warehouse on the corner of that street. The warehouse is only fifty yards or so from the hammock house but will still fully conceal the cars.

"After we park, we'll advance on foot to our scouting locations—teams of two, five minutes apart. There's hardly any traffic where we'll be parking, so we shouldn't be observed. Alpha team will set up a recon position in the empty lot on the other side of the T-intersection, just across the street from the hammock house. Bravo team will set up in the alley across the street from the junker house.

"We should try to blend a little more than we do now.

Kamaal, do you have any clothing we could borrow? It might help make us look a little less conspicuous."

"Yes. I have a couple of jackets. I hope they are big enough. I don't have anything for the ladies to wear, though."

"I saw a burka and sweater in Mastana's duffle bag," said Mallory. "Fahima and I can use those."

"Good," said Alton. "It's not going to win us covert ops team of the year, but it's better than nothing.

"Now for equipment. Everyone take earphones, mikes, and binoculars. There's no telling how late we'll be there, so let's also take the night-vision goggles."

"We should bring weapons, too," said David. "I know we're trying to stay under the radar, but there's still a chance we'll engage with Al-Qaeda while we're there."

"Good point," said Alton. "The SIG Sauers have suppressors. Let's bring those."

"We should also bring the A-fours, just in case all hell breaks loose," said Mallory.

"Also a good point," said Alton. "Let's bring both. We'll need to leave the A-fours in the car, though. We can't exactly walk down the street carrying assault rifles. We'll bring the SIG Sauers with us. Hanif, why don't you take a Sauer for Bravo Team, and I'll take another for Alpha Team?"

"Yes, I will take one."

Alton rubbed his chin. "Since there's six of us, we'll

need to take two cars. Hanif and Kamaal, are you all good for driving?"

They replied in the affirmative.

"All right, let's gather the equipment and roll in five."

Thirty minutes later, they arrived at the agreed-upon side street, half a block away from their stakeout locations. Alton called the other car. "We're going stealthy as of now. Turn off your cell phones and turn on your mikes and headsets. Everyone test your mike to make sure the others can hear you."

After everyone had completed the equipment check, Hanif called Alton. "Kamaal and I will go first."

"Okay. Two more will deploy in five minutes. David and Fahima, why don't you all go next? That way, we'll get our Pashto speaker in place right away."

"Okay," said Fahima, whose face was crossed with worry. Alton couldn't blame her. While this mission was about reconnaissance, not combat, it still carried some risk. Her background was less suited for this type of mission than that of the others, all former soldiers or law enforcement.

"You'll be fine," said Alton. "You have David with you. If you encounter Al-Qaeda members, he can always incapacitate them with one of his jokes."

"Nice," said David with a roll of his eyes. "Are you ready, Rose of Kabul?"

Fahima giggled. "Yes."

Within fifteen minutes, all six of the team members had deployed to their designated spots. Alton and the rest of Alpha team crouched behind a thick clump of dying blackberry bushes. Peering through the thistles, they had a nice line of sight to the hammock house yet remained well-concealed. Alton had to look for a minute before he spotted Hanif and Kamaal ensconced behind a pile of garbage in the alley, keeping a close eye on the junker house.

Both teams had maintained a vigilant but uneventful watch for nearly an hour when a Mazda Demio pulled up to the curb in front of Alpha Team's hammock house.

"Heads up," murmured Alton into his sub-vocalization mike.

Exiting the car was a man wearing a white turban and traditional khet partug clothing, a knee-length linen shirt combined with loose-fitting, pleated pants. The man looked to be about the right age to be Mastana's uncle.

Alton raised a pair of binoculars to his face, but the man circled around the car, turning his back to Alpha Team.

"C'mon," whispered Alton. "Turn around."

The man turned back to open the door to the car's back seat.

"Damn. I think that's him, guys!" said Alton. He

brought up Dani's photo on his cell phone. "Affirmative. The photo is a match."

As Alton spoke, Dani bent down into the back seat and began pulling out an object. Fahima gasped as the item came into view.

Dani lugged a rolled-up blanket with a person inside, someone of a small stature. The blanket had been swathed with silver duct tape, trapping the unlucky person inside. Dani attempted to throw the blanket over his shoulder but was confounded by the prisoner's constant struggling.

"Al, that could be her—Mastana!" hissed David. "Let's go get her."

Alton hesitated. "What if we've been spotted? Al-Qaeda could be trying to lure us into the open. It seems too lucky that we'd stumble across Mastana the first hour we're here."

"Maybe, but I doubt it. Let's assume we *haven't* been spotted. What if there's more of Dani's Al-Qaeda buddies in there? Let's stop him before he goes inside. At least out here we have him outnumbered. We can't let this chance slip us by. There's no telling who or what we'll encounter if we let him escape into the house."

Dani finally hoisted his load onto his shoulder and turned towards the house, staggering a bit under the weight.

Alton activated his mike. "Hanif and Kamaal, come quick. Dani is here. He's carrying a prisoner, and we're moving in!"

CHAPTER 36

"Let's move!" said Alton. "Fahima, you stay here. Mallory and David, advance toward Dani. I'll cover." Alton withdrew the SIG Sauer from his waistband.

Dry weeds covering the ground in the lot betrayed their movement.

Dani spun. His eyes grew wide as he saw Mallory and David running towards him. He scurried back to his car and threw his prisoner into the backseat. Withdrawing a pistol from his jacket's pocket, he crouched behind the car and lined up a shot in Mallory's direction.

Alton could see Dani through the windows of the car, but he couldn't risk shooting through them. The shot might ricochet and hit Mastana instead. Rather than take that chance, Alton shot the engine compartment.

Dani jumped in surprise as the bullet impacted the Mazda with a resounding thud. He peered over the car, trying to figure out from where the shot had originated.

At the sound of the Alton's shot, Mallory peeled off to the left to take cover behind a telephone pole, while David threw himself behind a parked car.

Alton took another shot at Dani's head but missed, instead burying the slug in the wooden frame of the house behind Dani. Crouching down, the terrorist swiveled and stared at the impact spot.

Alton fired again. Another miss, but a least he was rattling the man. Maybe Dani would run off and leave Mastana behind.

Dani spun back in Mallory's direction and fired. He turned towards David and fired again. Luckily, both shots missed, but the terrorist used the opportunity to enter his car through the passenger door. He crawled to the driver's side and roared the engine to life. Alton lined up his pistol in the direction of the rear tire, but the car lurched forward just as he squeezed off the shot, causing the round to bounce harmlessly off the road.

Dani squealed the tires on his Mazda as he careened down the street. He spun the car around the T-intersection and revved the engine as he accelerated along the straightaway.

Hanif and Kamaal arrived just in time to hear Alton yell, "Back to the cars!"

They bolted for their vehicles. Alton's limp caused him to fall behind, so he shouted, "Hanif, pick me up when you head back over here."

"I will," replied Hanif in full sprint.

The others disappeared, turning into the warehouse parking lot where they had parked their cars. Moments later, Kamaal—traveling solo—roared past in his Corolla, giving chase to the underpowered Mazda.

Alton halted at the side of the road, gasping for breath as his heartbeat pounded out a steady rhythm in his damaged leg. Seconds later, Hanif pulled alongside. Alton jumped into the car, which never came to a complete stop. "Go! Don't lose him!"

The old Merc C200 powered up, shrinking the distance to Dani's car. The sidewalk soon became a blur. For the first time, Alton felt grateful for the Afghani police's indifference toward civilian crimes. If potential kidnappings didn't capture their attention, what were the odds they would care about a few speeding cars?

Dani made a series of turns in an unsuccessful attempt to shake his pursuers.

"He's only turning to the right," said Fahima. "If he keeps doing that, we can turn onto one of these alleys and come out in front of him."

"Good thinking, Babe," said David.

Dani turned a corner, and the Merc squealed as it followed him around the hard turn. Hanif punched through the gears, reaching top speed in seconds.

"Kamaal, can you hear me?" Alton asked into his microphone.

"Yes, there's some static, but I hear you."

"Okay. Stay on Dani. We're going to turn onto another street to try to get ahead of him."

"I will try." The interpreter sounded nervous. Alton was impressed with the man's resolve. Kamaal wasn't letting fear get in the way of pursuing the terrorist.

As they sped down the thoroughfare, Fahima eyed the side streets. "There! Turn onto that one!"

Hanif jammed on the brakes, releasing them just as he skidded around the corner. He punched the Mercedes into low gear and accelerated out of the curve.

Fahima chattered to Hanif in Pashto and pointed. Hanif stopped the car next to a brick building, leaving only its hood visible to the four-lane road's crossing traffic.

"This will be a good ambush point," said Hanif.

Alton snatched his cell phone from his pocket, praying Kamaal had likewise activated his. He hit the speed-dial number and silently rejoiced when the interpreter answered his phone. "Kamaal, we're concealed behind a building. Do you see a shop with a picture of a bed frame on it?"

"No, I don't see—wait, yes, I see it. Dani is almost there."

"Back off. We're right behind that building, and we're going to ram him."

"But what if you hurt Mastana?" asked Fahima.

"It's a risk we have to take. What will happen to her if

we don't stop Dani?"

Nobody spoke.

Alton peered down the street. "Here he comes. Ready? Gun it!"

Revving the motor, Hanif shot into the road but still nearly missed the speeding Mazda. He caught the rear bumper just enough to send the terrorist's car into a 360-degree skid before it smashed into a streetlight in the yard-wide median.

Wisps of steam began to rise from underneath the Mazda's hood. Hanif pulled his car up to the wreck. All its occupants piled out and raced for the Mazda.

Dani moaned as blood dripped from a gash in his forehead.

"Leave him," said Alton. "Let's free Mastana and get out of here before his Al-Qaeda cronies show up."

The rescuers pulled the prisoner, still tightly wrapped in a blanket, from the car and carried the bundle to the curb, out of the way of Kabul's rather psychotic traffic.

Kamaal's car pulled up beside them while eager hands ripped away the packing tape that had secured the prisoner in a woven jail. Alton tore away the last piece of tape and unwrapped the blanket as fast as he could, nearly sending the occupant into a spin.

Alton removed the last fold of blanket, and the group fell into silence. Inside was a teenage girl—terrified, bewildered, shocked…but not Mastana.

"Damn!" said Alton. "Let's go back to Dani! He may be keeping Mastana somewhere else."

They raced back to the steaming car.

Alton turned to Kamaal. "Ask him where Mastana is."

As the interpreter spoke, Alton withdrew the SIG Sauer from his waistband and jammed the silencer into Dani's stomach. The terrorist's eyes grew wide, and he produced a rapid-fire reply.

"He says he doesn't know where that little…well, he called her some bad names," said Kamaal. "He says he asked the students and teachers at her school in case she told someone there, but nobody knows where she is."

"Who's the girl in his car just now?"

After another exchange with Dani, Kamaal summarized the answer. "He says the girl is the daughter of a friend. He says the girl's father was angry with her for misbehaving and had banished her to another house for a few days. He didn't tell me, but I think his friend is Al-Qaeda. If so, then maybe they were going to use this girl to attack Camp Eggers."

"Makes sense, now that Mastana's gone," said Alton. "And that would confirm Dani's contention that he doesn't know where Mastana is. Otherwise, he'd still use her. He'd have no need for the new girl."

"I think you are right," said Hanif. "We should take this new girl with us. She's not safe here."

Mallory turned to Alton. "That's well and good, but if Dani didn't kidnap Mastana, who did?"

CHAPTER 37

The clang of a distant door roused Mastana from an exhausted slumber. She wondered how long she had been asleep. With no change in her cell's light conditions, she had no way of tracking the passage of time. How long had she been imprisoned here? Two days? Four?

Prior to sleeping, she hadn't heard or seen anyone for hours. At least the interval had given her time to devise an escape plan.

The door down the hall from her cell closed, stirring up a growing panic in Mastana's breast.

Her cell door swung open, and Ghoyee entered. "You said you'd like to see me again."

Mastana released a quiet breath of relief. "Indeed I did. I am glad you have returned."

"Why is that?" The man looked skeptical.

"I'm surprised you'd need to ask, a big man like you. I imagine you have a lot of lady friends?"

Ghoyee shrugged and tried to look modest. "Here and there."

Mastana had recognized her captor's lustful stares. "But none quite like me?"

"What do you mean?"

"None as young as me?"

"No, none."

"And wouldn't you like to have me with you all the time?"

Ghoyee licked his lips and ran his gaze down the length of her body. "Sure, I'd like that. But there's a little problem. You're in here."

"Not if you took me out. I could stay in your home with you, be with you all the time, and…show my gratitude."

Ghoyee laughed. "Nice try, little one. You're a beauty. I'll give you that. But you can't give me what Divband does."

"What is that?"

"A nice, fat paycheck. And freedom to spend time alone with the girls like you—not to do everything I'd like, but there are other women for that anyway. Maybe they aren't as…fresh…as you, but they'll do."

Ghoyee left the room. Mastana could sense the man's temptation, but something—fear of his master?—had restrained him from acting on his lustful impulses.

Mastana pondered her next step. She had little time for contemplation, however, for Divband entered her cell a quarter-hour later.

"You're an enterprising young woman, aren't you? Trying to seduce away my right-hand man."

Mastana attempted to still her heart. Assuming as disinterested a countenance as possible, she said, "Well, you know he is not the man I really wanted anyway."

"Oh, really? And who *did* you want?"

"The man in charge, of course. There's nothing more attractive than a man with power, who knows how to command the respect of others."

"Someone like me? You find me attractive?"

"Indeed I do, my Lord."

"So if I released you, you would stay?"

Mastana knew she couldn't appear too desperate. "If you promise not to hurt me."

"And why wouldn't you run away?"

"Did Ghoyee tell you where I was living before he brought me here? A tiny house with a man I barely knew."

Divband cocked his head. "Why were you with this

man, if you barely know him?"

Mastana couldn't think of a lie, so she divulged as much of the truth as necessary to convey a believable story. "I used to live with my Uncle, who is a member of Al-Qaeda. My mother is sick—very sick. She will be dead in a matter of days if she is not already." She paused a moment to find her voice. "My uncle commanded me to wear an explosive vest into the Americans' military base in Kabul last Saturday."

"And you did not want to do this?"

"No, I did not, so I ran away."

"And why did you go to this man's house, if you barely knew him?"

"When I was injured from the bomb blast, the one I told you about before, this man worked as an interpreter in the American hospital where I recovered. I do not know him well, but I have no other family. He was the only person I could think of." She didn't mention the more recent interactions with her American friends. There was no reason to divulge everything. Instead, she tried to remember some of the lewd comments the boys in her old neighborhood sometimes called in her direction. "As you can see, I need a place to stay, with a real man, someone who is not a friend of the Americans. And I think you would like to have a girl who is eager to please you."

Divband's face hardened. "I do not think you would like the things you would have to do to please me. My proclivities are not the same as most."

"My Lord, there are many tastes in the world, are there not? Some people like grapes, while others prefer dates. There is no right or wrong. There is only the grape and the date. Perhaps my tastes will be the same as yours."

Divband studied her face. "What is your name?"

"Mastana, my Lord."

For a moment, he did not speak. "I will think of these things you have said. You are a little lynx, aren't you?"

"I think we are interested in the same thing—a person who can make us happy, no?"

Without speaking again, Divband closed the cell door and locked it, then meandered down the hallway, as if deep in thought.

Mastana could only hope the ideas she had planted in the soil of his mind would take root. She hated the false innuendos she had planted there but felt a growing certainty that remaining in her cell represented a pathway to death. She had to escape this prison before her time ran out.

CHAPTER 38

"Let's get out of here," said Alton, surveying the wreck of Dani's car. "We'll discuss Mastana later."

He and the rest of the band left the median, running back to their cars and the young kidnapping victim, who seemed to be in shock.

"I don't know for sure what Dani's true plan was for this girl, but it obviously wasn't anything good," said Alton. "I agree with Hanif. We should take her with us."

Fearing the arrival of other Al-Qaeda members, they beat a hasty retreat back to Kamaal's house. The interpreter prepared green tea for the girl, while Mallory wrapped her in a warm sweater from her luggage.

Once the girl seemed reasonably collected, Fahima gently questioned her, while Kamaal provided a running translation of the dialogue for the Americans.

"What is your name, my dear?" asked Fahima.

"I am called Nafisa."

"Nafisa, can you tell us how you came to be with that man—Dani?"

The girl drew in a deep breath, exhaled, and spoke with a trembling voice. "My father is Al-Qaeda, like Dani. I heard them talking a few nights ago. I heard Dani say that his niece was supposed to carry out a jihad against the Americans, but she had disappeared. Dani could not find her, so he asked my father for help.

"Today, my father approached me and said he had a 'great mission' for me, a great jihad. He told me an explosive vest, one to be worn under the clothes, had been prepared for Mastana, but she wasn't available to wear it. He told me *I* should be the one to wear it instead. I…did not want to do this thing. My father and I got into a great fight. He commanded me to wear the bomb, and I refused. He held a wet handkerchief over my mouth, and I became dizzy. After that, he grabbed a blanket from his room and called Dani. Together, they imprisoned me in the blanket and put me in Dani's car."

"But if you said no, why was Dani taking you away?" asked Fahima.

"My father yelled that Dani would 'make me understand my duty.' I suppose he thought I would eventually agree to carry out their jihad if I was away from my home and family—and if Dani continued to drug me with the medicine in the handkerchief."

"I see. I don't think you should go back to your father. Do you have someone else you can stay with?"

"Yes, my grandmother lives in Jalalabad, east of here. She does not like Al-Qaeda, either. She will let me live with her, I'm sure."

"What if your father comes looking for you?" asked Fahima.

"My grandmother will not tell him I am with her, especially after I tell her what happened today. She will protect me from my father."

Fahima's shoulders relaxed. "I'm glad you have a place to go."

"Nafisa, can you give me your grandmother's phone number?" asked Hanif. "I will call her to arrange your transport to her house."

"Yes," said the girl, replying with the number.

"Ask her if she knows Mastana," prompted Alton.

Fahima passed along the question.

"No," said Nafisa, "I know the name, but I do not know the girl. But I can tell you that Dani was very angry because he couldn't find her. As I said, he told my father that Mastana ran away."

"I see," said Fahima. She eyed the teen. "You look tired. Would you like to rest for a little while?"

"Yes, that would be nice. Thank you."

Avoiding the undisturbed crime evidence in Mastana's former bedroom, Fahima led Nafisa to Kamaal's room and returned moments later. "She is exhausted, poor thing. Her eyes closed before I even left the room."

"I'm glad we extracted Nafisa from the clutches of Al-Qaeda," said Alton, "but regarding Mastana, we're truly back to square one. How do we find out who really *did* kidnap her?"

Mallory looked thoughtful. "You know, we've been thinking about this all wrong, believing Dani and Al-Qaeda took Mastana. Now that we're faced with a 'normal' kidnapping, we should consider a normal kidnapper's profile."

Hanif nodded.

"What do you mean?" asked Kamaal.

"Many kidnappers act serially, meaning they abduct multiple victims. Remember how we saw earlier kidnappings when we did a search in the local papers? I wonder if Mastana's is connected to those."

"Makes sense," said Alton, "although the newspaper articles were pretty sparse. I think we'd have to have access to police records to have enough evidence to establish a true pattern." He turned to Hanif. "Do you think Poya will let us look through his case files?"

"I don't know," said Hanif. "He is not crazy about Americans, so I don't think so."

"What if you asked on our behalf?"

"Ha! That would be worse. He would tell me to put my uniform back on if I want that kind of information."

"Okay, so are police records kept in paper files or

computers?" asked Alton.

"A little bit of both. Minor crimes are recorded in paper files. Violent crimes, including kidnapping, would be stored in the computers."

Mallory grinned. "I see where you're going with this."

Alton acknowledged the statement with a nod and turned back to Hanif. "Do you still have access to those police record-keeping systems?"

"I doubt it, but I can try. But wait…if I try to log on to those systems, won't they know it was me based on my user name? Poya would love to have a reason to arrest me, and accessing restricted police records would give him the perfect excuse."

"Good point. We'll just have to look for a back door."

Hanif looked doubtful. He stood and began to pace the room. "You want to break into the police's computer systems? How are you gonna do that?"

"That's something of a specialty of mine. I'm a cryptologist, so this is right up my alley."

"I'm not crazy about breaking into police systems," said Hanif, "but I don't know how else we can get that information. The more I think about it, the more I'm convinced Poya won't let us access the records. When I worked for him, he was very by-the-book about those sorts of things."

Alton placed his laptop on the table and booted it up.

"This shouldn't take too long. You give me the URL, and I can take it from there. I don't even need to know your user name. In the meantime, there's a low-tech approach we can use to see if any new kidnappings occur—monitor the police scanner."

"I still have one of those back at my house," said Hanif. "I can go get it while you are working."

Less than an hour later, Hanif returned with the scanner, which Kamaal set up on the kitchen counter.

Alton called Hanif over to the dining-room table. "Any word from Nafisa's grandmother?"

"Yes. I spoke with her on the way to my house. She will be here in a couple of hours to pick up Nafisa."

"Good."

"How is your work coming along?" asked the former policeman.

"I just got into the police systems a few minutes ago. Of course, everything's in Pashto. I could break out the kind of translation software I used when I was stationed here with the Army, but it'd probably be quicker for you to review the records yourself and tell us what you see. Plus, you know how the records are organized, right?"

"Yes. Give me a few minutes to look over the kidnapping files."

A quarter-hour later, Hanif called the others around. "Over the last three months, nine teenage girls were reported missing. Five of their bodies were eventually found in the desert north of Kabul."

"Do the records indicate the kidnappers' MO?" asked Mallory.

"A little. It says all the victims were all abducted while alone, usually in or around their house. All the kidnappings occurred in the afternoon or evening, never in the morning. In three of the houses, police found rags with traces of Ketamine on them. Ketamine is a liquid used for anesthesia, so they think it was used to subdue the victims. One more thing...I saw the girls' photos. They were all quite pretty."

Mallory looked at Alton with a grim expression. "It sounds like regular old perve kidnappings, all right. And it seems to me that the same guy did all the kidnappings."

"I agree," said Hanif.

"I recommend we look for more patterns in the kidnapper's behavior," said Mallory, "ones that could help us narrow down the search."

"That sounds reasonable," said Alton. "Did you have anything particular in mind?"

Mallory turned to Hanif. "Have the police brought in any suspects or made any convictions?"

"No, none. But they did have a surveillance video from an ATM machine. One of the girls was kidnapped while using it. It was located just a block down from her house."

"Let's watch that video," said Mallory. "Maybe something will pop out."

They gathered around Alton's computer. Hanif started the security video. They watched in somber silence as the silent, grainy video showed a pretty teen approach the machine and insert a card. As she entered information into the screen, a large man wearing a black mask and robe approached from behind. He grabbed her with one beefy arm and held a rag over the girl's face with the other. The teen was still struggling when the assailant pulled her out of the frame.

Everyone remained silent for a moment when the video ended.

"This was the second teen kidnapped," said Hanif. "Her body was discovered at the foot of the mountains a month and a half ago."

"We're not gonna let that happen to Mastana," muttered David. "Not if I have anything to do with it."

"You got that right," said Alton. "Is there any useful information we can glean from that video?"

"We know the kidnapper is a huge guy," replied Mallory. "Did you see the size of him?"

"That's true. Anything else?"

Hanif rubbed his chin. "The man is wearing a mask and a plain black robe. I don't think there is much we can do to identify him. But did you see him put the cloth over her mouth and nose? I think the video confirms that he used a substance—probably Ketamine—to subdue the girls."

"How many places in Kabul sell Ketamine?" asked Alton. "We could ask them if they have any repeat customers that resemble the Incredible Hulk."

"I have no idea where to buy Ketamine," said Hanif, "but is good idea to check like you say."

"Okay, I'll do a search on likely businesses tonight," said Alton, "and we can visit them tomorrow morning."

"That might be difficult," said Fahima. "A lot of supplies in Kabul are sold on the black market. I used to buy some of my liquor at Gandamak's Lodge that way."

"Really?" said David. "You never told me that."

Alton smiled. "All right, folks, let's stay focused. Hanif, did the police records include crime scene photos?"

"They did, but I haven't reviewed them yet. I was anxious to share the case summaries first."

"Why don't we review the photos next, then? Let's take them in chronological order."

"The police never found the body of the first girl," said Hanif. "I will start with the second girl, the one in the ATM video."

A collective gasp arose from those gathered as Hanif brought up the first photo.

"Holy shit!" said David. "What did he do to her?"

The teen had been eviscerated, her torso a tangle of shredded skin and intestines. Alton had instinctively turned his head away, but he turned it back now. The grisly scene sent a torrent of memories from the day of the IED explosion in his mobcom van. Some of those under his command had undergone a similar level of destruction. As he stared at the photo, Alton could feel his chest constricting, making breathing difficult. God, the carnage...

"Sweetie?" asked Mallory, laying a hand on his back and breaking his reverie. Her look communicated a mixture of love and concern.

Alton collected his thoughts. "Hanif, let's keep going."

The ex-policeman scrolled through the photos, lingering on each long enough for everyone to scrutinize the details.

"Okay, let's go to the next victim," said Alton. Hanif brought up more pictures.

"It looks almost identical to the first," said David, mirroring the thoughts of everyone.

"That's not unusual," said Mallory. "We count on that, actually. People like this psycho usually have a set routine they follow. Once we figure out the routine, we're one step closer to catching the bad guy."

"Hanif, stop on that picture for a minute," said Alton. "What's that along the edge of the wound? There's something dark on her skin, right where the incision is. At first I thought it was dried blood, but you can see blood that dripped down her side, and it doesn't look the same."

"I see it," said Mallory. "You're right. Hanif, can you zoom in on that?"

The picture expanded, showing faint swirls and brushstrokes in the black substance adjacent to the wound.

"It almost looks like the killer painted a guide on her stomach, then cut along the line," said Alton. "But why?"

"How can we know why a crazy person does something?" asked Fahima.

"We only need to discern the pattern," said Alton. "I've read about victims in Mexican drug wars being pretty mutilated. Could this be some kind of turf war between tribal leaders? Perhaps one sending a message to the other by killing young women this way?"

"I don't think so," said Hanif. "Tribal leaders have a lot of power in the north and south, but here in Kabul, the national government has pushed them out. Plus, they usually kill the men, not teenage girls. This looks like something different."

"Okay," said Alton. "Let's look at the rest of the photos and try to get a better sense of the overall pattern."

As they reviewed the photos of the fourth victim, Mallory spoke up. "Stop. This girl's stomach isn't as mangled as the rest. It looks like the black substance forms a pattern on her stomach."

Hanif zoomed in again. "You're right. It looks like a star. Let me go back to the other victims and see if there are traces of this same design."

He pulled up the previous photos, then scrolled through those of the final victim. His face clouded. "We're seeing the same star pattern on all of them—a star inside a circle."

"Were there any ransom demands to the families?" asked Mallory.

"No. None," replied Hanif. "The girls went missing and were then found dead a few weeks later."

"That settles it, then," said Alton. "The motive isn't greed. We're looking for a serial killer."

CHAPTER 39

Ghoyee's last conversation with Mastana had occurred three days ago, yet the teen's alluring comments had continued to plague him.

Wouldn't you like to have me with you all the time? He had laughed off her question at the time, but the insinuation in her voice and seductive gaze in her eyes had lit a fire that continued to burn.

Why did the girl have to tempt him so?

Yesterday, an idea had presented itself to Ghoyee's mind: take the other girl, the one Divband had rejected in favor of Mastana. Once the idea took root, it quickly grew, crowding out all other thoughts.

And why not? Thanks to the Brotherhood, Ghoyee was well-versed in the art of kidnapping. But unlike his previous "collections," there was no need to involve Divband in this one. The new girl wouldn't be delivered to the Brotherhood. Rather, she would be Ghoyee's own special prize. For the same reason, however, he couldn't enlist Meskin's help as he had previously. This would have to be a solo operation.

By the time dusk set in, Ghoyee had watched the girl's house for nearly an hour. From his vantage point, he overlooked a rear corner of the brick-and-mud abode. The only movement inside occurred in the girl's bedroom. He had seen her young, budding figure in the window, moving in the dim light. Some might say thirteen was too young, but he had no objection to her years. In fact, her innocence spurred him to action.

Ghoyee opted against using the house's front entrance. It lay on the opposite side of the structure from the two bedrooms. If the girl heard him enter, she would have plenty of time to run, possibly even escape through a bedroom window as Mastana nearly had.

The other bedroom—the one across from the girl's room—had been dark throughout Ghoyee's vigil. It seemed to be the perfect entry point, a spot providing him with the element of surprise yet denying his target sufficient time to escape.

Using an old turban to construct a makeshift mask across his mouth and nose, Ghoyee crept towards the house, thankful for the cover provided by a series of brick walls abutting the property in the rear and side yards. The walls did have an open spot in the corner to allow access to a small alley, but a witness would have to stand motionless in that spot to have any line of sight to the house—and Ghoyee's activities.

The cultist reached the unoccupied bedroom's window and slid it open. Placing a linen cloth over the frame to cushion any potential noise, he squeezed through the opening.

Tiptoeing as quietly as possible for a man his size, Ghoyee reached the empty bedroom's door and cracked it open. He couldn't restrain a small grunt of surprise in seeing the door to the girl's bedroom standing wide open and the light switched off. What bad luck! The girl had remained in her bedroom the entire time Ghoyee had watched her from the scrub brush.

The girl must have moved to another part of the house. When Meskin participated in the collections, he would enter from another door and help Ghoyee herd the target into a dead end. Without his crony, Ghoyee had to make his way into the hall and head for the front of the house, all the while hoping the child wouldn't see him and run screaming from the front entrance before he could reach her. Thankfully, the hallway was dark enough to hide his lumbering form—at least he hoped so.

He reached the end of the hallway and peered across an open area in the front of the house into a small kitchen. There was the girl, chopping something on the counter. Perfect!

A sudden noise startled both the girl and Ghoyee. The front door swung open, and the girl's father strode into the house.

"My darling!" said the cursed father.

Ghoyee backed away, ducking into the shadows. He could always return on Wednesday at an earlier time of day, before the father returned from work.

"Who is there?" shouted the father, staring into the moving shadows on the wall.

Terrified of being seen, Ghoyee bolted down the hallway. Reaching the end of the hall, he grabbed the doorframe to stop his momentum, then pulled himself into his entry-point bedroom. After slamming the door shut and locking it, he scrambled to the window and dove through as a furious pounding erupted from the door.

Ghoyee fell into the dirt of the backyard with a thud. He righted himself and bolted down the alley. He twisted through a maze of tightly-packed houses in the neighborhood. As he ran, he pulled the mask off his face.

He reached a wide thoroughfare and plunged into the crowd streaming down the sidewalk. For the first time, he stole a glance behind him. The girl's father hadn't followed, probably opting to remain with his distraught daughter to console and question her.

Ghoyee cursed his luck. Of all the times for a collection to go wrong, this was arguably the worst. Perhaps he would try to collect another girl in the future, but for today, he rejoiced in having escaped from the target's house with his identity undiscovered.

CHAPTER 40

Mastana's heart accelerated as she heard the door down the hallway open. She felt guilty praying that, if one of the prisoners were to be taken, it would not be her.

The door to her cell creaked open, causing a chill to run down her spine. Divband stepped into the gloom.

"My Lord," said Mastana, bowing her head.

Divband studied her for a full half-minute. "How do I know I can trust you?"

"How indeed, my Lord? I am chained to the floor. Such restraint does not afford one an opportunity to demonstrate trustworthiness."

He frowned at her. "Yet if I give you freedom, you could betray me."

"A man like you does not rise to power on the basis of poor choices. I trust that your decision regarding me will be wise, my Lord."

Divband paced the narrow confines of the cell, muttering to himself. A myriad of conflicting emotions flitted across his countenance.

He stopped pacing. "We can take this in stages. I will allow you a bit of freedom. Exercise this freedom responsibly, and you will gain my trust...and a little more freedom."

"As you wish, my Lord. I thank you."

Divband turned on his heel and exited the cell. After pulling the door shut and locking it, he leaned his face against the bars in the window, obscuring most of the feeble light from the hallway. "Mastana, if you lose my trust, you will never get it back. Do you understand?"

There was no point in attempting this charade without a willingness to fully commit to the role. "Completely, my Lord. I will not fail you."

Five minutes later, a guard entered her cell. "Divband has ordered me to remove your chain." The man grabbed her arm and inserted a key into the shackle. With a twist, it fell free.

Mastana rubbed her wrist. The elation of this bit of freedom threatened to overwhelm her, but she maintained an icy stillness as the guard rose. If the man reported back to Divband, he should not observe so exuberant a reaction as to suggest the potential of an eventual escape attempt. "I thank you, sir."

The guard grunted and left the cell, locking it behind

him.

After waiting for the guard to leave, Mastana walked to the door and, for the first time, peered through it. The hallway looked as she imagined it, a narrow, stack-stone tunnel lit with a string of florescent lights, ending at a massive wooden door with steel plates banded across it.

She stepped back into the interior of her cell, a cacophony of thoughts battling for attention in her mind.

Divband had given her a bit a freedom. Had he ever done that before?

The weakest glimmer of hope arose in Mastana's mind. Was she guilty of wishful thinking, or was the path to her salvation, once dark, now illuminated with a flicker of hope?

CHAPTER 41

"I don't think we're looking for a serial killer the way you are imagining," said Hanif, his face a mask of worry as he surveyed the others around Kamaal's table.

"What do you mean?" asked Alton.

Hanif rose and began to pace. "This may not be the work of one crazy person. The markings we saw on the bodies, a star within a circle. I have seen it before."

"You know," said Mallory, "I thought I had too, but I can't remember where."

"Back in college," said Hanif, "I studied the history of my country. This symbol was used by an ancient cult, one that existed before Islam began."

Alton rubbed the stubble on his chin. "Do you think there's a connection between the crimes and this cult?"

"Certainly the use of this symbol makes me wonder."

"Or it could be some lunatic that's latched on to this symbol as a representation of his evil urges," said Mallory.

"Yes, that is quite possible," said Hanif.

"Plus, didn't you said the cult was ancient?" pressed Mallory.

"Yes, but a few months ago, I heard whisperings of this cult reemerging. I did not know if this rumor was true. I hope it is not."

"Why?"

"The Brotherhood of Stones was different from other cults. Most religions seek to connect with the benevolent forces of the universe. This cult sought a darker path. They pursued the power of the black *jinnd*."

"Black *jinnd*?" asked Alton.

"The *jinnd* are spirits. As the name implies, white *jinnd* are good, and black *jinnd* are evil."

"And this group, this Brotherhood, worshiped the evil ones?" asked David.

"That is correct. The Brotherhood believed in the blood sacrifice as an offering to Iblis, the most powerful black *jinnd*. In your culture, you would call this *jinnd* Satan."

"That's where I've seen that symbol before," said Mallory. "There are groups of Satan worshipers in the US who use something similar."

Hanif continued. "The Brotherhood's sacrifices were

always females, which is consistent with our recent string of crimes. If they are indeed returning and are responsible for Mastana's abduction, we must find her soon. Otherwise, she may end up the next sacrifice."

Mallory leaned back in her chair. "I'm surprised someone on the police force hasn't already made the connection between the symbol and the Brotherhood of Stones."

"Well, that cult was pretty obscure. I really liked that college class, so I studied all the cults, including the Brotherhood. But today, not many people have heard of them."

"I'm glad you know these things," said David. "We'd be up the creek without you."

"I don't see how we can know just yet whether these kidnappings are the work of a new and improved Brotherhood of Stones or only one individual," said Alton, "but we should look into the possibility that the Brotherhood is involved. Some of us should follow up with Captain Poya tomorrow, see if he's heard anything about this cult."

Everyone agreed.

Alton looked at his watch. "Man, it's nearly midnight. Why don't we get some shuteye, and let's plan on getting started at nine tomorrow morning."

"I think I will go with you to the police station tomorrow," said Hanif. "I would like to be part of the conversation."

"Thanks, Hanif," said Alton. "Like David said, we'd be dead in the water without you."

Hanif departed, and with the exception of Alton, the others began to prepare makeshift beds scattered around the front of Kamaal's house. As they did so, Nafisa's grandmother arrived. Thanking the rescuers, she spirited the girl away, back to the relative safety of Jalalabad.

"Sweetie, don't you think you'd better get some sleep, too?" asked Mallory, resting her arm on Alton's shoulder as he worked on his laptop.

"I will in just a minute. I'm going to look up vendors who sell Ketamine in Kabul. Even if it's a long shot, we should still try to track down the shop where our kidnapper has been buying his stuff."

"Okay. Don't take too long. You won't be good for tomorrow without rest." She leaned down and pressed into a lingering kiss. "Remember our wedding night, when I said you're my hero? This is why. Think about what you're doing. You're halfway around the world working yourself ragged, searching for a girl who isn't even related to you. Not many people would do that. But I'm not surprised at all that my husband is."

"Thanks, Honey. But I think on this mission, we're all equally in the hero business."

"Well, I'm going to get my hero self in bed. Don't be long."

"I won't."

As he searched the internet for Kabul's Ketamine

vendors, Alton's mind wandered. He didn't feel like a hero. His return to Afghanistan had been more difficult than he had anticipated. Since arriving in Kabul, an undercurrent of latent anxiety had continued to trouble his mind. Also, the pain in his leg had grown progressively worse. Yes, he had been forced to run earlier in the day, but his leg's deterioration had started before then. He wasn't sure why, but he felt an odd certainty that if he could just find Mastana and leave Afghanistan, his limb would return to its typical level of discomfort.

The next morning, Fahima and David left to visit the largest medical supply stores, using the list Alton had compiled the night before.

Meanwhile, Alton, Mallory, Kamaal, and Hanif went to see Captain Poya. The desk sergeant ushered them back to Poya's office.

The captain smiled when he saw the group but took on a more grim expression when he spotted Hanif. "You helping these guys, Hanif?" asked Poya, apparently using English as a courtesy to the Americans.

"Yes, they came to me and explained their case, and I said I would help this one time."

"I'm glad. But Hanif, you should have stayed on the force. We could use a good cop like you."

Hanif's expression looked pained. "We've discussed this before. I…can't. Not all the time. It is too much."

"Whatever you say," grumbled Poya. "Now, tell me why you are here today. It's about the kidnapping case, right?"

"Yes," replied Alton, hoping to defuse the tension between the officer and his former lieutenant. "We have a few specific questions we're hoping you can help us with."

"Tell me your questions."

"We were wondering if you've heard of any recent crimes associated with a cult called the Brotherhood of Stones."

Poya rubbed his chin in thought. "I don't think so. Why?"

"We think they may have been involved in multiple kidnappings, similar to the one Mr. Blackwell is investigating," said Hanif. He provided a summary of the information they had acquired the previous day.

"You know a lot about the police reports," said Poya. "How did you find this out?"

"I…uh…asked some of my former colleagues on the force."

Poya frowned. "You know you're not supposed to do that. If you want police information, you have to be a policeman or submit an official request." His expression softened. "We could use you, Hanif. Come back, and you can get this kind of information anytime you want it."

"Sorry, I can't. But you'll still let us know if you get

any information about the Brotherhood, right?"

"Sure. In fact, let me ask my sergeant." He picked up his phone. "Sergeant Majid, can you come into my office for a minute?"

A moment later, a beefy man entered.

"Sergeant Majid, have you heard of a criminal organization called the Brotherhood of Stones?"

Majid looked from face to face with an uneasy expression. "No, I have not heard of such a group. Why?"

"Hanif and his friends think this Brotherhood group may be involved in some kidnappings. If you hear of anything pertaining to that group, can you let me know?"

"Of course, sir."

"Thank you, Sergeant. That will be all."

Majid exited the room, and Poya turned back to the others. "I will let you know if I hear anything." He nodded and turned to his computer monitor.

That seemed to be the cue for them to leave.

"Thank you, Captain Poya," said Alton as they slipped out the office door.

Mallory leaned over to Alton. "Holy crap! Did you see the size of that sergeant?"

"Yeah, I wonder if he has his uniforms custom made. Sergeant Schwarzenegger reporting for duty."

Early that afternoon, both groups reconvened around Kamaal's table. He served them a light lunch while they compared notes.

"Did you find anything at the medical supply stores?" asked Alton.

"Nope. Not a damn thing," said David. "Maybe Fahima was right, the kidnapper is buying Ketamine on the black market."

"It'd certainly be harder to trace," said Alton. "If I were trying to cover my tracks, that's what I'd do."

"So, what about you guys? Any luck?"

"Not really. Poya hadn't heard of the Brotherhood. He said he'd let us know if he hears anything, but you heard him talking about civilian crime the other day. Unless the Brotherhood somehow gets involved in terrorist crimes, I don't think they'll get a lot of attention from the police."

"Agreed."

"You know, that makes me think, though," said Alton. "What about Colonel Rand at Camp Eggers MI? Can you see if he's heard of these guys?"

"That's a thought," said David. "Military Intelligence might have heard something, especially if the Brotherhood is operating in Kabul. Let me go call Rand now."

David called Camp Eggers. After three transfers, he finally connected with the colonel. After posing the question to Rand, he spent most of the remaining portion of the conversation listening. He thanked the man and ended the call.

"So?" asked Mallory.

"Pretty much the same as Poya. Rand hasn't heard of the Brotherhood but he'll let me know if he does."

"That's too bad."

"Yeah." David pursed his lips. "You know, it seemed like Rand was holding something back."

"Like what?" asked Mallory.

"I can't say exactly. Remember a long time ago I told you that growing up on a cattle ranch in Wyoming helped me develop a good sense for JDFR?"

"'JDFR'?" asked Kamaal.

"'Just doesn't feel right.' Back when I worked the ranch, the cattle would generally know when something was up. After a while, I started to pick up the same kind of subtle cues they did. When I was talking with the colonel, I got that same vibe."

"We'll just have to hope that if he does have any information about the Brotherhood, he'll share it with us," said Alton. "Mastana's time is surely running out."

CHAPTER 42

Mastana estimated she had enjoyed freedom from her floor shackle for a day. Of course, she couldn't be sure exactly how long she had been unchained, but her body's circadian rhythm suggested a twenty-four hour interval.

The heavy clang of the hallway door and the approach of footsteps raised Mastana's anxiety, as it always did since her arrival in this dismal place. She backed herself into the darkest corner, praying the tread would continue past her door.

The sound of a key in the lock refuted her wish. Divband entered the cell. Until now, he had always appeared in a black robe, but today he wore a more modern look, sporting a shirt and pants made of linen. Did the relaxation of his attire in her presence denote a loosening of other attitudes respecting her?

Divband wrinkled his nose. "By Iblis, when is the last time anyone emptied your chamber pot?"

Emerging from the shadows, Mastana hung her head in affected shame, as if she had anything to do with the timing of the filth's removal. "I do not know, my Lord. Many hours, I believe."

"We must get that taken care of. But that's not why I'm here. I came to ask you how you've enjoyed your taste of freedom."

Praise the heavens, no walk down the hall! "I have enjoyed it very much. I thank you, my Lord."

Divband smiled. It seemed no amount of false praise was too much. "Yet the guards tell me you have hung back, that you have not made a show of your freedom from the chain."

"That is true. I believe my Lord would prefer a companion capable of exercising restraint."

"A companion? And where did you get such an idea?"

"I apologize, my Lord. I merely meant for those moments we share together in this cell, I hoped my Lord would find my conduct pleasing to his taste."

The man nodded, and Mastana breathed a silent sigh of relief that her attempt to suggest the possibility of a deeper relationship between them hadn't backfired.

"And yet, if I *were* to choose a companion, I would value such restraint. The companion of a leader must not outshine her man."

No, her suggestion definitely hadn't backfired.

"Indeed, my Lord."

Divband took two steps towards her. "And how would you feel about a little more freedom?"

"I am content in any measure of freedom my Lord finds pleasing."

"Come, come. You'd like to have a little more, wouldn't you?"

She brightened. "Yes, my Lord. Perhaps I could use it in service of you."

"How so?"

"That would depend on the nature of my freedom, my Lord. I cannot say until I know what privileges I would be allowed."

"Fair enough." Divband tossed a package on the floor, a small parcel wrapped in brown paper. "I brought you a clean garment, but I must say that another freedom comes immediately to mind," he said, glancing at the chamber pot once more. "How would you like access to the bathroom?"

"I would like that very much."

"You'd have to be escorted by a guard."

"Of course, my Lord."

"Very well—it's decided. I'll send Walid down here to empty that pot. And I'll instruct him to escort you to the bathroom. He'll check with you every couple of hours to see if you have the need."

"You are generous, my Lord."

The man smiled, and Mastana wondered how much unmerited praise she would have to heap on his head before he became suspicious.

Divband left and locked the door behind him. Although the illumination from the narrow hallway's florescent bulbs hadn't changed, the light in Mastana's cell nonetheless seemed of a brighter hue.

CHAPTER 43

Divband sat in his office, lost in thought. Until now, he had rejoiced at the screams and terror of the brides of Iblis as they had been sacrificed. Why not? Their repulsion showed in every look and action. They were just the sort of harlots who would laugh at him if they knew the truth about his condition.

But this new girl, Mastana, was different. Of course, a sexual relationship with her remained out of the question, but she had a pleasing, compliant way about her. And although intercourse wasn't an option, there were other forms of intimacy that were satisfying in their own way, methods the teen had all but suggested.

What would it be like to have someone like Mastana around? The Brotherhood only allowed men to join their ranks—this was Divband's own regulation—but the leader could be allowed a companion, just as his followers had their wives and girlfriends at home.

He recognized that the teen could not yet be trusted.

She would have to prove herself over time. But the current timetable could be a dilemma. Following the normal protocol for the brides of Iblis, Mastana would soon be starved, then sacrificed. Divband had half a mind to stay this sequence of events in favor of giving her the opportunity to demonstrate her trustworthiness. Worst case, she would fail and be sacrificed, no different from the current plan.

As he mulled over this course of action, Ghoyee and Meskin arrived at his office.

"Master, you sent for us?"

Divband sighed. He would have preferred to remain alone, contemplating Mastana, but being available to his followers, including those who answered a summons at an inconvenient time, was a price of leadership. "Yes, come in."

Meskin bowed again and again, while Ghoyee entered in silence.

"We are now two days away from performing the next bride-of-Iblis ceremony," said Divband. "As you know, the ceremonies proceed more smoothly when the bride is weak from hunger. You've already put the next bride on half-rations, right?"

"Yes, Master," said Ghoyee. "And may I tell Meskin of our earlier conversation, the one about the Americans?"

Divband nodded.

Ghoyee turned to Meskin. "Some Americans were

inquiring about the Brotherhood."

"Why were they asking?"

"They're trying to track down one of the brides. I guess they're friends of hers."

Meskin looked worried. "What do we do about this?"

"Oh, it'll be taken care of," interjected Divband. "Some of our Brotherhood members are, shall we say, uniquely placed in the government. We'll soon hear the details of the Americans and their investigation. I don't think they'll learn anything useful, but if it turns out they do, well...I'm sure Iblis would like to have a few more servants in his kingdom."

CHAPTER 44

Grateful for the chance to wear clean clothes, Mastana immediately discarded her old rags and put on the new garments.

Recognizing the need to avoid appearing overanxious, she declined a trip to the bathroom the first time it was offered. The second time, she accepted yet made as meek a show of the journey as possible, walking with her eyes cast down to the floor and completing her time in the public latrines in the space of two minutes. On this first visit, she scarcely looked around the building. Her priority lay with giving all indications of abiding by Divband's rules. Such an impression should raise the odds of success if she eventually had an opportunity to attempt an escape.

Several hours later, shortly after a meal of rice, *naan*, and water, Walid peered through the bars of Mastana's cell door. "Would you like to go to the bathroom?" The man wore a frown, apparently unhappy with this new responsibility. He reeked of beer, the influence of which probably did little to improve his mood.

"Yes, thank you."

Again, Mastana kept her gaze fixed to the floor. As she reached the threshold of the bathroom, she turned to her male captor. "I am sorry, but this may take a little longer. The meal, you know…"

"Fine, just get on with it."

Mastana passed to the left of one crumbling, stacked-mudbrick wall, then to the right of another, finally entering one of the ancient temple's public baths. The building's architects had been ahead of their time. Behind a row of vats used for bathing lay a trench, a sloped indentation on the floor used as a latrine. A narrow stream of water flowed into the trench from the right side of the room, and gravity did the rest, carrying away the waste through a small opening on the left wall.

Mastana examined the cavity through which the rivulet exited the room. The opening was only several inches high, but the wall around it was made of stacked mudbrick rather than the indestructible granite stones used to construct the exterior walls. She could see cracks in the mudbricks, and some pieces had already broken away in places.

Bracing herself, she kicked the wall, hoping her captor could not hear the dull thud. Since this might be her only opportunity to escape, it was a risk she had to take. On the third kick, a jagged crack nearly two feet long lanced up the wall. Mastana wiggled the mudbrick at the edge of the crack until a fist-sized piece came off in her hands.

She repeated the procedure on the other side of the crack, widening the opening a little more.

The building's architects had been advanced, but even they had no remedy against the deteriorating effects of two millennia on clay masonry. Ever-widening chucks broke off in Mastana's hands. She laid them inside one of the bathing vats, hoping to minimize the pile of rubble near her escape route. In the space of three minutes, she had enlarged the hole to roughly two feet high and wide.

She glided back to the bathroom's entrance to ensure her guard had not started calling for her. If so, she would have to make some excuse for needing a few more minutes. Otherwise, the alarm would be sounded too soon for her to escape. She didn't hear anything at first, but then she cocked her head at a strange noise. Was that snoring? It was. What an enormous stroke of luck! She decided she didn't detest the smell of beer so much after all.

Mastana hurried back to her escape hole. Suppressing a gag, she lowered herself into the trench, wiggling herself through the hole as her stomach slid through the filth. She pulled her legs through the hole and stood up, finding herself in an unlit storage room.

Using the faintest trace of light from around the doorframe, she felt her way to the door, which—thankfully—seemed to lie on a different hall from the one from which she had entered the bathroom. She pulled open the storage-room's door and tiptoed down a narrow hallway, scarcely daring to breathe for fear of alerting someone to her presence.

Mastana continued skirting down a series of narrow passages, heading away from any source of light or noise, all the while thankful for dark shadows that enshrouded most of the ancient structure like a crypt. In under five minutes, she reached a room containing a speaker dais, a collapsible table, and a wheeled rack of folding chairs—but no exit from the building. The items seemed oddly out of place in the aged building.

Pressing forward through the darkness, Mastana detected the faintest hint of external light. In seconds, she reached a small room with a fire pit and, directly above it, a narrow hole cut out of the ceiling. Peering up, she saw a splash of stars twinkling through the gap.

Although the ceiling was quite low, it was nonetheless too high for Mastana reach from the floor. She cast her gaze around the room but saw nothing she could use as a makeshift ladder. Remembering the previous room, she returned to it and lifted a folding chair off the rack. Making her way back to the second room, she unfolded the chair and placed it in the fire pit. She reached for the ceiling, praying it would prove to be more durable than the bathroom's wall. Fortunately, the ceiling's construction held firm as she struggled to pull herself up through the hole.

Emerging through the opening at last, Mastana squatted down and swiveled to take in her surroundings. Her building seemed to lie near the center of some type of large, aging compound. A nearly-full moon illuminated a frosty mountain range in the direction of the North Star. To the east and west lay desert, and behind her rose another, smaller mountain range. She decided to make for the desert, figuring she could put the greatest distance between herself and this compound on such terrain. Plus, the buildings between here and the western desert were all dark, suggesting the absence of occupants who might spot her escape.

Her next step, though, involved getting off this roof without being detected. She low-crawled to the roof's edge, raising and lowering each limb with deliberation in order to minimize noise. At the first roofline, she encountered a straight drop. Jumping from the squat building at this height wouldn't hurt her, but it could quite possibly make too much noise. She crawled to an adjacent roofline and found a retaining wall running away from the building. After studying the surrounding area to ensure her privacy, Mastana slid from the roof onto the wall. She then lowered herself off the wall, her feet dangling a mere twelve inches off the ground. She dropped in almost perfect silence and bent into a crouch.

The buildings in the direction of the western desert remained dark and silent. Hugging shadowed walls and swiveling her head almost constantly, Mastana worked her way from one building to the next. As the edge of the compound neared, she forced herself to not let the proximity of escape lead her into recklessness.

She reached the last building. Only then did she see the security perimeter, a series of small huts located about a hundred meters outside the compound proper. She plotted a path between the two huts that seemed to have the greatest distance between them. Using a large boulder in the distance as a landmark, she crawled on hands and knees across the ground, determined to avoid capture with the prize so close. A straight route would have been quicker, but she turned time and again to avoid patches of dried Calligonum desert shrubs, the rustling of which could betray her presence.

Were they already looking for her? She imagined that had her escape already been discovered, someone would have sounded an alarm. But she couldn't count on this assumption. She had to maintain a stealthy escape.

Desert winds sent a chill down Mastana's spine. More determined than ever, she slipped between the two guard shacks without incident. She could hear the faintest murmuring of music on the radios of both locations, confirming her absence from the bathroom had not yet reached the guards' ears.

As she moved past the shacks, she heard a great noise erupt from the compound. Intermittent shouts mixed with curses. In seconds, the phones in both guard shacks rang simultaneously. Mastana couldn't make out the conversations, but she had a pretty good idea they revolved around her.

While the desert still represented the best ground for making good time, Mastana knew better than to walk in open terrain in such close proximity to the compound, recognizing that her silhouette could give her away. She spotted a dried creek bed off to the right, leading in a southwesterly direction, and headed towards it.

Mastana entered the channel. By bending forward slightly at the waist, she dropped out of sight of her pursuers. Balancing the need to move quickly with the necessity of minimizing noise, she settled on a quick walking pace. As she strode, the drone of noise from the camp grew louder. Once or twice, the beam of a spotlight flitted over her head, illuminating dust motes kicked up by the evening breeze.

After fifteen minutes of brisk walking, Mastana peered over the top of the riverbed. In the distance, lights continued to flash and a hum of noise could still be discerned. None of the searchers, however, appeared to be headed in her direction.

Feeling an irresistible urge to put as much distance as possible between herself and her captors, Mastana emerged from the riverbed and dashed toward the open desert—and freedom.

CHAPTER 45

Minutes earlier, Divband had been roused by a frantic visit from Walid, the guard.

"Master, the girl has escaped!"

"What girl?"

"Mastana, the one allowed to visit the communal bathrooms."

Divband cursed. "Why weren't you watching her? That was your job."

The man flushed. "I was, Master, but she…she attacked me as I stood guard at the door to the bathroom." Walid cast his gaze to the floor, unable to meet his leader's eyes.

Divband studied the man. He looked to be lying. Probably the escape had involved something less dramatic, but it hardly mattered now. "Do you have any idea where she is?"

"No. She fled into the halls. She could be anywhere."

Divband turned to Ghoyee, who had arrived at the sounds of confusion. "Alert the perimeter guards. Don't let her slip past them." He faced Walid again. "Did Mastana change into her new clothes?"

"Yes. She wore them to the bathroom."

"Where are her old ones?"

"Still in her cell. I saw them when I took her out."

"Go get them, and take them to the bathroom. Hurry!" Turning back to Ghoyee, Divband continued. "Collect the dogs and take them to the bathroom. We'll give them a good smell of her old clothing, then let them track her down from there."

Ghoyee nodded and raced down the hallway, nearly colliding with a zealot headed in the opposite direction.

Scarcely five minutes later, Divband's phone rang.

"It's Ghoyee. The dogs are on her scent. She made it off the west end of the building."

"Good, but you must hurry. Don't give her a chance to escape into the hills, or even the dogs may not be able to find her."

"Don't worry. If she made it outside the compound, I'll pursue on horseback. She won't go far."

Divband ended the call. He paced his office's

cramped space, running through scenarios in his mind. If the teen made it to freedom, would she be able to lead authorities back here? That is, would she have time to do that before *other* authorities, those in the Brotherhood's membership rolls, eliminated her?

He continued to pace, wondering how this crisis would play out.

CHAPTER 46

Through a blur of tears, Mastana looked into Divband's furious face. She had eluded the Brotherhood's human members but had been unable to find any water to put the dogs off her scent. She had returned to the dry riverbed, but the dogs had hugged her trail, leading the horse-mounted Ghoyee directly to her.

Several supplicants had dragged her into their master's presence and dropped her onto the floor, grinning at their trophy.

"Leave us," ordered Divband.

Once alone, he raised a hand as if to slap her, then let it drift to his side. "It wouldn't do to leave a mark," he muttered more to himself than to her. "My followers might consider you an unsuitable bride for Iblis if I did." He fixed his gaze on her and scowled. "You are deceitful—the curse of your gender. I blame myself for wanting to trust you, wanting to believe your eyes could hold a glimmer of truth."

Mastana said nothing, certain any words would enflame his wrath.

"I told you you'd get only one chance," he said, his eyes raw with betrayal, "and you've used it."

He stepped into the hallway. "Guards, come here."

Three followers entered the small office.

"Search her. Ensure she has no weapons or objects on her, then return her to her cell—fully chained on all four limbs."

A guard, the husky one, ran his hand over Mastana's body as commanded. The damp, clammy surface of the man's fingers made her skin crawl.

"Master, look at this," he said, handing over a stone bearing a sharp edge.

"Where was it?"

"In the rear band of her undergarments."

Mastana continued to remain silent with averted eyes. Resistance would only fan the flames of Divband's anger.

"Take her from my sight. I will not see her again until the day of her marriage to Iblis."

The trio of guards led Mastana back to her cell. The husky one secured the shackles around her ankles and wrists, then attached them all to the chain bolted to the cell's floor.

As the guard slammed the door shut, Mastana hung

her head and wept. Yes, she had escaped the jihadist schemes of her uncle, but did she await a similar fate in the hands of these madmen?

CHAPTER 47

The following morning, Kamaal served a breakfast of *naan*, apricots, pistachios, and tea to his American friends. Hanif had once again taken the morning off from his job at the electric utility, opting instead to help them in their search.

The dawn song of a swallow provided a tranquil, natural score to their meal. As sunbeams spilled through an open window and took the chill out of the air, Alton's optimism warmed as well. Surely today they would make some progress tracking down Mastana—they had to.

Reaching for a piece of fruit, he received a call from Captain Poya.

"I wanted to let you know," said Poya, "I did some checking in my department to see if anyone has heard anything about the Brotherhood of Stones, but no one is familiar with the name. I wish I had better news to tell you."

The Devil's Due

"I appreciate the follow-up," said Alton. "I know you've been given marching orders to focus on terrorist crimes."

"That is true, but I thought during morning report, it wouldn't take much time to ask all my policemen if they know this group. No one said anything. But I will keep checking and will let you know if I learn anything."

"Thanks again, Captain. Who knows? Maybe something will turn up."

Alton ended the call and shared the content of his conversation with the others.

"Well, Miss FBI agent, what do you recommend next?" Alton asked his wife.

"That's *missus* FBI agent now...and I've been thinking about that question," said Mallory as she chewed on the end of a pen. "Kamaal, do you have a map of the city?"

"Yes, in the spare bedroom. Let me go get it."

"What do you have in mind?" asked David. He stirred the green tea in his mug with a dejected look, one that spoke of a need for coffee.

"Old-school charting," said Mallory. "Let's mark the location of each kidnapping on the map and see if any visual patterns jump out at us."

"Kamaal," called Alton. "Do you have any thumbtacks?"

"Yes, I will bring them."

They soon had the map of Kabul tacked to the wall. Alton accessed the violent-crimes database of Kabul's police department. Once in, Hanif pulled the date and location of each of the nine reported kidnappings. As he called out the information, Kamaal located the spot on the map, which Mallory marked with a thumbtack while scribbling the date of the attack next to it.

When all the thumbtacks had been placed, they surveyed the pattern.

"It's pretty random," said Mallory, "but there is a bit of clustering in the northeastern section of the city."

"Northeastern section, you said?" asked Hanif.

"Yes, why?"

"When Alton was pulling the kidnapping files out of the database, I noticed a report of an attempted break-in last night at a residence in the Pule Charki neighborhood. This is in the northeastern part of Kabul."

"So you're wondering if the criminals were trying to burglarize it or had a more sinister motive?"

"Yes."

"Let me log back in so you can see what additional information the report contains." Alton's fingers flew over the keyboard, bringing up the police system in the space of thirty seconds.

Hanif accessed the record and scanned it. "There's not much more. It just says someone broke into a first-floor bedroom. When the father entered the house, the burglar ran away."

"I wonder if there's a teenage girl in the family," mused Alton. "Does the report list the family members?"

"Yes, there is a mother and a son of nine years in the family, but they were attending a soccer game. The family also includes a father …and a girl of thirteen years."

Alton's blood ran cold. "So before the father entered and scared away the burglar, the girl was there by herself?"

"It reads that way."

"Just like Mastana," said Mallory.

"Do you all think it'd be worthwhile to swing by the house and see if there was any evidence left behind?" asked Alton. "Based on Poya's comments, I doubt the police spent much time on-scene, if any."

"It won't hurt," said Mallory. "It's the only promising lead we have, even if it is a long shot."

CHAPTER 48

Divband called Ghoyee into his office. The man hadn't been himself lately, and Divband intended to get to the bottom of it. He couldn't afford to have the mind of his right-hand man wandering.

"You called for me, Master," said Ghoyee as he poked his head through the opening of Divband's office. Ghoyee's countenance seemed to match the gloom of the narrow space.

"Yes, come in."

The sidekick entered but did not meet his master's eye.

"You missed the initiation ceremony for the new members two nights ago."

"I'm sorry, Master."

"You know how important that meeting is. Why

weren't you there?"

Ghoyee's hangdog look grew more pathetic. "I will not lie to you, Master. I was visiting the home of the girl we rejected in favor of Mastana."

"The skinny girl with thirteen years?"

"Yes."

"Why? What were you doing there?"

"Do you remember how Mastana tempted me by asking me to take her home?"

"Yes, and you did the right thing to tell me at that time."

Ghoyee nodded without meeting his master's gaze. "I kept thinking about her words. They drove me wild with desire. Then I remembered the other girl we didn't choose, and I came up with an idea, a perfect idea, I thought. I already knew much about the other girl. Since you had rejected her, I decided I could collect her for myself."

"And did you?"

Ghoyee sighed. "No, master. I made it into her house, but her father returned, and I fled."

An alarm bell sounded in Divband's mind. "Did they see you?"

"No. At least…I don't think so."

"Ghoyee, I can see something else is troubling you.

What is it?"

The man shuffled his feet, looking for all the world like an oversized schoolboy who had been caught stealing money from the teacher's desk. "I entered the girl's house through a window in an empty bedroom. When I heard the father come home, I scrambled back out the window. I am afraid I may have touched the window sill."

"And left fingerprints," concluded Divband. "You may have been collecting the girl for your own benefit, but if you're caught, you could lead the police back to us. Did you leave prints anywhere else?"

"I…I don't know. When I heard the front door open, I ran. I may have touched the wall. Maybe the bedroom doorframe, too."

Divband knew he had to take decisive action. "Take Meskin and the rest of Alpha Squad. Burn down the house."

"Master?" Ghoyee looked shocked.

"It's the only way of ensuring all potential evidence is destroyed. And take your weapons. We can't run the risk of your being caught in the middle of committing an act of arson. If the father comes home again, *he'll* be the one running."

CHAPTER 49

Kamaal, Hanif, and the married couples departed for the house of the recent break-in within minutes of connecting it to the string of recent kidnappings.

"What kind of evidence are we looking for?" asked David as Hanif's Mercedes bumped over the ill-maintained roads of Kabul.

"Anything, really," said Mallory. "Hanif, you don't have a fingerprint kit, do you?"

"No, not anymore."

"Well, there may be other forensic evidence left behind, right?"

"I hope so. We can also ask the family what they saw. Perhaps they witnessed something that wasn't included in the police report."

As the two cars approached the house, they spotted a clutch of men in dark robes and masks circling the exterior of the property.

"Do you see that?" asked Alton. "Hanif, keep going. We don't want them to spot us."

"Do you think they came back for the girl?" asked Mallory.

"If they did, we're not going to let that happen," said Alton with grim determination. "Not again."

Hanif sailed past the house, as did Kamaal in his Corolla. They pulled into an alley a block away and huddled between the two cars.

"What was going on back there?" asked Kamaal.

"We're not sure," said Alton, "but we think the kidnapper came back for the girl."

"Make that kidnappers—plural," said Mallory. "There must have been seven or eight of them. Maybe more, if there were any in the back yard."

"That's about what I counted, too," said Alton. "I wonder if it's the Brotherhood of Stones. Whoever they are, they're armed. I saw rifle straps on the ones closest to the street."

"What do we do now?" asked Fahima, her eyes wide.

"We still have all our combat supplies in the trunks of these cars," said Alton. "I say we treat this like a military operation. We move in. Capture them if possible, kill them if not."

David and Mallory nodded.

"Fahima and Kamaal, you stay here and call the police. Let them know what's happening. Hanif, I know you didn't sign up for…this," said Alton, gesturing his hand back in the direction of the masked men. "Can you go to the end of this alley and put eyes on the back of the house? We could use some intel."

"Yes, I can do that."

"Okay, let's gear up before those guys leave. We'll need to coordinate our movements, so be sure to put on mikes and earpieces."

Alton, Mallory, and David slipped on the communication equipment. They snapped on web belts and stuffed the pouches full of thirty-round magazines, then slung A4 rifles over their shoulders.

Alton glanced at the afternoon sun glowing behind the victims' house. "We'll arrive at the southern edge of the property line separating the front yard on the left from the street on the right," he said. "David, there was a drainage ditch between and yard and the street. Can you low-crawl through it to the northern edge of the property?"

"Sure, Al. I was hoping I'd have a chance to do some low-crawling today."

"Good. We'll have the advantage once you're in position. If they try to escape out of the front yard, we'll have them trapped in overlapping fields of fire.

"Mallory, I'd like to send you to the back of the

house. I noticed a fence between the girl's house and her neighbor's. But even if you travel on the other side of the fence, those goons will see you if you try to crawl over. So, can you wait with me on the southern edge of the front yard? If Hanif says the fence has a gate or door, you can move down there and be in position without being spotted."

"Okay."

"Everyone ready? All right, let's roll."

Alton performed a mike check as they traveled to the house. He also asked Hanif, who had already moved down the alley, to look for a gate in the fence.

In a flash, the terrain changed, and Alton could only see Gazib, the Afghanistan desert in which he had been stationed four years ago when the IED had ended his Army field command. He stopped and looked around, incredulous.

"Sweetie, are you okay?" asked Mallory. "Is it your leg?"

He snapped back to Kabul. "Sorry—I'm fine."

They continued walking at the fastest pace Alton could muster, reaching a garbage dumpster at the house's southeastern border. The dumpster emitted a horrendous smell but provided first-class cover and concealment.

"You ready, David?" said Alton.

His friend nodded and dropped to the ground. Alton was surprised at the speed David made low-crawling

The Devil's Due

along the bottom of the ditch.

Alton peered around the dumpster, studying the hostiles. What were they doing? They lugged plastic containers that created sloshing sounds when moved. He turned to Mallory and whispered. "What's in the containers, do you think? Gas?"

"I don't see what else it could be, but why? How does that help them with a kidnapping?"

"I don't know."

"The parents' car isn't here," said Mallory. "Maybe they plan to grab the girl—or maybe they have already—and are planning to torch the place once they leave."

"It looks like it, but I still don't see why. Unless maybe they're afraid they left evidence the other day during the botched kidnapping."

"Alton, we need to be careful. If they have the girl, she could be caught in the crossfire."

"Good point." He raised David on the mike. "Watch out for the girl. They may have her. Don't fire unless you have clear line of sight on the target."

"Roger, Al."

At that moment, a dilapidated Accord pulled up to the house. It started to pull into the driveway, then stopped. Alton could see the wide eyes of a boy of nine years and a girl of thirteen in the back, while the children's parents occupied the front seat. The father had spotted the activity in his yard and seemed undecided how to react.

"C'mon," murmured Alton. "Get the hell out of there."

The robed thugs turned at the sound of the car and froze. All except one, who pulled an AK-47 assault rifle off his shoulder. The father jammed the car into reverse and pealed out the driveway. After shifting gears again, the man lurched the car forward and careened down the dusty road.

"So why did the kidnappers come back, if not for the girl?" asked Mallory.

"Maybe it's just about the evidence they left behind. Perhaps they needed to get rid of it."

"Al," said David over his mike. "The girl got away, so do we still engage?"

The chatter of multiple AK-47s erupted before Alton could answer. Two of the thugs lay flat on the ground and kept a steady stream of rounds pouring into David's position.

David hugged the ditch, pinned down, but Alton had no such problem. He and Mallory slipped to the right side of the dumpster. Setting his carbine for three-round bursts, Alton aimed for the closest attacker and opened fire. The thug's head snapped sideways, bits of his cranium scattering into the dust.

The second attacker swiveled in their direction just in time for Mallory to put a bullet through his eye. He slumped to the ground, motionless.

The Devil's Due

Their success drew the attention of the other attackers. A fusillade of rounds poured in from three directions, pinging off the dumpster with a deafening clatter.

"Around to the other side," Alton told Mallory, motioning with his head to the left edge of the dumpster. "Maybe we can catch them by surprise from there."

A ricochet bounced within inches of Alton's right hand. He instinctively snatched it back towards safety. The sour odor of gunpowder wafted into his nose, bringing with it a collage of horrific memories.

"What is happening?" called Hanif over the mike.

"They spotted us," said Alton. "We took down two, but the rest are laying into us pretty good. What do you see from your position?"

"There were four of them in the backyard. They all headed to the front when the firing started."

"Wonderful." He turned to Mallory. "We need to put down suppressing fire or they're gonna move around and flank us. From what I can hear, it sounds like two of them are already making their way along the left fence. Let's take them out first."

She nodded.

"You go low, I'll go high. Ready…now!"

They swung their weapons around the edge of the metal container. Peeking their heads around just enough to line up the attackers in their sights, they opened up with a pair of bursts. One of the goons fell against the fence but continued firing. The other turned and fled back towards the house.

A compact pineapple landed in the dust a dozen feet away.

"Grenade!" screamed Alton. "Get around to the other side!"

The couple leapt behind the rear of the dumpster, landing on the ground with a thud just as the device exploded.

"That was a Russian F1," said Alton. "These guys are certainly well-equipped."

He glanced over to David. His friend occasionally peered above the rim of the ditch and fired, but pulsing gunfire from the hostiles kept him pinned down.

"How you doing over there?" asked Alton into his mike.

"Just dandy. Wish we'd brought more firepower."

"I hear you, brother. You'd better fall back. Keep going north along the ditch. They know you're there, and it's just a matter of time before you get a pineapple headed in your direction, too."

"Roger."

"Alton, how are we going to get out of here?" asked Mallory. "We won't make it five feet in the open, and they'll just keep chucking grenades at this position until they get lucky."

Alton nodded, his mind racing to devise an effective solution. "The best defense is a good offense. Let's go back to the right side. Three-round bursts. Focus on the driveway. If I were trying to flank our position from that side, that's where I'd go—behind that little berm along its edge."

They swung around and fired, their rounds chewing up the driveway's dirt surface and kicking up a cloud of dust. Alton heard an attacker cry out in agony. He didn't know how severely the man was injured—hopefully enough to take him out of the fight.

A blast rocked the front of the dumpster, sending shards of metal spraying out on both sides. Alton's ears rang, and the sounds of combat in his left ear were suddenly dampened.

"Ah, damn!" cried Mallory.

Alton looked over to his wife. A slow drip of blood emerged from between three fingers she pressed onto her left forearm.

"Mallory! You're hit?"

"It's not bad. I think a piece of the dumpster caught me on the last blast." She waved a hand back in the direction of their adversaries. "Let's reengage, or this will be the least of our problems."

Alton nodded. He scanned the side yard, spotting no one, then looked over to David. His friend had crawled forty or fifty yards along the depression—a good thing, too, for another grenade landed at the top of the ditch at David's original location and dribbled down the incline.

"Fire in the hole!" yelled Alton into his mike.

David pulled his arms under his body as the device exploded. Alton heard him grunt over the mike and saw a crimson stain cloud the side of his shirt.

"Shit. David's down."

"Alton, catch!" came Hanif's voice over the mike.

Alton turned to see the ex-policeman standing behind the wooden fence on the edge of the house's property. Hanif swung a pouch over his head and sent it flying in Alton's direction. The bundle almost hit Mallory as it landed at their feet.

As Alton hurried to unsnap the canvas flap, he heard gunfire from Hanif's direction. He looked over to see the former policeman lying in a prone position, looking through his rifle's sights. "Alton, there's a hostile at the southeastern corner of the house, and another low-crawling directly behind the trash container. He's almost in range to throw another grenade."

"Thanks, Hanif," replied Alton. He opened the pouch and discovered a cache of squat bullets. "Awesome—rounds for the M two-oh-threes," he said, referring to their rifles' under-the-barrel grenade launchers. He studied Mallory's face. "How are you holding up?"

Mallory gave her arm a shake. "It stings like a mother, but it's okay."

"Good. In that case, let's load up."

He and Mallory slammed rounds into their weapons.

"Split up," said Alton. "You to the left, me to the right. I'll take the guy right in front of the dumpster. We'll both take the guy on the corner of the house. Stay low."

Hearing them over the mike, Hanif spoke up. "Count down, and I will lay down suppressing fire."

"Roger. On my mark…three, two, one, now!"

Alton and Mallory swung around opposite ends of the metal container, launching their grenades and unleashing a blitz of rounds towards the corner of the house. The man positioned there jerked as if on marionette strings, then fell to the ground in a heap.

Alton's grenade exploded, eliciting cries of agony from the thug who had approached their position head-on. The man sounded too injured to toss any more Russian grenades.

The remaining goons returned fire with a fusillade of their own. How many were there? A stream of rounds pinged off Alton's side of the dumpster's metal wall, and a hail of bullets sliced through the wooden fence behind which Hanif had taken cover.

Ducking behind the dumpster, Alton heard the sound of labored breathing in his ear mike. He looked toward David, but his friend had rolled onto his side and had his rifle pointed in the direction of the combatants, ready to fire if approached. He didn't seem to have any difficulty breathing.

So who was injured? It must be Hanif, but Alton would have to survive this firefight first before he could assist the man.

"Reload," said Alton to Mallory. "Don't give them a chance to catch their breath. You aim for the left side yard, I'll aim for the right."

They punched in two more M203 rounds, then turned and fired. One of the masked men went to catch Alton's round, perhaps with the intent of throwing it back towards them, only to be blown to bits as the impact-detonated grenade landed at his feet.

A burst of fire from two or three AK-47s pinged off the front of the dumpster, setting Alton's ears ringing again.

As suddenly as the firefight had begun, it stopped. Alton and Mallory hung back, suspecting a trap.

"I don't see anyone," said Alton as they both reloaded their M203s, "but they could be coming right up the front, where we can't spot them. We'll have to swing around again from both sides. On my mark…ready, go!"

They pivoted around opposite edges of the container, only to find the yard empty of the living. An explosion from the back of the house sent a plume of black, oily smoke into the air.

"They've detonated the gasoline," said Alton, noticing the blast had occurred too far from the house to ignite it.

He scanned the front and side yards and heard the sounds of men scaling the wall in the backyard. "They're escaping."

"Alton, we can't pursue," said Mallory, her breathing still heavy from the ordeal. Sweat tracked down her face, creating trails of clean, pink skin through the layer of dust that had accumulated there. A line of blood dripped down her arm, staining her pants with crimson drops.

"I know. Let's take a look at your arm."

"I'll be okay. We need to look after David first."

"And Hanif. I think he's down, too." Alton wiped the sweat streaming down his own forehead and ignored the pain lancing down his left thigh.

"Okay," said Mallory. "I'll take Hanif, you take David."

Alton nodded and began hobbling toward his friend. He activated his mike. "Fahima and Kamaal, can you hear me?"

"Yes, we hear you," said Fahima, "Is David all right? How bad is he hurt?"

"I'm heading over to him now. The kidnappers are taking off, so it should be safe for you all to come over here now. Can you bring two of the medic kits? One for David and the other for Hanif and Mallory?"

"Yes, we have them. We are coming."

Alton reached David's side. His friend grimaced. At least he was conscious.

"How you feeling?" asked Alton, kneeling.

"I've been better."

Fahima raced up and fell to the ground, cradling

David's head in her arms. "Oh, my love, my husband!"

"Careful not to jiggle him just yet. David, can you feel this?" asked Alton as he pinched David's toes.

"Ow—yes."

"That's good. It means your spinal cord is still working. I need to roll you over to assess the wound, but we need to go as slow as possible, just in case your spine took a hit."

David's jocularity evaporated, and he seemed too afraid to breathe while Alton and Fahima rolled him onto his stomach.

"You're in luck, dude. It mostly hit a love handle."

"What love handle?" David's eyes narrowed into slits.

"Uh…the ones you've been working on since you married your bride here." Alton removed antiseptic, gauze, antibiotic cream, and bandages from the medic kit, treating David's wound with a field dressing in the space of two minutes.

Alton turned to Fahima. "Can you stay here with David for a minute? I'd like to go see how Mallory is faring with Hanif."

"Yes, I will stay."

Alton limped through the yard and across the decimated front of the dumpster, arriving at the wooden fence the former policeman had used for cover.

He stepped around the fence to see Hanif lying on

the ground behind it, just as he had feared.

"How's he doing?"

"Alton," said Mallory, looking up with tears in her eyes. "Hanif is dead."

CHAPTER 50

Mastana's mind reeled. After her brief taste of freedom, the confines of her cell seemed more oppressive than ever.

She couldn't help but replay the scene of her recapture in her mind. Could she have done something differently? Perhaps she should have used the sewer to her advantage, using it to disguise her scent rather than avoiding its foul contents. But she hadn't known Divband would employ dogs to find her.

The sound of snoring interrupted her musings. The guard on duty, the fat one, often slept on the job, and tonight seemed to be no exception. With a shackle on each limb and two locked doors between herself and the guard, though, Mastana couldn't see how she could use the man's dereliction of duty to her advantage.

A new sound mingled with the snoring—the sound of a girl crying. It seemed to be coming from the adjacent cell.

"Hello?" called Mastana softly. "Is someone there?"

The crying stopped.

"Najia, is that you?" whispered a voice through the cracks.

"No, my name is Mastana. Who is Najia?"

"She was in your cell until a few days ago. Then the guards took her away. I have not heard from her since then. I was hoping she had returned."

A sense of dread filled Mastana's heart. When would it be her turn?

"What is your name?" asked Mastana.

"Sita."

"How did you get here?"

The guard's snoring stopped for a moment, and the girls fell silent. Mastana held her breath. Perhaps the man had merely needed to reposition himself, for his nocturnal blasts resumed within seconds.

"My school is not far from my house, so every day I would walk home after school. About a week or two ago—I am not sure exactly how long—someone grabbed me from behind. I could not see this person, but his arms were very large. He put something over my face, and I passed out. When I woke up, I was here in this cell. I have not been out since then."

"I am here in the same way. A man entered my house when I was alone. Actually, it wasn't *my* house. I was staying with a friend. In any case, a large, brute of a man caught and drugged me, too."

"I am sorry for you."

"Thank you. Sita, what became of Najia?"

"I do not know. But whatever happened to her must surely be our fate, too."

"The guards never speak to you of their plans for us?" asked Mastana.

"No, never."

The muffled sounds of chants from several rooms away reminded them of the menacing presence of their captors.

"Do you have family or friends who might be looking for you?" asked Mastana.

"I am sure my parents are worried and doing all they can, but how would they ever find us? By the time I awoke from the drugs, I was already chained up here inside this room. I do not know where we are. Even if I found a cellphone, I would not know where to tell them to go. What about you, Mastana? Do you think your family is looking for you?"

"My parents are dead," said Mastana, omitting the details of her mother's recent decline. "I have friends who are clever, but as you said, how would they know where to look?"

The teens fell into silence for a minute.

"Sita, do you know if there are others like us in this place?"

"I think so. I believe I heard a girl crying a few days ago, but I cannot be sure. She was too far away for me to call out without the guards hearing."

"I wonder how many of us are here."

"I do not know." Sita's breathing became ragged, as if she were fighting her emotions. "Mastana, I am afraid of this evil place."

"Me, too. If one of us has a chance to escape, we must promise to help the others."

"Yes, I promise."

"As do I," said Mastana. "Now we must hope such an opportunity arises."

But what were the odds of that? Mastana leaned her head against the wall and, exhausted, fell into a fitful slumber, an interval interrupted by recurring dreams of crying, curses, and a bright, blinding light.

CHAPTER 51

Alton's mind reeled. Hanif—dead?

"Are you sure?" he asked, kneeling down.

Mallory nodded, unable to speak as tears tracked down her face.

Alton examined the body. A shot had severed one of Hanif's carotid arteries, causing him to bleed out in a minute or two. Even if Alton had been with him and applied medical treatment the moment the injury occurred, Hanif wouldn't have survived the wound.

Alton felt a sickening sense of déjà vu. Once again, a man under his leadership in Afghanistan had died in combat. He could only stare at the dead man's face.

"Alton," said Mallory. "It wasn't your fault. You gave him the chance to stay away. He came to help us of his own accord."

"But once he arrived, I was happy to have his help. Should I have told him to back off? Or was I too worried about saving you and me?"

"He was a combat-trained policeman who made a personal decision. If you had told him to leave, do you think he would have?"

Alton mulled over the question. He hadn't known Hanif for long, but he had grown to understand the man enough to tender an answer. "Probably not."

"So let's make sure he didn't die for nothing. Let's collect whatever evidence we can from the yard."

"Yeah," said Alton, standing. "You're right. But first let's take care of your arm." He opened the medic kit, cleaned the wound—a light gouge running across the middle of her left forearm—and applied a bandage.

"Good as new," said Mallory.

Alton counted his blessings that the injury hadn't been worse. He turned to Fahima and Kamaal, who stood nearby. "How's David?"

"He is telling his jokes, so I think he will be okay. But I think he will need rest for a few days."

"That's a relief." He looked around the scene of destruction and bloodshed as fire crackled in the backyard. "Did you call the police?"

"Yes, just as you said," replied Fahima.

"I wonder why they're not here yet. This is about as violent a civil crime as you can get."

"I will call them again."

"Wait, why don't I call Captain Poya?" said Alton. "That'll probably get a faster response."

Alton called the police office and was put on hold. As he waited, he walked over to the body of the closest thug. He raised the man's mask to reveal a fellow with a nondescript appearance. Then he rummaged through the dead man's pockets but found nothing but a few banknotes.

Captain Poya came onto the line. "Hello, Mr. Blackwell?"

"Yes. Captain, we just had a major firefight with a band of thugs."

"What? Where?"

"I don't know the exact address here, but we're in the Pule Charki neighborhood."

"What happened? Why are you there?"

"We…uh…read in the paper about a break-in at a house here a couple of days ago. We wondered if it was related to a recent string of kidnappings—including Mastana's—and decided to come here to check the yard and maybe talk with the family, to see if they had any information that could help us track down the kidnappers."

"I see. So how did this turn into a big fight?"

"The kidnappers were already here, a band of ten or twelve men. It looked like they were pouring gas around the house, presumably to burn it. Our guess is that they must have left some evidence behind when their first kidnapping attempt went awry."

"That makes sense, but how did the fighting start if you were just watching them?"

"We established recon positions on the street. The family came home and saw the men in their yard, then left. Just as they pulled away, the kidnappers opened fire on us. We had to return fire just to live."

"I understand that, Mr. Blackwell, but why didn't you call me before the fight started? In a case like the one you're describing, I would have sent policemen."

"We did call, before the fighting began. At least we called the police station. So you never got the word yourself?"

"No. These types of reports come up through my chain of command, but certainly news of a band of men like you've described should have reached my ears. I will have to investigate to see where the communication broke down. For now, I will send officers to the scene."

"Okay. Do you want me to put on Kamaal so he can give you our exact address?"

"Yes. And Mr. Blackwell, please don't touch the crime scene. My men will do that. I don't want the evidence disturbed."

"Understood," replied Alton, handing the phone to the interpreter and walking over to join Mallory as she continued to search the bodies of the dead men.

"Poya says he doesn't want us to disturb the crime scene."

"Once he collects evidence, how much help can we count on from him in the kidnapping case?" said Mallory. "I think we should keep checking."

"Agreed. I'll check out the driveway."

For the first time, Alton assessed the scene of the battle. The destruction and carnage wrought in the space of a few short minutes boggled the mind. Bullet holes pock-marked the house, fence, and driveway, while grenade blasts had sheared away the front and left side of the dumpster as if by a malevolent giant. The bodies of five thugs lay sprawled about the front yard and driveway, while the obliterated remnants of a sixth lay scattered in the vicinity of Alton's second grenade.

They had won the battle, yet it had been a costly victory. David and Mallory were injured, and Hanif was dead. Alton remembered Mallory's entreaty to make use of the battle and hurried to gather evidence before Poya's policemen arrived.

He moved to the driveway and rifled through the dead man's pockets, withdrawing an interesting assortment of items from within: a wallet, a ballpoint pen, and, most importantly, a cellphone. He slipped the items into his own pocket.

He rejoined Mallory. "Did you find anything?"

"Yeah, the guy next to the corner of the house had this." She opened her fist to reveal a few common Afghani coins and, in their midst, a pendent bearing the same pattern they had observed on the victim's bodies: a pentagram within a circle.

"Let's hang onto that. You never know, right?" Alton showed her the items he had collected.

"A cellphone? That could be a goldmine."

"That's what I was thinking. I'm going to work on this as soon as we return to Kamaal's house. But first, we need to visit Hanif's wife. We owe it to her to explain what happened."

An hour later, Alton and the rest met with Ara, Hanif's widow. He described the course of events and the sacrifice her husband had made.

"I'm so sorry, Mrs. Hanif. He told me he quit his job as a policeman to avoid this kind of danger. When we saw the criminals, I directed him a safe assignment, but he saw that Mallory and I were in trouble and came to our aid. I don't think we'd be alive right now if he hadn't intervened."

An initial flash of anger transformed into a look of heartsick resignation. Tears tracked down Ara's face. "That sounds like my Nur. Being a policeman was the occupation he loved. He took the job with KE for me and our children, not for himself."

"If I had known things would turn out like this, I never would have asked—"

"Mr. Blackwell," said Ara, "If Nur did not want to be

there, helping you, he wouldn't have been. I am sad he is gone…so sad. But he has—he *had*—a strong belief in protecting the innocent from evil. That is why he agreed to help you in your investigation."

"If there's anything we can do, please let us know."

"Alton, we'll need to call a cab," said Mallory. "We can't all fit in Kamaal's car." They had left Hanif's Mercedes parked outside.

"Would you like to use the car until you finish your investigation?" asked Ara. "I will have family with me for the next week or so to help with the…arrangements. I will not need it for a little while."

"Thank you. That would help us a lot, Mrs. Hanif," said Alton. "I can see why you and your husband were attracted to each other. You seem a lot alike."

After a few more words of condolences, they departed, leaving behind a grieving widow and bewildered children. What had Mallory said? Make sure Hanif didn't die in vain? Alton promised himself that wouldn't happen.

When the group arrived back at Kamaal's house, Mallory and Fahima helped David inside, where he eased himself onto a futon.

Kamaal placed a kettle of water on the stove to boil. "Would anyone like some green tea? It's good for the nerves."

"Dude, I've been shot," called David. "You got any beer?"

"Technically, it was shrapnel from the grenade," said Alton, "which reminds me…I'd like to take a look at it, if you don't mind."

"Fine," grumbled his friend.

Alton peeled back the hastily-applied field dressing, then swabbed out the antibiotic gel he had squirted into the wound.

"Overall, it doesn't look too bad, but I think you have a piece of metal in there. We need to take you to the ER to have it removed and get you stitched up."

"I don't really think—"

"David Dunlow," said Fahima, "your friend gives you smart advice. I know a good hospital. They will take care of you."

"Plus, we need to get you on an antibiotic so the wound doesn't get infected," added Alton. "Otherwise, you might spend a lot longer in Kabul than you planned."

"Okay, fine. Let's get this over with."

"I will use Hanif's car to take David," said Fahima.

"Do you mind if I stay here to work on this cellphone we recovered on scene today?" asked Alton. "The clock is still ticking for Mastana."

"No, is better if you keep working."

David and Fahima left, and Alton turned his attention to the dead man's cellphone. Luckily, the phone itself wasn't locked. He checked for photographs, but the phone contained none. He brought up the list of phone contacts, which, as expected, were written in Pashto.

"Kamaal, can you help me with this?" Alton asked. "I'd like to record the names of the people listed."

A puzzled look crossed the interpreter's face as he scanned the list. "This is just gibberish. It doesn't mean anything."

"It must be in code, which probably means the phone numbers are encoded, too. Whatever organization this guy was a member of—the Brotherhood, or something else—they took their security seriously. Why else would they have a boatload of Russian rifles and armaments, encrypted contacts, and no photos on their phones?"

"True," said Kamaal. "So is there anything you can do with this phone?"

"Yes. My next step is something I did back when I was in the Army: decrypting enemy messages. In fact, I'll fire up my translation and decryption program now," he said, booting up his laptop.

"Where'd you get the software?" asked Mallory. "You didn't keep a copy from the Army, did you?"

"Naw. The Army software was good, but we've developed a better in-house version at Kruptos."

Alton connected the phone to his computer and downloaded the information from its contacts list. The translation portion of the program converted the original letters to their English equivalents, then the decryption module searched for possible ciphers to the encoded words. As the job ran, Alton dialed the first four phone numbers on the contacts list.

Mallory wandered over, green tea in hand.

"Well, the phone numbers are encrypted, too," said Alton. "They're not real."

"Can you decrypt them?"

"That's challenging, because the only way I can test a decrypted phone number is to call it. Even if someone answers, it doesn't prove it's the *right* number, the one the dead guy intended to save. It only proves I called a functional number."

"That sucks. What about the names on the phone?"

"There we might have more success. Let's see what my program spits out."

Mallory joined Kamaal in the kitchen to help him prepare a light afternoon meal.

As Alton watched the slow movement of the progress bar in his decryption program, his mind was drawn inexorably back to his role as a cryptologist in the Army.

"Captain Blackwell," said a voice.

"Lieutenant Anders? Is that you?" Inexplicably, Alton found himself in his Army "mobcom"—mobile communications—van once again, the van in which he had nearly died when an IED had exploded inside it.

"Yes, sir. Can you give me a hand with the new signal scramblers?"

"But I thought you were…" Alton looked around, disconcerted.

"Alton!" said a female voice.

The mobcom van faded, and Kamaal's kitchen snapped back into focus. Mallory stood over him with a distinctly worried look on her face. "What was that all about?"

Alton sighed. "Can you sit down for a minute?"

She lowered herself into a seat.

"I've been having these…flashbacks, I guess you'd call them, ever since we arrived back here in Kabul. One second I'm sitting here working on a phone, the next I'm back in the mobcom van."

"Oh, Sweetie. Why didn't you tell me?" She laid her hand on his.

"They only last a few seconds. I didn't want you to be worried."

"Anything that affects you like that—even if just for a few seconds—is going to worry me, as it should. What can I do to help?"

"I'm not sure. I wish I knew. One thing I don't understand, though, is why now? I worked here for six months after the mobcom explosion and never had anything like this happen back then. Plus we've worked three dangerous cases together since then."

Mallory pursed her lips. "I'm no psychologist, but perhaps it's because once you left Afghanistan and the Army, you put this part of your life behind you. Maybe coming back, being here physically, has triggered those memories in a more profound way."

"Mm…maybe you're right. I do remember feeling a little overwhelmed as soon as I got off the plane. One thing I can think of that will help…getting the hell out of this country. But first, we find Mastana."

"Yet another reason to find her as quickly as possible."

The laptop beeped.

"Looks like the job finished," said Alton. "Kamaal, can you come take a look at these results?"

"Sure."

"The program lists the five most likely decryptions of each word. If none of them looks right, I'll bring up the next five."

"But these words are in English," said Kamaal, peering at the screen.

"True, but they're simply English renderings of Pashto words. Can you see if any of them look familiar?"

"Yes, I will do that." He ran his finger down the computer screen as he reviewed each line of the program's results. "The names on this fourth row are words in Pashto, but they are not the names of people."

"Could they be nicknames or code names for real

people?"

"I suppose, but why?"

"Same reason the phone numbers are encrypted—to protect the true identities of those involved in this organization."

"I see. In that case, this is probably the correct row. All of the words listed are real."

"But that still leaves us with a dilemma," said Alton. "If these aren't the people's real names, we're back to square one in tracking down Mastana's kidnappers."

CHAPTER 52

Divband drummed his fingers on the hard surface of his desk.

Ghoyee had reported in a few minutes ago. The man had made a shambles of the operation to destroy the house of his failed kidnapping. Six followers were dead with another critically injured. At least Ghoyee himself had made it through unscathed.

This was the work of the Americans, the ones looking for Mastana. They had proven to be more trouble than he had expected. He would have to look for an opportunity to remove them—permanently.

In the meantime, he had to decide how to proceed to correct Ghoyee's failed mission. Should Divband assume that responsibility himself, or should he order Ghoyee to make a second attempt? Perhaps the latter option, which would at least give his right-hand man an opportunity to redeem himself.

With that settled, Divband mulled over the question of ridding himself of the Americans. He would have to devise a strategy to eliminate them before they disrupted any more of his plans. He wasn't yet sure how he was going to pull that off, but he knew he had to do something. The foreigners had turned into a problem he could no longer ignore.

CHAPTER 53

David and Fahima returned from the hospital. Alton couldn't help but notice that David's face seemed more relaxed.

"So, did they get you all fixed up?" asked Mallory.

"You know, yeah, they did," said David. "I'm glad you all talked me into going. The docs took out this one shard that was pretty uncomfortable. It wasn't that big, but it kept digging into me at the wrong angle. Once they removed it and put in a few stiches, I felt a lot better. And I got some antibiotics."

"It sounds like you've improved quite a bit."

"Yep. I should probably lay off the marathons for a while, but otherwise I'm pretty good."

"Cool. I'm glad you're recovering," said Alton. "We could use you." He explained their lack of progress with the cellphone.

"We know we're not going to throw in the towel," said Mallory, "so what are our next steps?"

"Fahima, you haven't had any success asking for information from your friends yet, have you?" asked Alton.

"No. They told me about a few Al-Qaeda attacks, but I am thinking that will not help us now."

"I agree. What about the Brotherhood of Stones? Have you asked them about that?"

"No. I don't think they would know anything about the Brotherhood, but I have another idea. I could ask my old friends at Gandamak's Lodge. When I worked there, I heard a lot of rumors from the customers. Maybe the workers there will know something. Plus, if we go to Gandamak's, I can also visit the bazaar down the street. If some of the workers I used to know are still there, I can ask them about the Brotherhood, too. They also hear a lot of things."

"Excellent," said Alton. "Since you won't need all of us for that, I'm thinking we should divide and conquer. Why don't the rest of us visit Jaweed Bina and see if he knows anything."

"Jaweed Bina?" asked Mallory.

"Yeah. He's the politician Captain Poya said his boss reports to, the governor of Kabul who ordered the police to focus their efforts on terrorism instead of civil crime. Since he's so focused on terrorists, perhaps he's heard of the Brotherhood."

"Sounds like as good an idea as any," said Mallory. "Why don't we eat a quick bite and be on our way."

"Okay," said Alton. "And by the way...we all need to be sure to arm ourselves. We don't want to be caught unprotected."

Thirty minutes later, David and Fahima left in Hanif's Mercedes, their somber silence during the drive marking the memories of their fallen comrade.

They pulled into a gravel lot at the rear of Gandamak's Lodge and stepped out of the car.

"This brings back some memories, doesn't it?" asked David. "That's the bush I hid in with Alton and Mallory the night those Al-Qaeda creeps abducted you."

"And now we are together," said Fahima, taking his hand. "It is a happy ending."

"It sure is. Let's go inside and see what your friends can tell us. Maybe they can help make it a happy ending for Mastana, too."

They circled around to the front of the building, then entered the dim light of its depths. Not much had changed, except the air conditioning unit looked even more dilapidated than before, a transformation David wouldn't have thought possible. A scattering of tables led to booths along the rear wall, and lazy ceiling fans rotated overhead.

At this early hour, only three other people occupied

the restaurant and bar. Things didn't start rocking here until late in the evening.

Fahima approached the smoke-stained oak bar. "Rafi!" she said, embracing her former co-worker as a friend would. The two spoke rapid Pashto in hushed tones for several minutes.

In the middle of their conversation, Fahima tensed.

"What is it?" asked David.

"Rafi says an Al-Qaeda man with a pistol tucked into his pants just entered the building, and another one is looking at us from outside."

David turned as casually as he could and leaned his elbows back on the bar. A man wearing a tightly-wound turban peered through the front window's dirty glass. He seemed to be staring at David and Fahima.

"How do you know they're Al-Qaeda?"

"He and the man who entered both wear the black sash of Al-Qaeda," said Fahima. "This is how they know one another."

"Why would he care about us unless…maybe Dani gave his terrorists friends a heads up and they've been on the lookout for us. Do you think they recognized Hanif's car out back?"

"I do not know, and I don't want to find out. The man outside looks angry."

"Got any good ideas for getting out of here?" asked David.

"Walk towards the exit, then when we reach the kitchen door, go through it. We can pass through the kitchen and out the backdoor into the parking lot where our car waits for us."

"Yeah, and hope these guys don't have any buddies waiting for us, too," said David, even as he began to follow Fahima's instructions.

As they neared the kitchen, David could hear the first terrorist approach from behind. Without warning, David spun and cold-cocked the man's jaw, sending him collapsing to the floor in an unconscious heap.

The couple bolted through the kitchen door. Running through the claustrophobic space, David grabbed a pot of some dark, bubbling liquid. "Insurance."

"But your Beretta—" began Fahima.

"Too loud," panted David as he held a hand to the wound on his back. "It'll alert anyone else in this area who might be looking for us."

They burst through the restaurant's rear door and skidded to a stop in the parking lot. Shouts coming from the building's nearest side indicated their pursuer had rounded the front corner and trailed them by only seconds.

David waited behind the rear corner of the building long enough to chuck the scalding liquid into the terrorist's face before joining Fahima in a sprint for their car.

They piled inside. David gunned the Mercedes'

engine, sending the vehicle spinning out of the parking lot as it sprayed a rooster tail of gravel. They shot down an alley and made a hard right onto a two-lane road.

As they turned onto a main thoroughfare, David slowed the car and turned to his wife. "You okay?"

"Yes. What about you?"

"I'm fine." He paused to let his frenetic heart rate subside and the pain in his wound recede. "Good thing there weren't any more terrorists. I'm fresh out of boiling oil."

CHAPTER 54

At the same time David and Fahima had departed for Gandamak's Lodge, the others had left to visit Jaweed Bina.

Kamaal parked in a visitors spot, directly in front of the municipal building. He, Alton, and Mallory entered the building, which resembled a slice of America in the nineteen fifties or sixties. Drop-panel ceilings joined plain, cinderblock walls. Each office door featured a glass window and a nameplate.

The three approached a main lobby desk, where Kamaal spoke with the receptionist.

"She says Governor Bina is busy all day. We will have to make an appointment for next week to see him."

"Tell her that we have information about a recent string of kidnappings and murders in Kabul," said Alton. "Tell her we believe this is the act of a new terrorist group, and we seek any information the governor may have about this new group."

After Kamaal relayed the information, the receptionist whispered into the phone, then spoke to Kamaal.

"We can go in now."

They traveled down the hallway, their footsteps echoing off dingy linoleum. Kamaal pointed to a door. "This is it."

Alton knocked. Not receiving an answer, he swung open the door. A thin man with pitch-black hair and metallic glasses glared at them from behind an imposing mahogany desk. He waved them to a cluster of small, plastic chairs facing him.

They took a seat.

"What do you want?" asked Bina in accented English.

"I'm Alton Blackwell. This is my wife, Mallory, and our friend Kamaal. We came to your city to look for a young friend who was kidnapped. While we've been looking for her, we've uncovered evidence of a new organization that may have kidnapped nine other girls and murdered at least five of them, maybe more."

"The receptionist said you had information about a terrorist organization, not some lunatic abducting and killing girls. Now if you'll excuse me—"

"Wait," said Alton. "This isn't one guy."

"How do you know?"

"We had a major firefight with the kidnapping

organization this morning, right here in Kabul. A friend of mine—a former policeman of yours—was killed in that firefight. The perpetrators were armed with AK-47s and grenades. That meets the definition of a terrorist organization in my book."

Bina studied him for a moment. "Do you know the name of this organization?"

"Just a guess. Based on the symbol they draw on the bodies of their murder victims, we think it may be an organization called the Brotherhood of Stones."

Bina drummed his fingers on the desk in front of him. "Would you excuse me for a moment? I would like to hear more, so I will need to reschedule a call that is supposed to begin in a few minutes." He paced to the corner of the room and activated his cellphone, speaking too low for them to hear.

He returned. "Tell me how you got into this firefight."

It seemed an odd way to begin, but Alton described the sequence of events.

"You Americans are all the same," said Bina. "You think you can come here and take over law enforcement. I have news for you. We have our own police for that. Civilians, including Americans, are not authorized to take police actions, especially against organized criminals."

"We called the police as soon as we saw the masked men," said Alton, "and we only returned fire after they started firing at us."

"So you say. I wonder if they would tell the same story."

"I'm sure a bunch of murderers wearing masks would tell the absolute truth," said Mallory, exasperated. "Of course, none of the living ones stuck around to make a statement."

"You are in my country, Mrs. Blackwell, so don't speak unless you are spoken to."

Alton could feel his hackles rise, but he forced himself to stay on task. He needed the man's cooperation if he was to rescue Mastana. "Governor Bina, have you heard of this Brotherhood of Stones organization?"

The man paused. "I have not. There was some kind of Stones cult that existed many centuries ago, at least that's what I was taught in school. But unless they have managed to rise from the grave, I don't think they are kidnapping anyone these days."

"We didn't fight ghosts this morning. Those were real people. Have you at least heard of this string of kidnappings?"

"I have not. I leave such civil affairs for my police force to handle."

"But the police are focused on terrorists—on your orders."

"Do you presume to tell me how to manage the affairs of my city?"

"No, sir. I come to you with the proposition that we

can help each other."

"I don't see what you have to offer that I would want."

"Your police didn't connect the murders with the Brotherhood of Stones," said Alton. "My friends and I did. And if you can put someone on your force to look into that lead and share what he learns, we'd be happy to share any additional information we uncover as well."

Bina steepled his fingers. "Here is my dilemma, Mr. Blackwell. Do you know how hard it is for a Shiite Muslim to rise to the position of governor in a country dominated by eighty percent Sunnis? Let me tell you, it is not easy. My detractors would love to have another reason to call for my removal. Giving two Americans jurisdiction over an investigation is something they would call into question."

"We're not asking for jurisdiction, just mutual cooperation."

"No, Mr. Blackwell, it won't do. You seem to think my police aren't capable of solving a major crime like this on their own, and I assure you that they are."

"Governor Bina—"

"That will be all, Mr. Blackwell. Or do I need to call security?"

The trio rose to leave.

"So if we uncover more evidence in this case," said Alton, "should we pass it along to your police force, or are they so good, they'll already have it?"

"You are very sure of yourself, but I don't think you'll learn anything new here."

They exited the governor's office and moved down the hall.

"That could have gone better," said Alton.

"You tried," said Mallory, grasping his hand. "I don't think there was anything else you could have said."

They climbed into Kamaal's Corolla and pulled out of the parking lot.

"Now what do we do?" asked the interpreter.

"Let's go back to your place," said Alton. "I've run some internet searches on the Brotherhood of Stones, but only on public domains. I'd like to try some government databases. Maybe Mallory can check with the FBI and see if they have anything on them."

"I already did," said Mallory. "It came up blank."

Kamaal drove onto a bridge spanning the Kabul River on the outskirts of the city. They had just reached the center of the structure when two cars pulled across the bridge, blocking both lanes.

"It's a trap," said Alton. "Turn around—quick!"

Just as Kamaal slowed and began turning his wheel hard to the left, a trailing car rammed into the side of the Corolla, sending it careening into the guard rail.

The Corolla died. Kamaal frantically twisted the key over and again, but the engine refused to start.

"Grab the A-fours, and let's get out of here!" said Alton, thankful that most of their cache of weapons lay ensconced in Hanif's Mercedes and Kamaal's house.

As Alton grabbed his rifle from the trunk and began to flee, he looked back over his shoulder. The trailing car that had smashed them, an older Taurus, had itself crashed into the opposite guardrail. A brute of a man leapt from the Ford and began to give chase. The distance was too great to discern the man's features, but Alton could see he was huge.

While Mallory and Kamaal probably could have outdistanced their pursuer, Alton knew he had no hope. He hobbled along the bridge's great span with the thug closing the distance every second.

Alton turned to fire his A4, only to find the pursuer had already begun to raise a pistol. Knowing panic would lead to an errant shot, he took an extra moment to line up his rifle. Before Alton could squeeze the trigger, though, a pair of booming shots rang out.

CHAPTER 55

Mastana awoke, her thoughts blurred from lack of nourishment. The shackles encircling each limb rendered her bouts of sleep even more uncomfortable than during her first interval of captivity.

She heard the slow tones of the guard's snoring. Perhaps she could talk with the girl in the neighboring cell.

"Sita," she called softly. "Are you there?"

Mastana waited a full sixty seconds but received no reply. She called again, yet still no answer.

Mastana dared to raise her voice a little more. "Is there anyone else being held prisoner here…besides me?"

Only the guard's incessant wheezing reached her ears. Were there other girls in nearby cells who couldn't hear her or were too frightened to speak? Or was Mastana truly the cell block's only occupant?

Mastana had never felt so alone. The feeling threatened to crush her earlier resolve to escape. But there remained in her the faintest hope that somehow, she might yet take flight from these evil people. She must never give up trying to figure out a way.

CHAPTER 56

From the bridge's pedestrian sidewalk, Alton had prepared to fire at his pursuer when a pair of gunshots rang out from behind.

The enormous pursuer spun sideways on the first impact and careened over the bridge's low railing on the second. Moments later, his body penetrated the water thirty feet below with a resounding *ca-whoomp*.

Mallory lowered her smoking A4. "It was him or you."

A shot ricocheted off the walkway's railing, while other rounds skittered across the surface of the bridge in front of them. The occupants of the two vehicles blocking the bridge had pointed handguns out their windows and were now letting loose a barrage of fire.

"Head for cover—back to the car!" cried Alton.

Flipping the safety switch of his A4 to three-round

bursts, Alton sent several volleys of hot metal into the blocking vehicles. The attackers ducked behind their doors, giving Mallory and Kamaal time to reach the cover of the disabled Corolla. They laid down suppressing fire from both sides of the vehicle, giving Alton time to join them.

Alton checked the chamber of his M203 to ensure the grenade round was still there. He had preloaded all of their rifles after the firefight that morning.

Taking aim, he fired towards the car on the left. The round dropped into the open window—a lucky shot, really—and sent the car expanding into a fireball of flaming wreckage.

While the husk of the first car burned, the motor of the second one roared to life. The driver spun the steering wheel and punched the gas, sending his vehicle squealing away from the Corolla. Alton and Mallory fired a few shots at the retreating car, but it soon disappeared into the traffic on the opposite side of the bridge.

"You all okay?" asked Alton.

They replied in the affirmative.

Alton surveyed the wreckage of this latest attack. He withdrew his cellphone from his pocket and dialed a number. "Connect me with Captain Poya, please."

"This is Captain Poya. Is that you, Mr. Blackwell?"

"Yes. I have to report a violent crime—again. Someone just tried to kill us."

CHAPTER 57

Working together, Alton and Kamaal managed to restart the Corolla, escaping the bridge before their adversaries could return with reinforcements and finish them off. They moved through heavy traffic, making their way back to Kamaal's house.

During the drive, Alton filled in Poya on the details of the attack. The policeman promised to send someone out to the bridge to investigate.

As they neared the house, Alton's phone vibrated. He took it out and scanned the message.

"Who's that from?" asked Mallory.

"David. He says his phone stopped working, so he picked up a burner. He says they've made an important discovery and want us to meet them at Bala Hissar," said Alton, referring to the city's well-known ancient fortress. "Wait a minute, though. Look at this." He handed his phone to Mallory.

She read it off. "'Hey, Alton. Phone is broken…'" She stopped and looked up.

"David never calls me 'Alton.' It's always 'Al.' And even then, he doesn't put my name in his texts. Someone's trying to lead us into a trap."

"Tell 'David' we'll be over in a few hours, after we run an errand," said Mallory. "That should buy us some time to continue the investigation until they realize we're a no-show."

"Good idea." Alton rubbed his chin. "You know, if these guys tracked down my phone number, they may be able to locate Kamaal's house, too. Perhaps it's time to move our HQ to a different location."

"I agree," said Mallory. "Let's touch bases with the real David and line up a rendezvous spot."

"I know a good place," said Kamaal. "There is an inn on the edge of town owned by my friend Sabir. Let's go back to my house to gather your belongings and weapons, then head to the inn."

"Sounds good," said Alton. "I'll text the fake David and tell him we've already left your place. That should keep them away long enough for us to gather our stuff. Then I'll call the real David and Fahima and get them up to speed."

They all arrived at Kamaal's house at about the same time. Happy that their friends had survived the latest round of battles, the members of the two groups embraced.

"Okay, let's gather our stuff and get the hell out of Dodge," said Alton.

"Alton, wait," said Kamaal as he stood near the police scanner Hanif had provided several days earlier. "I think they are talking about you all."

"What—?" began Alton, but Kamaal waved him quiet, listening with his head cocked. "Poya has issued an arrest warrant for Mallory."

"Why?" said Alton. "We were the ones attacked."

"The man she shot…he was a policeman. Just before Mallory shot him, he radioed in he was chasing criminals on the Behsood bridge. Now no one can reach him on the radio."

"Why would he say that?" said Alton. "Unless…"

"What?" asked Mallory.

"Our attacker, the policeman, must have been one of them, one of the Brotherhood of Stones members," said Alton. "What else explains it? We weren't even speeding."

"But how did this policeman know where to find us?"

"Remember how Governor Bina made a call right after we mentioned the Brotherhood in his office? Maybe he's mixed up in this somehow, too. Once we arrived and announced our intensions of looking for the Brotherhood, he must have called his buddy on the police force."

"Wait," said Kamaal, holding up a hand again. "They

are also calling for a search for the missing policeman, in case he wasn't the one shot, I suppose. He is Sergeant Gutzar Majid."

"Majid!" said Alton. "That's the guy who works for Poya. Remember the other day, Poya asked that guy if he'd heard of the Brotherhood of Stones? He said 'no' but looked kind of weirded out at the time. Now I understand why. And now that I think about it, Majid was a huge guy, just like the man who pursued us on the bridge. It has to be him."

"I agree," said Mallory, "but this whole turn of events is going to make the search for Mastana even tougher. Instead of helping us, the police will be looking to arrest us."

"Then it's a good thing I have access to the police's databases," said Alton. "Anyway, it's not like they've helped us much so far."

"True."

Alton turned to the others. "Before we leave, we'd better activate our shroud apps."

"What's that?" asked Kamaal.

"My company recently finished work on an app to block a phone's GPS locator. If we turn it on, the authorities can't trace our location through our phones. Kamaal, you'd better take the battery out of your phone, or they'll trace us through you. Or you could download the app."

"I don't want to disable my phone. I will install the

app."

"Okay, I'll send you the link."

Kamaal's fingers danced over his phone, installing and activating the program. "We had better leave," he urged. "We don't want the police to arrive while we're still here."

They gathered their suitcases and the weapons they had stored in the house, packed everything into the two vehicles, then drove off into the dusty haze of Kabul.

An hour later, as they settled into the plain, cozy rooms of the inn, Alton's phone chimed. He snatched it from his pocket to read the incoming text message.

> I see you discovered our earlier deception concerning your friend David. I will give you this warning only once: leave Afghanistan, and never return, or you and your friends will die. There are forces aligned against you that you cannot imagine. You will not win—I promise. How could a crippled, ex-soldier ever hope to defeat an entire organization? Remember: leave or die.

CHAPTER 58

Alton showed the message to his friends. As he expected, it did nothing to deter their resolve to track down Mastana.

They all agreed that Kamaal and Fahima, being the most inconspicuous members of the team, would collect their meals. With this assignment in mind, the two left to acquire a much-needed dinner.

While they were out, Alton's cellphone rang. "Now what?" he said to Mallory as he brought the device to his ear. "Hello?"

"Why did you do it?" asked Captain Poya. "Why did you and your friends kill my sergeant?"

"Now wait—"

"I just received word that they recovered Sergeant Majid's body from the Kabul River—with two bullet holes in his chest."

"He ambushed us when we emerged from Governor Bina's office," replied Alton.

"A policeman 'ambushed' you? That's called an arrest, not an ambush."

Alton began to pace the narrow room. "He wasn't wearing a uniform, and he drove an unmarked car. And once he ran into *our* car and disabled it, he shot at us without making any kind of statement or command at all. That doesn't sound like something a cop would do. You said yourself your men worry about only the most violent civilian crimes, so why would a policeman take the time to track us from Bina's office? What was his purpose?"

The first note of conciliation crept into Poya's voice. "I don't know. He didn't say why he was there, just that he was trailing criminals."

"Why would Mallory shoot a cop, or anyone, for that matter, other than in self-defense?"

A note of steel returned to Poya's voice. "Who knows? I don't care. I know she did it, and that's enough."

"But she did it in self-defense. He was trying to kill us."

"Sergeant Majid may have been a little reckless and hardheaded at times, but he was a good policeman. He would not chase you unless you were doing something wrong. And I will find out what you were doing."

"I've already told you exactly what we were doing: speaking with Governor Bina about Mastana's kidnapping. You can confirm that with Bina, unless he's one of them himself. If you truly want to get to the bottom of this, you might want to start with asking why Sergeant Majid was waiting for us outside Bina's office. We all saw Bina make a call just after we told him about our search for the Brotherhood of Stones. He must have called Majid. How else would the sergeant know we were there?"

"If you turn yourself in, I will check into these claims. I really don't think Governor Bina is part of this Brotherhood cult. He's not the type to get mixed up in that sort of thing. But I warn you, if you are right, and Bina *is* involved, is not good for you. He is the top politician in Kabul. He could have a hundred men looking for you if he wanted."

"I appreciate the heads up about Governor Bina, and I'm sorry your sergeant got himself killed, but we're not turning ourselves in, not while Mastana's life hangs in the balance."

"Then it will be my job to find you…and bring you to justice."

CHAPTER 59

After dining in their rooms at the inn, Mallory turned to Alton. "Will you be able to track the threatening text message back to the sender?"

"I was just getting ready to try that."

Alton opened his laptop and brought up a Kruptos program. Using a USB cable to connect his cellphone to the computer, he download his texting information to the program, which then tapped into the local phone network.

The laptop emitted a chime, indicating the tracking program had finished.

"What's it say?" asked Mallory.

"Rats. The message was sent by a burner phone. Whoever sent it has probably already chucked it in the trash by now."

"That's too bad, but not really a surprise, right?"

"No. The sender would've been a complete moron to use their own phone for that kind of message. But you never know—sometimes you get lucky."

Mallory drummed her fingers on the table. "Since we don't know who sent the message, we need a new lead. Now that we have a confirmation that the cop who tried to kill us was Majid, can you break into his e-mail account and review his messages? Maybe they'll lead us somewhere."

"That's a good idea," said Alton. "I'll start working on that now. Kamaal, if I'm able to break into his e-mail, I'll need your help translating."

Despite his exhaustion from the day's activities, Alton attacked the problem of cracking the dead policeman's e-mail account with all of his mental acuity, knowing Mastana's life might depend on the success of his efforts.

After two hours, he leaned back in the rickety chair he had drawn up to the room's tiny desk. "Got it."

"You're in Majid's e-mail account?" asked Kamaal.

"Yep. Now it's your turn. Can you tell me what this says?" said Alton, gesturing to the Pashto script filling the screen.

Kamaal spent the next half hour reading the man's messages. Alton used the interval to assess David's wound. It had bled a little during his flight from

Gandamak's Lodge, but the stitches had held, thankfully.

"There is no doubt," announced Kamaal. "Sergeant Majid was a member of the Brotherhood of Stones."

"How do you know?" asked Mallory.

"The names used by the people—many of them are the same ones Alton decrypted from the phone he recovered off the dead fighter this morning. They are the same *code* names, not the real names of the people."

"So we know both dead men knew the same Brotherhood members," said Alton, "we just don't know who those members are, right?"

"That is correct," replied Kamaal.

"So once again, we're back to square one."

CHAPTER 60

"Maybe we should redirect our research back to Sergeant Majid," said Mallory.

"What do you mean?" asked Alton. "He's dead."

"Exactly. We might learn more from him dead than alive. Poya won't share any details about his own man's death, at least not with us. But he might put a lot of investigative details into his department's criminal database."

"Which I can access online," said Alton. "It's worth a shot. And since Majid worked for him, you know Poya's going to fast-track the investigation, which means we shouldn't have to wait long for information to show up in the database. In fact, I'm going to check now."

Alton accessed the police records, then requested Kamaal's help to track down and translate the details of the investigation into Majid's death.

"Here are photographs of the items in the policeman's possession," said Kamaal.

"Good, let's take a look," said Alton as Mallory joined them.

"What are we looking for, exactly?" asked Mallory.

"Anything out of the ordinary."

Alton began scrolling through the items, lingering long enough to study each one. Most of them were unremarkable, but one stood out from the rest.

"What's that?" asked Mallory as Alton brought up the anomaly.

"Looks like some kind of old coin." The white-hued, circular item depicted the silhouette of a soldier wearing a tall helmet.

"Do you think we should follow up on this?"

"Probably. It's not like we have any other leads at the moment. Let's look at the rest of the photos and see if we find anything more promising."

The final two pictures showed only a pen and a condom, so they returned to the photo of the coin. Alton copied the image onto his laptop, then sent it to his phone.

"Kamaal, do you know anyone who can help us make heads or tails of this coin?" he asked, snickering at his unintended wordplay.

"Dude, you talk about *my* jokes!" called David from

across the room.

"I do not know what you mean, 'heads or tails'," said Kamaal.

"What I mean is, do you know someone who can give us some details about this coin? Maybe Sergeant Majid purchased it at a particular market. If so, perhaps we can track his movements backwards from that location."

"I see. Well, there is a famous…how you say… archeologist who teaches in Kabul University. He specializes in the study of Afghani antiquities."

"Do you trust him?" asked Mallory.

"Yes, I've known Professor Aziz for nearly ten years. He's an academic, not a violent cultist."

"In that case, he sounds perfect," said Alton. "Let's go see him."

"I should let you know. He is known for being a little…unusual."

"Do you mean he won't see us?"

"There are many requests for his time. We must explain why he should honor our request."

"It's getting pretty late," said Mallory, glancing at her watch. "Do you think he's still at the university?"

"There is only one way to find out. I will call him."

Kamaal looked up a number on his phone, then dialed. Once connected, his speech grew more impassioned, then calmed as the call ended.

"Well?" asked Mallory.

"We will meet him in his office at nine o'clock tomorrow morning."

The band of would-be rescuers arrived at the university well in advance of the appointed time, entering the grounds by passing under an arched sculpture depicting waterfowl in flight. Kamaal walked them to the Humanities building—a plain, brick affair—then led them through a series of twisting hallways to the proper office.

He swung open the door to another world. Trinkets and artifacts of all stripes—pottery, jewelry, tools, old currency, and a myriad of other items—seemed to inhabit every flat surface not already occupied by scores of books. Rusty wind chimes and delicate talismans hung from the ceiling, and a dozen or so bulky stone statues created a reasonably-challenging obstacle course as one attempted to navigate across the floor. Dark wood wall panels put the finishing touch on the room's natural, almost wild, ambience.

Buried beneath the collection of artifacts sat a modest desk with an older man hunched over it. He had a small stature, almost childlike, but the lines of many years under the hot sun were etched upon his kindly, bronze face. Upon hearing the noise they made nearly tripping over a smiling Buddha parked in the middle of the floor, the man pushed a pair of spectacles higher on his nose and rose to greet his guests.

The Devil's Due

He conducted a brief conversation in Pashto with Kamaal, then turned to the others with an extended hand.

"I am Professor Aziz. I am sorry for ignoring you, but I have not seen Kamaal here for some time."

"It's a pleasure to meet you, Professor," said Alton, grasping the man's hand.

"Thank you. Likewise, I'm sure." He introduced himself to the rest of the party. "Ah, Kamaal, I have not seen you since the last time you took one of my classes. How long has it been? Nearly eight years, no?"

"I believe so, Professor," replied the former student with a smile.

"Ah, what a fine archeologist he would have made," said the Professor, flapping his arms in excitement, somewhat in the fashion of a duck. He turned to the others. "Four classes of mine he took—four! Who takes so many unless they will be working in this field?"

"Perhaps someone with a deep interest in the subject, Professor," replied Kamaal, clearly enjoying the reunion with his former instructor.

"Now, I am happy to see you, Kamaal, and the rest of you, too, but I do have a schedule to keep. I understand you would like to consult me about an artifact."

"That's right, Professor," said Alton.

"Why don't we get started, then? Now, I must tell you…Kamaal whetted my appetite last night by saying you had an urgent question, the answer to which could be a matter of life or death. I understand he may have exaggerated, so I won't hold it against you when you explain the true nature of your inquiry."

"I don't think he was exaggerating, Professor Aziz, but I'll let you be the judge of that."

Intrigued by Alton's claim, Aziz performed a quick duck-flap of excitement as he resumed his seat at the desk. "Do tell me."

"We came to Kabul to help find a teenage girl named Mastana. She's a friend of ours and was kidnapped last week. But the kidnapper wasn't acting alone. He was part of some shadowy organization called the Brotherhood of Stones."

This comment merited another duck flap on the professor's part.

"This Brotherhood organization has kidnapped nine other teenage girls in the last few months and killed at least five of them," continued Alton. "They engaged us in two separate battles yesterday, which leads us to believe we're coming closer to learning the truth about their organization and, hopefully, finding Mastana."

"My word!" said Aziz, producing a duck-flap of extended duration, accompanied by a slight shake of his left leg. "This is the most remarkable thing I've ever heard! But…what can I do to help you?"

Alton pulled his cellphone from a pocket and showed Aziz the picture of the dead man's coin. "This was in the pocket of Sergeant Majid, a member of the Brotherhood who was killed in one of yesterday's firefights. We were hoping you could give us some background on it, perhaps where it might have been purchased. Anything that could help us track this artifact back to other members of the Brotherhood would be helpful."

Aziz studied the picture. "I haven't seen one of these in decades. It looks like something that would have come from Bagram."

"Bagram?" asked Alton, "The city where the US military runs a prison?"

"Yes, but Bagram is an ancient city. It used to lie on the Silk Road to China. Long ago, Alexander the Great captured the city, and it has changed hands many times over the millennia."

"Interesting, but does the coin point definitively to Bagram, or could it have come from some other site?"

Aziz cocked his head and examined the artifact's photo once more. "This is not a coin. It is a plaster cast of a Greek soldier. The only place I have seen one like this is from Bagram—the ancient city, not the one people live in now."

Alton shot a glance at Mallory, perplexed. "So there are *two* Bagrams?"

"The modern Bagram is about sixty kilometers north of Kabul," said Aziz. "The ancient city lies on the western side of the foothills that surround the modern city."

"So they're close to each other?" asked Mallory.

"Well, yes, but it is difficult to reach the ancient

Bagram site. You must travel on dirt roads over the foothills. It can be dangerous, especially at night. That's why people don't go there anymore. Plus, the site was pretty thoroughly excavated in the nineteen-sixties, so people in my profession moved on to more promising locations."

"So let me make sure I'm getting this straight," said Alton. "You believe this plaster cast came from the ancient Bagram?"

"Yes. At least, the only other cast I've seen that's identical to this relic came from that city."

"Let's operate on the assumption that Majid's cast came from the ancient Bagram," said Mallory: "What else can you tell us about that site?"

Aziz warmed to the subject, letting a slight flap escape. "Oh, it is quite fascinating. Archeologists have found all manner of statues and plaster casts and totems and pottery, artifacts spanning thousands of years."

"Wait," said David. "You said totems—as in items of worship?"

"Yes. Because of the city's location on the Silk Road, many religions and cults set up their houses of worship there. In fact, as the city was conquered, the same central temple was appropriated by different religious groups over the centuries."

"What about the Brotherhood of Stones?" asked Mallory. "Did they ever set up shop there?"

"Permit me to make a small observation. In academic

circles, we refer to this group as the *Cult* of Stones, not the Brotherhood of Stones."

"Why don't you tell us about the Cult of Stones?"

Suppressing another movement of his appendages, Aziz continued. "The Cult of Stones existed long before Islam. Its members emphasized certain rock formations, especially the type found in abundance in Bagram, as dwelling places of *div*."

"'*Div*?" asked Mallory.

"A *div* is a special class of *jinnd*. The *jinnd* are spirits. They can be either benevolent, the white *jinnd*, or malicious, the black *jinnd*. The worst of these black *jinnd* are called *div*—demons, in English. The leader of the *div* is Iblis, who you would call Satan.

"The leader of the Cult of Stones held the title of 'Divband,' which means binder, or ruler, of demons. Despite the lofty title, this leader did not truly rule Satan and his minions. Rather, legend says the Divband entered into an uneasy truce with Iblis, an agreement in which each provided for the needs of the other."

"I'm guessing this truce had something to do with human sacrifice," said Alton.

"I'm afraid so," said Aziz. "The cultists were promised powers in exchange for the sacrifice of unspoiled women, who were considered the brides of Iblis."

Alton turned to his companions. "That sounds a hell of a lot like the kidnappers we're facing now, doesn't it?"

"Absolutely," said Mallory. "The Brotherhood must be some modern incarnation of this ancient cult."

"I can see the appeal two thousand years ago," said Alton, turning back to the professor, "but how would anyone buy into that crap today?"

Professor Aziz looked thoughtful. "When Islam began to spread throughout this region in the seventh century, many elements of pre-Islamic beliefs integrated with the new religion, creating a unique belief system in Afghanistan. This belief system has perpetuated until this day. In many ways, the native Afghani manifestation of Islam is closer to the beliefs of the Cult of Stones than it is to the imported Islam of the Taliban and Al-Qaeda. Many of my countrymen resent the unnatural Islamic beliefs of these terrorist groups and would welcome a return to the traditional ways."

"I get that, but resurrecting the practice of human sacrifice seems pretty extreme," said Alton.

"Yes, but after years of oppression and helplessness, I think some people, perhaps many people, would accept that as the price of reinstating our core beliefs."

Alton pulled from his pocket a pendant depicting a pentagram inside a circle, the one he had acquired from a dead assailant the previous morning. He handed it to Professor Aziz. "Is this symbol associated with the Cult of Stones?"

"Yes, exactly. And several other groups that came after them, too."

"One thing I don't understand," said Mallory.

"Modern satanic groups around the world use this symbol today. How is it that this group used the same symbol so long ago?"

"Remember," said the professor, "this part of the world is the cradle for three of civilization's major religions: Judaism, Christianity, and Islam. It is also the birthplace of a number of other belief systems, including the worship of Iblis, or Satan. This symbol, the pentagram inside a circle, originated with Satan worship in these parts over two millennia ago and has been used ever since."

"I see," said Alton. "Is there anything else can you tell us about this cult?"

Aziz studied the ceiling, deep in thought. "Most cult members were assigned a nickname as part of their transition into the organization. This served as a way of separating the member from their old life and establishing a new identity within the cult."

David snorted. "Sounds like boot camp."

"By any chance," said Alton, "could this be one of those nicknames?" He used his cellphone to show Aziz a photo of a symbol: ثور.

"Why, yes. This is 'Ghoyee,' meaning 'bull' in Pashto. Was this assigned to a large man?"

"You have no idea. This was Sergeant Majid's nickname. That guy was huge."

"It makes sense," asked Fahima, "but how do you know this is Majid?"

"Remember how I took the phone off the guy who died outside the girl's house yesterday morning? Well, I saw this symbol in its contacts list. Then, when I saw the personal-effects photos of Majid's stuff online, I noticed he had the same symbol etched onto his cellphone case." Alton turned to Aziz. "Professor, you said people stopped excavating the ancient Bagram site in the sixties. So no one is there now?"

"I don't think so. I haven't heard of any excavation work there for years."

"And Professor Aziz would know," added Kamaal.

"I think we should check out that site," said Alton. "Maybe it's been reoccupied recently." The others nodded. "Care to come with us, Professor?"

"You make me wish I were young again. It sounds exciting, but I'm too old and fragile for that kind of adventure. My bad back could not withstand the roads leading over the foothills. And I don't know the front end of a gun from the back."

"We'll miss your expertise, but I certainly understand. Since you can't accompany us, do you have any maps of the area?"

"Yes, I do—maps of the roads leading there and of the ancient city itself." Aziz scurried to a grey, metal filing cabinet and withdrew a folder overflowing with yellowed papers. Laying the folder on his desk, he flipped through its contents, eventually picking out two pages. "This is a map of the road leading to the ancient city. The modern Bagram is here on the right, the ancient city is on the left. This next sheet shows the organization of the compound itself. This outer perimeter is composed of a series of guard posts—small, stone buildings. Inside the guard posts lies the inner perimeter, really nothing more than a dirt path encircling the edge of the temple complex."

Alton studied the documents. "Is this large room where they would meet for their ceremonies?" he asked, pointing to a spacious chamber pictured in the compound's centermost building.

"Yes—and perform sacrifices."

"Does the compound contains prison cells?"

"Yes. That was a standard feature of temples at that time. The cells are located here, on the southeastern side," said the professor, pointing to a rectangular structure on the map. "The entrance is aboveground, but the cell block itself lies partially underground."

Alton committed the building's location to memory. If Mastana were being held at the compound, chances were she occupied one of those cells. "Thanks, Professor Aziz. I can't tell you how helpful your expertise has been…and these maps, too."

"I can make copies, if you like."

"That would be perfect," said Alton. "Next stop, the temple of ancient Bagram."

CHAPTER 61

Mastana's eyes opened only with difficulty. Was that distant noise real or a product of her recurrent nightmares?

Any unnecessary movement now required too great an expenditure of precious energy, so she remained motionless on the floor. The sparse rations provided during her first round of captivity had tapered off to almost nothing, rendering her weak in the extreme from lack of nourishment.

She longed to speak with Sita, yet every attempt to reestablish contact with her neighbor had failed. Had Sita been taken away while Mastana slept? She prayed this was not the case.

When was the last time she had heard a friendly voice, or taken a sip of water or had a bite to eat? Hours? Days? If they needed her for some grand purpose, why did they allow her to decline so? What purpose could she serve if she perished?

CHAPTER 62

Alton and the others returned to their quarters at the inn to regroup.

"Our first order of business should be acquiring new vehicles," said Alton. "Al-Qaeda probably tracked down David and Fahima yesterday by spotting Hanif's Merc, and it's a pretty safe bet the police are looking for our cars, too. Plus, Professor Aziz said the roads over the foothills around Bagram are pretty rough. Jeeps or SUVs would be more suitable for that kind of terrain."

"So what's the best way to get some off-road vehicles?" asked Mallory.

"There is a place near the airport," said Kamaal. "But I am a little worried. Even if I pay in cash, I will still have to give my name. If the police have my identity, they will know what types of rental cars to look for."

"Why don't I ask my friend Rafi to rent the cars for us?" said Fahima. "The police aren't looking for him."

"That would be better," said Mallory. "Can you call him up now?"

"Yes."

"While Fahima is taking care of that," said Alton, "I have another question. Kamaal mentioned that the police are looking for us, but only because they're suspicious of the circumstances surrounding Majid's death. I think they'd still want to bust the kidnapping ring if they had sufficient evidence. So here's my question: should we tell Captain Poya what we've discovered? That the Brotherhood of Stones is very likely operating in the ancient Bagram site?"

Mallory tucked a strand of hair behind her ear. "Part of me wants to say yes, for the reasons you just described. But on the other hand, once Poya knows, what if he tells the wrong person?"

"Like Governor Bina?"

"Possibly, or someone else who turns out to be a cult follower."

Alton nodded. "I agree. Right now, we don't know who to trust, so we keep this to ourselves. Plus, once the police know the location of the Brotherhood of Stones, any hope of us mounting our own rescue operation would be out the window. The police would wait for us at Bagram."

"Speaking of a rescue operation," said Mallory, "we need to make sure we're ready, starting with the route to the site."

"Yeah, good idea." Alton pulled out the maps Professor Aziz had provided. He also downloaded contour maps of modern Bagram and the surrounding countryside. The group set about studying the assembled materials.

After fifteen minutes, Alton sat back and tried to stretch some of the discomfort from his damaged leg. "Man, Professor Aziz wasn't kidding about the terrain. It's rugged, all right."

"Fahima, what kind of vehicles was Rafi able to line up?" asked David.

"Two Jeep Grand Cherokees."

"Good—plenty of room. And better for the kinds of roads we'll be on. Do we need to go pick them up?"

"No. He and his sister will bring them here."

"Okay, good." David turned to Alton and Mallory. "Let's put the local jackets back on. They may not make much difference, but we might as well try to blend in as much as possible."

An hour later, the friends busied themselves packing their cache of weapons and other combat gear into the cargo spaces of the rugged Jeeps. Once complete, they covered the ordinance with green, canvas tarps to render it less alarming to outside observers. To appear as inconspicuous as possible, the two Afghanis, Kamaal and Fahima, drove the vehicles.

They swung by a market to stock up on food supplies, then turned onto the A76 highway leading north out of Kabul. As the traffic thinned, they sped up the winding mountainous road to Bagram, praying they would arrive in time to save their young friend.

CHAPTER 63

At the thirty kilometer mark, Alton could see the traffic ahead beginning to slow. In seconds, all vehicles came to a stop, and the Jeeps became part of a line of cars snaking along the highway.

From the rear vehicle, David called Alton's cellphone. "What's up?"

"It looks like a police roadblock," replied Alton, who occupied the rear seat of the lead vehicle. "Everyone except Kamaal and Fahima should take cover underneath the tarps. If this stoppage has anything to do with us, we don't want to give them a reason to become suspicious."

Kamaal called Fahima on his cellphone. "In case the policemen ask me any questions, it would be good for you to listen to my conversation when I go through the roadblock. I will leave my microphone on. Turn on your headset and leave it in your ear until I am through the roadblock."

Alton and Mallory folded down the rear seat, squirmed their way into the little remaining space in the cargo area, and then pulled the seat back to its upright position. They were forced to assume awkward angles just to fit into the cramped space. Once positioned, they smoothed the tarp over their heads as flat as possible.

"I liked the bungalow in Bora Bora better," said Mallory.

"Oh, I don't know," replied Alton. "You can't beat this for intimacy."

"Quiet," hissed Kamaal. "We are almost at the checkpoint. Do not talk again until I tell you."

"Have your Beretta ready," Alton whispered to Mallory. "If they look under here and see us with a bunch of weapons, they might fire first and ask questions later."

As Mallory pulled the handgun to her side, Alton stilled himself in the darkness under the tarp.

Without warning, Alton's world mutated into another cramped space at a different time. He was inside the component-access crawlspace of his Army mobcom van, just after the IED had detonated. His left leg felt numb. "Sergeant Dawson! Report! Are you all right?"

Pressure on his forearm brought Alton back to the present. Mallory squeezed his limb, the full saucers of her eyes acting as mute enjoinders for him to remain silent.

He gave her an "I'm back" nod, and she caressed his cheek, leaving her hand there. Did she suspect the physical sensation would keep Alton grounded in the present? If so, her supposition seemed pretty close to the truth.

Kamaal pulled the Jeep several feet forward and came to a stop. A guttural voice asked a series of rapid-fire questions, which Kamaal answered in a placid voice. Alton had to hand it to Kamaal. For a man whose day job involved translating conversations and the written word, he seemed to handle himself in dangerous situations with aplomb. The interpreter's inflection gave every indication of a traveler annoyed with the delay.

The conversation stopped. Had something gone wrong? Had some oversight on their part raised the policeman's suspicions? Alton scarcely breathed.

The Jeep moved forward with a lurch, and Alton dared to fill his lungs to capacity. His eyes met Mallory's and found the same relief there.

They drove for a few more seconds, picking up speed, before Kamaal spoke. "Wait another minute or two, then you can come out."

The couple did as instructed. After emerging from the cargo space and helping Mallory do the same, Alton looked behind their vehicle and saw Fahima's Jeep just discernable in the distance. Mercifully, it too had passed the roadblock.

Alton leaned forward to Kamaal. "Everything go okay back there?"

"Yes. The policeman asked me if I had seen any vehicles carrying Americans. He also asked if I had noticed an older, grey Mercedes Benz, one just like Hanif's, on the road today. Of course, I told him no. Fahima just radioed me. They asked her the same questions."

Alton turned to his wife. "I guess the roadblock was

Bina's doing."

"Or Poya's."

"Maybe, but I doubt it. Presumably, the police have these checkpoints on all roads leading out of Kabul. I have a hard time imagining Poya committing the kind of resources needed to do that for just for one dead man, even a dead cop—not after everything he's told us about how limited his resources are for non-terrorist crimes."

"True."

"We know one thing. It couldn't have been Al-Qaeda."

"Unless they disguised themselves as policemen. They've been known to do that before as an infiltration tactic."

"Well, whoever was behind the checkpoint, we slipped through. I'm glad we ditched the cars, or it might not have gone so well."

The pair of Jeeps sped straight up the highway toward the ancient city of Bagram. After another ten minutes, they turned left onto a narrow, two-lane road. The road's surface changed to dirt just as it led to the base of a foothill covered with stone pine and larch, along with a scattering of olive trees. Constant mountain winds blew tendrils of dust across the road. If any vehicles had traveled this way, their tracks would have been obscured within minutes.

As they plowed up the incline, the road's initial potholes widened into great chasms spanning much of its width. Kamaal did his best to maneuver around the holes, but Alton nonetheless felt like the subject of an insidious physics experiment run amuck as his skeleton rattled within his body. They crested the foothill and began a winding trek down the other side.

"Okay, we should be getting close to Bagram," said Alton, leaning closer to Kamaal while shading his eyes from the late-day sun. "Take it slow. If the site is occupied, we'll need to stop far enough away so the sound of our vehicles doesn't reveal our presence."

They reached the halfway point down the slope. Kamaal pulled under a dense grove of pine trees, and Fahima pulled up next to him. A clump of wild gooseberry bushes underneath the conifers provided a measure of concealment for the Jeeps. To enhance the camouflage, Alton and the rest of the team used the tarps to cover the Bagram-facing front of the vehicles.

Alton, David, and Mallory pulled out binoculars. Walking around the bushes to the unobstructed road, they scanned the compound. A scattering of cars and SUVs joined a couple of ramshackle buses in a dusty field on the eastern side of the temple.

"It looks pretty active for a site that's supposedly been deserted the last fifty years," said Mallory.

"Yeah, no kidding," said Alton. "Something tells me Mastana is down there somewhere."

"I agree," said David. "We need to talk with the others about our next steps, especially who goes down there and who waits up here."

"Yep. Let's finish the recon first," said Alton, panning his binoculars from left to right. "There are major guard shacks at the twelve, three, six, and nine o'clock positions, and I see smaller huts between them. I can see guards in two of the huts, so presumably they're all manned. Getting in there won't be easy."

"What's that in the window of the one at six o'clock?" asked Mallory.

Alton studied the hut through his field glasses. "It looks like a machine-gun barrel. Great, so the site may be ancient, but the defenses aren't. Let's hope they don't have motion detectors or Claymore mines, or we'll be up the creek."

The three former soldiers returned to the others.

"I think it's safe to assume that the folks down there are members of the Brotherhood of Stones, right?" asked Alton.

"Yes, I think so," said Mallory as several others nodded.

"Okay, that means there's a pretty good chance Mastana's down there, if they haven't already…you know." Alton couldn't bring himself to say the words, not after coming this far to save her.

"We need to devise a rescue strategy," he continued. "We don't know exactly how many Brotherhood members are down there, but based on the number of vehicles, I'd guess at least ninety or a hundred—maybe double that if they carpooled. So, we can't make a direct, frontal attack. That would be a suicide mission. We'll have to try to infiltrate the compound with stealth. Agreed?"

They all nodded.

"It'll be nighttime soon, so we'll wait until we have the full cover of darkness. In the meantime, we need to decide who goes on this mission and who stays with the Jeeps. As former soldiers, David, Mallory, and I will definitely go. Fahima, I recommend you stay here."

Fahima's countenance hardened into one more determined than Alton had ever witnessed. "Mastana helped save my life. She did not stay at home when things were dangerous. She went into a band of Al-Qaeda terrorists to help me, a person she had never met. With this debt, how can I stay here during her time of need? I will go with you."

David looked to be on the verge of arguing, but his wife's steely resolve seemed to silence him. "Okay, the more, the merrier. I'm glad I showed you how to use my Beretta back home."

"Right," said Alton. "Kamaal, I'd like for you to go, too. I have a special mission in mind for you."

The interpreter swallowed. "No problem. I was planning on coming with you." Alton admired the man's courage. This was far outside the range of his experience.

"Al," said David. "One thing we haven't discussed… when we're down there, if we run up against Brotherhood members, do we shoot to kill?"

Alton pondered the question. "None of us like the

idea of killing someone else. But these lunatics have brought the danger upon their own heads by starting a kidnapping and murder spree. If there's as many of them down there as the vehicles indicate, we can't try to take prisoners. If we can avoid killing, I'll take that option. If not, we do what we have to do. Is everyone okay with that?"

They all nodded.

"Okay, let's talk about our route." Alton had transferred the map of the compound onto his phone, and he brought it up. "It looks like the widest distance between guard huts is between the two at the eight and seven o'clock positions. Plus, those huts are smaller, so perhaps they'll have a smaller contingent of guards. We'll descend the hill fifty meters off the road and proceed north until we're about a klick from the huts. Then we'll head northeast, right between them."

"Then what?" asked David.

"The biggest buildings lie in the middle of the compound, so that's probably where most of the Brotherhood members will be. Once we're inside the line of guard shacks, we'll stick to the compound's inner perimeter, away from the central buildings. We'll make our way around the southern rim of the inner perimeter until we reach the prison building, here at the five o'clock position," he said, pointing to the southeastern corner of the map. "From there, we'll overpower the guards and free Mastana."

"We'll need to be careful when we do that," said Mallory. "If we go in there blasting, the whole compound will know we're here. That would make it problematic getting out."

"Exactly. We'll need to bring the SIG Sauers. They have silencers. And we should each pack a field knife, too."

"So what about the rest of our gear?" asked David. "We're not leaving it, are we?"

"Absolutely not. My hope is that we get in and out with none the wiser, but if we're detected, we need to have enough firepower to blast our way out."

David seemed relieved. "Speaking of getting out, what happens after we grab Mastana?"

"We retrace our steps—make our way back around the southern arc of the inner perimeter, then head back between the guard shacks at the eight and seven o'clock spots."

"Sounds like a plan, boss."

"Any questions?" Nobody spoke. "In that case, let's gear up. Don't forget face paint and night goggles. And everyone mike up. We'll need to stay in constant contact."

They started by applying camouflage to each other's faces, slipping on flak jackets and helmets, and setting up their mikes and earpieces. The former soldiers each packed an A4 carbine and Beretta, along with extra ammo and grenades for the M203s mounted below their rifles. They finished by strapping field knives to their web gear and stuffing frag grenades into cargo pockets. Kamaal and Fahima tucked Berettas, knives, and extra ammo into their pockets and waistbands. Alton then distributed the SIG Sauers to several team members.

As they packed, Mallory approached Alton. "Sweetie, are you sure you're good to lead this mission?"

"What do you mean?"

"The flashbacks…" She let the rest of the sentence drop.

He nodded. "I know. Honestly, I'm worried, too. This whole flashback thing is so frikkin weird. But everyone is counting on me to lead them down there. Can I really just tell them I'm going to sit this one out?"

"No, I guess not. But what if a flashback hits you while we're down there?"

Alton pondered the question. "When you put your hand on my face in the Jeep on the way here, there was something about your touch that brought me back. If you see me slipping away, touch my face again, and I think I'll come back."

"Okay, Sweetie. Let's hope I won't need to do that."

Alton kissed his wife. "You know, part of me hates that you're here, in this kind of dangerous situation, but another part of me is grateful we're in this together. I know that doesn't make much sense, but it's the truth."

"It makes perfect sense. It's how I feel, too."

Alton turned back to the rest of the group to assist in their preparations. "Everyone ready?" he asked when they had finished a quick mike check.

They nodded in the affirmative.

"Stay on my ass. Keep your mikes on, but no talking unless absolutely necessary. If you see danger, tap your mike three times so the rest will know to stop." He took a moment to explain the plan he had devised for Kamaal.

As the last rays of the setting sun faded in the western desert, the comrades snaked single file down the slope of the foothill. By the time they reached bottom, the sun and temperature had both dropped, rendering them comforttable despite the heavy loads they carried.

"Okay, everyone," whispered Alton into his mike, "switch to the Kamaal plan."

The group members shifted positions into a new formation, widening a little.

Alton looked at the compass app on his phone. "Turn to forty degrees," he whispered to the others. "Try to stay between the guard huts."

Angling to the right, the group traveled in silence, picking their way across the ground to avoid the noisy scrub brush littering the arid landscape.

They had just passed between the guard huts when Alton heard an ominous double-click, like the bolt of a rifle being drawn and released.

A man wearing black robes emerged from behind a wall extending from the rear of a guard shack. He barked a command in Pashto. With the cultist's AK-47 trained directly on the group, Alton knew he had no chance of drawing his SIG Sauer before the guard would mow him down.

In the pale moonlight, Alton could see the glow of yellowed enamel as the man smiled.

CHAPTER 64

Mastana dragged her head off the floor at the sound of her cell door swinging open.

"Mastana," said Divband. "Today is a special day."

"Special?" Even the act of speaking drew energy from Mastana's feeble reserves, exhausting her.

"Yes. You are to be the guest of honor at a ceremony. I don't normally visit the guests ahead of time, but in your case, I decided to make an exception."

"I thank you."

"Shut up!" Specks of spittle flew as he chopped off the words. "Don't try to flatter me! That trick doesn't work anymore."

Mastana wanted to reply but couldn't muster the strength.

Divband turned to another man the doorway. "Meskin, take her to the chamber and secure her, then meet me in my office." He departed as the man, whom

Mastana didn't recognize, entered. Meskin unlocked each of the four shackles on her limbs and held open the door.

Mastana tried to rise but couldn't. She hung her head in exhaustion and terror.

"Come on!" said Meskin, pulling her up. Had he not maintained a rough grasp on her arm, Mastana felt sure she would have fallen. With his help, Mastana shuffled across the stone floor. She wanted to call out to Sita, her neighbor, but fatigue from lack of nourishment rendered her too weak to do so.

Passing through the doorframe, Mastana remembered the many times she had prayed to depart from this cell. Now leaving it represented her greatest fear. All her instincts told her she would not return, but not because she had been granted freedom.

Meskin wound Mastana through a maze of tunnels and hallways, nearly carrying her by the time they emerged into a large, circular chamber. He took her to the edge of the room. After looping her arms around a column carved with mythic creatures, he bound her wrists together on the other side with a thick rope.

Mastana summoned the strength to speak. "What am I to do now?"

"Nothing," replied Meskin. "There's nothing you can do."

CHAPTER 65

"Keep walking!" came Kamaal's voice from behind Alton and the rest of the group.

To their left side, the Brotherhood guard swiveled his head in time to see Kamaal marching his band of "prisoners" in the direction of the buildings. Keeping his A4 trained on the group, Kamaal hailed the guard and began a rapid dialogue in Pashto. According to Alton's plan, Kamaal was to tell the guard he had captured a group of infiltrators just after arriving at the compound.

The tone of the guard's voice relaxed, and his grip on the AK-47 loosened. Kamaal approached the man and, judging from the intonation of his voice, seemed to ask the man a question.

The guard turned and used sweeping hand gestures in an apparent attempt to give directions, keeping his eyes on the prisoners but not Kamaal. As the guard turned to point out a pathway between two nearby buildings, Kamaal slipped the SIG Sauer from his waistband and fired twice. With the pistol's silencer in place, the shots sounded much like a dog's whimper. The guard collapsed to the ground without uttering a word or crying out.

"Quick," whispered Alton. "Get him back behind the fence."

Grabbing the guard's arms and legs, Kamaal and David shuffled the corpse to the indicated spot, then rejoined the group.

Alton scanned the ancient compound. As expected, lights blazed from the larger, interior structures, but the small buildings on the outskirts remained dark.

"Let's head for the inner perimeter's southern arc," he said. "Avoid any buildings with lights. They're likely to be occupied."

Leading the procession, Alton wound his way along the edge of the compound, remaining just inside the buffer zone in which the thick desert bush had been cleared, a route that produced a minimum of noise yet lay well inside the rim of guard huts.

Alton held up a hand, warning the others to stop. They froze in the moonlight while the muffled tones of a conversation passed from right to left. Two cultists traveled across a courtyard lined with paver stones and entered a large stone building that lay closer to the compound's epicenter.

Releasing his breath, Alton brought up the compound's map on his phone, shielding it with a small square of charcoal-lined cloth to avoid creating a visible light signature. Switching off the phone and slipping it back into his vest pocket, he located the target building, then motioned the others forward.

They hugged the wall of a nearby edifice while approaching a squat structure at the five o'clock position, on the compound's southeastern edge. The target building's stone walls seemed thicker here than elsewhere, and Alton could see no windows. As Professor Aziz had indicated, this seemed to be the prison cellblock.

Alton withdrew the SIG Sauer from the holster on his web gear. He turned to Fahima and David. "Wait here and stay sharp. If we need you, we'll wave you forward as soon as we've taken care of anyone inside. Otherwise, stay here and watch our backs."

Alton, Kamaal, and Mallory fanned out into a V formation and advanced towards the prison building. Checking to ensure the absence of any cultists, they darted across a ten-foot open space and approached the structure's lone entrance.

Alton pulled open the heavy door. A young guard turned in their direction, his eyes widening in surprise as he spotted the unexpected visitors. His eyes darted to an AK-47 leaning against a corner, but Alton jammed his SIG Sauer into the man's stomach before he could move.

"Ask him where Mastana is," he told Kamaal.

Kamaal traded a few sentences with the guard. "He says she is no longer here. She left an hour ago."

"Bullshit," said Alton. "Tell him to take us to her cell or we blow his brains out."

Kamaal spoke, and the guard began to raise his voice in protest. Alton raised his pistol to the man's chest. "Tell him either he'll quiet himself down, or I'll do it for him."

The guard lowered his voice but continued to babble.

"He insists Mastana is no longer here," said Kamaal. "He says he can show us the cell she was in."

"Okay, tell him to take us there."

The guard crossed a small foyer about the size of a walk-in closet. He lifted a set of keys off a large hook on the wall and unlocked a thick interior door fortified with strips of steel.

He led the threesome into a long, narrow hallway lined with cells. As he walked, the guard often turned to cast a fearful gaze on the weapon in Alton's hand. At first, the man's obvious youth spurred a twinge of sympathy in Alton's breast. But Alton reminded himself that despite his age, the guard had willfully joined an organization dedicated to killing random female teenagers. The man's hands were stained with the blood of innocents.

The guard stopped at an open door. Alton waved the man into the cell with his pistol and followed him. Alton's gaze landed on a set of four unlocked shackles attached to a chain, itself bolted into the floor.

Had Mastana truly left only minutes ago, or was the guard simply trying to save his skin? Pressing forward represented the only path to answering that question.

"Ask him where they took Mastana to," said Alton.

Kamaal passed along the question. "He says she went to the chamber for tonight's ceremony."

"What ceremony?"

"Her marriage to Iblis."

Icicles gripped Alton's heart. "We've gotta get moving. Tell him to remove his shirt."

The guard did so. Alton motioned for him to lie on the floor. Not relishing the idea of killing the guard, despite the fact that the man participated in the torture and murder of teenage girls, Alton used the shackles and chain to hogtie him. Alton ripped the shirt into strips, stuffing one into the man's mouth and using the rest to secure the gag in place.

"What if he starts thrashing around?" asked Mallory. "If another member of the Brotherhood comes into the building, he'll hear the noise."

"Good point." Alton used the butt of his A4 to cold-cock the man, sending him into unconsciousness. "Let's head for the chamber…and pray we're not too late."

CHAPTER 66

Dozens of candles cast an eerie glow on the walls and columns of the ceremonial chamber's round shape. For how many minutes had Mastana been the room's sole occupant? Thirty? Sixty? Fighting exhaustion, she couldn't be sure.

Divband entered the room at the head of a procession of followers. Streaming in, they stood two deep in a great circle around a central altar. Rousing her intellect, Mastana wondered how these people allowed themselves to be tricked into following this madman.

The leader motioned to Meskin, who unshackled Mastana and pulled her to the altar's horizontal stone slab. Laying Mastana on her back, Meskin and another cultist tied a length of thick, black cloth around her wrists and ankles, then somehow secured the restraints to the floor. They used another black cloth to gag her mouth. She tried to struggle against her captors, but the lethargy of near-starvation hindered her efforts.

Divband began an incantation which his followers began to repeat.

The Devil's Due

One of the zealots, an old man, stepped forward and placed an ornate knife, a small bowl, and a wooden paintbrush on a short table set up near the altar. Divband used the blade to slash an opening across Mastana's plain, linen dress, seeming to take pleasure in the effort. He cut vertical slits on each side of the dress, then rolled up the fabric like a rug, revealing her abdomen.

Divband removed the silver bowl from the table and placed it on the altar. Dipping the brush in the bowl, he painted a black circle on her stomach, pausing periodically to replenish the brush's ink. He then began painting an abstract pattern within the circle that, when finished, revealed itself to be a star of some sort.

The alternating chant between Divband and his followers swelled in volume. The growing blood-lust in the room assured Mastana she would not live through the night's activities. Her mind raced to devise an escape, but the hopelessness of her plight seemed to crush her imagination.

"Light the incense," said Divband.

Four members of the Brotherhood set smoldering urns on the corners of Mastana's slab. The burning substance in the small bowls emitted a heavy, sickly smell that sent waves of nausea through Mastana's frame.

Was it time to die? Would this madman and his fellow lunatics kill her without mercy?

Divband faced his followers, allowing his gaze to linger on each one before advancing it to the next. "The anointing is complete. As we have been taught, we must leave the future bride for an interval, to allow the black *jinnd* time to sense her presence and respond. Let us retire to the chamber of meditation.

"The ways of the black *jinnd* are beyond man's understanding."

"Powerful are the black *jinnd*," replied the throng in unison.

Divband began an ancient hymn. His followers soon joined the ritualistic chant, a low murmur echoing off the walls.

He leaned over Mastana and spoke in a whisper. "You could have been my partner, inferior in power only to me. But you suffer from the eternal curse of your gender: a natural instinct to lie…to demean…to trick. It will be my pleasure to eradicate such a filthy, lying whore as you from this earth. You can ponder the error of your ways while awaiting your eternal union with Iblis."

Divband turned and exited the room. Several minutes were required for the last member of the Brotherhood to file out behind him, leaving Mastana alone with her terror.

Could her life truly end like this? Were all her youthful aspirations in vain? Having escaped the lethal intentions of her uncle, Mastana could scarcely believe she was embroiled in the deadly schemes of an even greater madman. The joy she had experienced at Kamaal's house, anticipating a bright future, seemed a lifetime away.

Despite the earlier promise to herself to weep no more, bitter tears ran down her cheeks. "Mother," she whispered, "I will see you sooner than expected. I rejoice in the reunion but mourn the loss of my earthly life, a life that could have been so full. I pray I will find tranquility with you at the end of today's journey."

She twisted her head toward the stone doorway through which the members of the Brotherhood had exited the chamber, fearing more than anything their return yet unable to pull her eyes from the ominous space.

CHAPTER 67

While still out of sight inside the prison building, Alton consulted his map of the compound. The building containing the ceremonial chamber was easy to spot.

"Look here," he said to the others. "This is our current location. We need to make our way up to this central building." He motioned with his finger in a northwesterly direction.

"Isn't that where we saw the most people on our way in?" asked Mallory. "It's going to be a challenge getting there without being spotted."

"Yes, but that's where Mastana is. So that's where we'll go."

David nodded in grim determination. "What's the plan?"

Alton studied the map. A pair of buildings to the south of their target sat close together, forming an alley between them. The narrow space seemed to provide plenty of concealment. "See how these two buildings have buttresses? Maybe we can use those to advance up this alley a little at a time. Once we get to the northern end of the alley, we'll have a clear line of site to the central building, the one containing the ceremonial chamber. We can plan our next step once we see the central building's access points, and if anyone's guarding them."

"Sounds like a plan," said Mallory.

"Let's turn our mikes on. We'll need to stick to sub-vocalization from here on out."

The rescue party plunged into the darkness. The night's absolute quiet proved more unnerving than noise would have been. Alton knew scores of cultists lay between his band and Mastana. But lacking the audible cues of his enemy's location, the soundless blanket that enveloped the compound felt suffocating.

Alton felt himself slipping away to another still night, a night in the deserts of Gazib several years ago, when he had traveled from his mobcom van back to his quarters.

As the stars in the sky shifted to that long-ago night, he felt a warm touch on his face. The heavens realigned to their proper locations.

"Sweetie?" asked Mallory, her worried eyes studying his face.

"Thanks. I'm good." Alton felt relieved that the rest of his band were busy turning on their communications equipment, oblivious to the exchange.

Alton moved to the front of the group. "Sawtooth

formation until we reach the alley between the buildings. Everyone who has a SIG Sauer, take it out. Those will be our primary weapons. Only use the A-fours if you have to."

They slipped their way back to the cleared trail of the compound's inner perimeter. Sliding southwest around the edge of the compound, they reached the alley without incident.

The map had proved correct. Alternating buttresses between the two buildings, while not large, nonetheless provided sufficient opportunities for concealment.

"Okay, advance by twos. One group covers while the other advances. Kamaal, you stick with me and Mallory."

They darted down the alleyway, Alton doing his best to limit the duration of his forays into the dim moonlight, despite his limp. Within minutes, they reached a pair of buttresses at the northern end of the alley.

The central chamber, a large building whose walls curved north in both directions, lay directly in front of them. On the wall to the right, enormous stone blocks framed a spacious door. Several cultists stood watch at this entrance. Several others lingered in the yard outside, and presumably more waited inside. It seemed an unlikely avenue for entering undetected.

To the left of them, on the building's southwestern side, lay a smaller door manned by two guards with no other cultists in sight.

Alton studied the building's defenses. Apparently, the Brotherhood had bet all its chips on defending itself via the series of guard huts. Except for the prison guards, none of the interior sentinels carried weapons, at least none that Alton had detected.

He motioned to his companions. "We'll go in through the left door."

"Do you have a map of the interior of the building?" whispered Mallory.

Alton brought up Professor Aziz's document. "No, it only shows the layout of the buildings within the compound, not the interiors of the buildings themselves. We'll just have to get inside and hope we can find her, before…"

Mallory nodded, not needing to vocalize the fear on everyone's mind.

"I'll take the one on the left," murmured Alton, motioning to one of the guards. "You take the guy on the right. On my mark…three, two, one."

The two silencers sighed in the night. Both guards fell, but the one on the right began to call out in agony. Alton and Mallory send a stream of silent lead in his direction, and the cultist fell still.

Scanning the thirty-yard gap between the buildings and seeing no one, Alton waved the others forward. They made a dash for the now-unguarded entrance.

"Pull the bodies inside," said Alton. Kamaal dragged one, while David pulled the other. They entered a hallway strung with florescent lights. A tiny room the size of a closet provided just enough space to dump the bodies out of sight.

"Where to now, boss?" subvocalized David.

"We're almost on the southern end of this building, so let's head north, to the left. That will take us to the rest of the building and, hopefully, Mastana."

Crouching down, they moved in silence along the curved, stone hallway.

Alton held up a hand. He discerned a curious sound, like the bubbling flow of water in a creek. "Do you hear something?"

"It sounds like a lot of people walking," said Mallory.

"That's right. We should follow that sound. If there's a ceremony going on, that's probably where they're going to."

"Or leaving from," added Fahima.

Alton didn't like to consider the implications of Fahima's observation. Had they struggled to find Mastana all these many days, only to miss the opportunity of saving her by the space of minutes?

He waved the group forward, moving as quietly as possible. As they glided up the hallway, the sound of shuffling feet, which had been growing louder, abruptly stopped.

Alton noticed a cutout entrance to the wall on the right. If their curved hallway surrounded the ceremonial chamber, the door should take them right to it.

The Devil's Due

He motioned with his head towards the entrance. Crouching down, they entered a large, circular chamber, finding themselves in one of many dark alcoves built into the wall.

Lit by dozens of candles, the chamber gave the appearance of another world—or at least another time. Scores of cultists in black robes stood along the walls, the closest only a dozen or so yards away.

Alton spotted a cultist making his way to an imposing stone altar in the middle. Unlike the other members of the Brotherhood, the man wore a sash of crimson red, probably denoting his leadership role in the organization.

Then Alton saw her. Already strapped to the altar was a teenage girl. Was it really Mastana, or was he guilty of wishful thinking? The crown of her head faced Alton, so he had no way of making a proper determination.

With his back towards Alton, the leader placed his hands on the girl's shoulders and mumbled an incantation. He withdrew some kind of pendant and placed it on the prone figure's body, then raised his head and began speaking to the assemblage.

"He says the spirits are here," translated Kamaal in the faintest of murmurs, a sound nearly drowned out by the cult leader's booming voice. "He says Iblis has agreed to make the usual exchange."

Remembering Professor Aziz's explanations, Alton knew what that meant. If he was to save the girl on the stone table, whoever she was, he had little time to act.

The cult leader moved around the altar and grabbed

an object off a small, adjacent table. As he turned back to the figure on the stone slab, Alton gave a start of recognition.

He had no time to ponder his surprise. Knowing he must act, Alton considered his tactical position. He and his friends had the element of surprise, but they were outnumbered in the chamber at least ten to one. He hadn't spotted any visible weapons on the members of the Brotherhood, but with their flowing robes, any one of them could be concealing an arsenal. It was a chance he'd have to take.

The cult members began to chant, and their leader—the Divband, Professor Aziz had called him—continued his oration as he placed a black cloth over the prone figure's face and raised an ornate knife over her body while making a bold proclamation.

"Young one, it is time for you to meet Iblis, your groom," whispered Kamaal in translation.

Without thinking, Alton emerged from the shadows and limped three paces forward. "How about you meet him instead, asshole?"

Alton brought the A4 to his shoulder and fired. The shot impacted Divband's temple, propelling the Satanist and his dagger away from the altar. The cult leader landed in a lifeless, bloody heap on the floor, brain matter spilling onto his red sash and blood oozing into the stone floor's bas-relief carvings of flying dragons and scowling soldiers.

The time for Alton to glory in his victory was short. The chamber erupted with shouts. In the chaos, a half-dozen members of the Brotherhood ran towards Alton, while another three sprinted for the altar on which the girl lay bound.

CHAPTER 68

Alton heard the blast of three-round bursts erupt from behind him. Their element of surprise eradicated, his companions had dispensed with the SIG Sauers and now pounded the cultists with their A4s. The advancing hostiles fell like wheat under a sickle.

Alton used his A4 to line up the three cultists advancing toward Mastana and took them out with several well-placed bursts.

Moving toward the altar in his fastest trot, Alton picked up the engraved dagger the dead leader had dropped to the ground and turned to the girl strapped to the table. Snatching the cloth from her head, he found himself face-to-face with Mastana—a few years older and clearly fatigued and terrified, but definitely her. The girl's eyes widened to a size Alton wouldn't have thought possible, and she began to struggle against her restraints.

Alton used the dagger to cut through Mastana's gag and the cloth straps binding her to the table, then passed her the knife with an enjoinder. "Hang on to this. You might need it." As he leaned over, Alton's helmet slipped off and nearly hit the teen as it tumbled to the floor.

Mastana struggled to stand, and Alton recognized her weakened state. Wrapping an arm around her waist to support her, he staggered back to his waiting friends, who had been laying down a barrage of fire to protect him during his rescue operation.

Now that the extraction of Mastana from the altar was complete, Alton refocused on the tactical situation. The enemy combatants had scattered at the first sounds of gunfire, most fleeing the chamber altogether. Alton assumed many of them had no military training and would not return, now that they faced a group of adversaries more formidable than a restrained teenage girl.

But some of them appeared to be regrouping. Now armed, several dozen streamed back into the room. These returning cultists clearly knew their business with weapons and launched into a counteroffensive.

"Back-to-back," Alton told the others. Their military training asserting itself, the three former soldiers ducked behind their alcove's waist-high stone wall. They formed a semi-circle around Fahima, Kamaal, and Mastana, protecting them and each other from a flank attack.

A group of armed cultists ducked behind the altar and began to send sporadic fire in the direction of Alton and his friends.

Alton lined up his rifle's grenade launcher and fired. A deafening explosion sent shrapnel and shards of stone-altar fragments ripping through the cultists.

The scene shifted, and Alton found himself in a Kabul market, lancing pain in his leg nearly incapacitating him as he struggled to bring a wounded civilian into Camp Eggers after a bomb blast.

Through the fog of pain, Alton could discern distant voices.

"Alton, are you hurt?" cried Mallory. "Where are you hit?"

"Maybe he can't hear you," said David.

"No," said Mallory. "It's PTSD."

As the noise of the cultists grew closer, a distant corner of Alton's mind screamed at him to move, to run. But despite his struggle, he could only stare into space as a waterfall of combat memories pinned him to the spot.

CHAPTER 69

An explosion from a Brotherhood grenade on their left flank sent shards of rock sailing in every direction. One of them grazed the top of Alton's head, snapping him out of his reverie.

Cultists were advancing towards their position. Bullets whizzed by like angry bees, the crack of their impact on the stone behind them testifying to the precarious nature of their location.

"Return fire!" said Alton, himself opening up with A4 bursts.

Seeing their leader reengaged in the fight, his comrades likewise poured a fusillade of rounds into their enemy's positions. In the enclosed space, the exchange of gunfire sounded more like cannons than firearms. The deep, explosive wave of each A4 burst nearly drowned out the smaller *pop pop* reports from the attackers' small-caliber sidearms.

"Fire your grenades!" shouted Alton as he launched two successive rounds from his M203 into the center of the chamber. Mallory and David fired simultaneously to the left and right. The blasts produced a deafening roar, and the shockwave sent a wall of heat and pressure rolling across their faces.

In the ensuing confusion, Alton motioned to the others to head for the door behind them, the one leading back into the hallway. He moved his hand to feel the wound on his head and encountered the warm, sticky sensation of blood. But the pain wasn't too bad. It was a flesh wound, not serious enough to slow him down.

"Alton," said Mastana, ensconced under his arm once again, "there are others—girls like me. We must help them!"

His indecision lasted only a second. "Can you show me where?"

"I don't think I can find my way back to that place. The other girls were prisoners, like me. We were in prison rooms near each other."

Alton realized he had stood within feet of the other prisoners without realizing it. Why had they not called out?

"Let's head back to the prison building," he told the others. "We'll use the same route, the alley between the two buildings to the south. These cultists might even lose us if we head that direction."

Firing to cover their retreat, they scrambled down the curved hallway toward the exit as fast as caution and Alton's limp would allow.

Bursting through the southwestern exit, they encountered a cacophony of shouts from all directions. Wasting no time, they raced across the open space, reaching the alley in seconds and darting straight down its length. Alton's leg protested the exertion by sending bolts of pain up and down his limb as he ran. At last, they arrived at the southern end of the alley.

"Let me help Mastana," said Kamaal, observing the deteriorating condition of Alton's leg. The teen staggered to Kamaal's side and grasped his arm.

Having reached the inner perimeter's southern edge, they dashed east, darting from building to building. They neared the prison block, and Alton came face-to-face with a bearded cultist whose lips curled into a snarl of fury. Reacting on instinct, Alton pulled his field knife from its scabbard and attacked. As he plunged the knife into the cultist's chest, the man's last earthly breath produced an abrupt exhale, and he crumpled to the ground.

In a few more steps, the group reached a dilapidated edifice located across the courtyard from the prison building. Alton could see a half-dozen cultists scouring the area, peering into the dark recesses of each ancient building. Recognizing they would never reach the prison unseen, he turned to David. "Lay down suppressing fire on my mark. Once Mallory and I reach the archway over the prison-building door, we'll cover so you all can join us."

Alton gave the command, and David began firing. Two of the cultists dropped, while the others scattered for cover.

Trailing Mallory, Alton reached the prison building, the pain in his leg lancing out in time with his heartbeat and causing sweat to pour down his brow, despite the evening's chill. Having no time to focus on his discomfort, he turned to Mallory, who had already raised her A4 into firing position. "Ready? Fire!"

They both opened up on the concealed members of the Brotherhood. Alton's A4 ran out of ammunition on the second burst. He reached into his web gear for a magazine and reloaded. Looking up, he saw that his cessation of gunfire had apparently emboldened one cultist, who sprinted towards the prison from Alton's side.

"Thanks for making it easy," murmured Alton as he took down the zealot with his first shot.

David and the others reached the prison. Alton turned to his friends, who all panted with exertion. "Mastana will guide me and Fahima to the cells. The rest of you set up a defensive position at this doorway. Don't let anything past."

With Alton's help, Mastana traveled back towards the prison's narrow, stone hallway. On the way in, Alton lifted the key ring off the hook on the wall.

Mastana shuffled down the hall. She looked around for a moment, then led Alton to a heavy door. "This was my cell."

"Yeah, I know."

Mastana gawked at him, incredulous.

"We were here earlier," explained Alton. "Sorry we missed you."

Mastana stepped to the left a few paces. "This is my friend's cell." She began calling out in Pashto.

"She is calling to someone named Sita," explained Fahima. "She is saying she is here with friends and we will rescue her, as she promised."

Alton hurried to join Mastana at the cell door. He began inserting random keys from the key ring into its lock, finding success on the third try.

Mastana stumbled into the cell and embraced the occupant, murmuring in the other's ear. She turned to Alton. "I feel as if we are sisters, but I have never seen Sita's face until now."

Noticing the girl's chains, Alton rushed over to free her. The girl pulled back, and Mastana spoke to her in reassuring tones. Despite the lingering fear made plain on her face, Sita remained motionless long enough for Alton to unlock her shackle.

Alton walked back to the hallway. "Are there any more in here?"

"I do not know," said Mastana. "Maybe." She emerged into the hallway and began calling out in Pashto once again.

"Why don't you call, too?" Alton asked Fahima. "If there are any other girls in here, they'll certainly respond more to a woman's voice in their native language than to mine in English."

Mastana had already started working her way down the right side of the hallway, so Fahima proceeded down the left. As they did so, Sita peeked out her cell door but retreated in terror upon spotting Alton.

"It's okay," said Alton, not sure if the teen could understand him. "I'm not going to hurt you."

"Alton, down here!" Mastana gestured from the front of another cell. Alton reached its heavy wooden door and soon found the proper key, swinging it wide open. A dirty face looked up at him. The prisoner appeared to be a couple of years younger than Mastana. Alton rushed to the girl's side and unlocked her shackle within seconds.

"Tell her to come with us," said Alton.

The teen looked blank, uncomprehending. Perhaps the shock of captivity had rendered her incapable of internalizing any more surprises.

"Alton!" called Fahima. "There is a girl in here!"

Alton limped into the hallway and joined Fahima, eventually freeing one more prisoner.

Mastana led the dazed, younger prisoner into the hallway, then coaxed Sita into the open as well.

Alton turned to Fahima. "Explain to them that we'll have to fight our way out. They'll need to stick close to us and obey our commands to have a chance of escaping alive."

Fahima raised her voice and communicated the information. The two older prisoners nodded, but the young one seemed to remain in a daze.

Alton noticed the frequency of gunfire from the front of the building had picked up. "We need to get out of here. Is that all the prisoners?"

"Yes," said Fahima. "I looked into the cells on both sides."

"Let's go, then, before we're completely cut off."

Fahima helped Mastana and Sita, while the other older prisoner grasped the hand of the young one. Alton led the group back to the building's entrance, where David and Mallory were firing almost continuously.

"We have three other girls besides Mastana," he told them. "Ready to roll?"

Before they could answer, the youngest prisoner darted past them, hurling straight into the open courtyard fronting the prison. Shots rang out from the left. David turned and fired, bringing down a cultist, but not before the young prisoner collapsed to the ground.

"Dammit!" said Alton. "Can we get to her without being shot ourselves?"

"Now that you and Fahima are back, yes," said Mallory. "We were waiting for you to return before we tried to punch our way out."

Alton passed a couple of frag grenades to Fahima and Kamaal. "On my mark, use these and your Berettas. We need to lay it on so thick that nobody will try to return fire when we leave."

"M two-oh-threes loaded?" asked Alton. David and Mallory confirmed, and Alton gave the command. "Fire!"

Bristling with weapons, they opened up with a salvo of grenades, following by a barrage of rifle shots. The walls of the surrounding buildings disintegrated as if a demolition company had been hired for the job. Bits of mud brick, wood, and human flesh flew in all directions as concussion blasts mixed with the steady pulse of gunfire.

"Let's go!" yelled Alton as the din subsided. They piled out of the door and turned to the left, aiming for the compound's southern edge once again.

With the smoke of armaments and debris dust heavy in the air, David veered into the courtyard and scooped up the young escapee. He rejoined the others as they reached the relative safety of a half-demolished building's interior.

"How is she?" asked Mallory, studying the girl with anxious eyes.

David laid her on the ground and felt her neck. "No pulse. Let's try CPR." Alton and Kamaal stood guard while David and Mallory knelt by the girl's side, administering the procedure. After working for two or three minutes, a time that to Alton in their precarious position felt like an hour, David sat back on his haunches. "It's not working. She's bled out." A dark pool of blood on the girl's side bore somber witness to the truth of his words.

David moved as if to pick up the body, but Fahima laid a hand on his arm. "There are other girls, living ones, who will need your protection to escape from this evil place. We must leave this one here."

David nodded and straightened the girl's arms by her side, then rose.

Alton noticed a bright stain on David's shirt, just over the site of his torso wound. The exertion must have torn open his stitches.

Alton flinched as a cacophony of shouts erupted from the nearby courtyard. Apparently, the cultists had sent reinforcements. He turned to the others. "We need to get moving. We're not out of this yet."

CHAPTER 70

Escaping with the teens was proving to be problematic. The former prisoners had all been deprived of proper nutrition, Mastana worst of all. While her spirit showed a fiery determination to escape, her body confounded that intention, sending her stumbling with almost every step.

"Kamaal, can you help Mastana again?" asked Alton.

Kamaal looped his left arm around his young charge, leaving his right hand free to grasp his Beretta.

As he limped along, Alton eyed Sita and the other escapee. They appeared fatigued but had no trouble matching his pace. The others seemed to be faring reasonably well, albeit disheveled and covered with dust and sweat. David paused for a moment to rest his hands on his knees, drawing a deep breath as the exertion took a toll on his torso wound.

Alton knew they needed an escape plan. Surely, all the sentinels in the guard huts would be on full alert, looking for them to escape from within. He spoke into his microphone. "Let's head for the guard hut at the eight o'clock position. Hopefully, the guard we took out there was the only one manning that spot. If so, we should be able to slip right through."

They hugged the walls of the closest buildings, fearful of stepping into the moonlight and revealing themselves to the guards and random search parties scouring the grounds for them.

Continuing along the southern arc of the compound's inner perimeter, they soon reached the spot corresponding with the eight o'clock hut. Alton glanced in its direction. Had the light inside the shack been on when they passed earlier? He didn't think so.

Alton turned to ask David and Mallory about this when the question was answered for him. The light from the hut winked twice as armed cultists emerged from within and passing in front of the hut's light fixture.

"Well, that option's out," he said. "Anyone got any bright ideas?"

"What about the main gate?" said David. "They may be so sure we wouldn't try to use it that they've deployed their forces elsewhere, to the more isolated spots where it'd be easier to slip through their lines."

Alton glanced to Mallory, who nodded. "Okay, let's try that," he said. "Plus, it's at the nine o'clock spot, just a little further down. I'm not sure how much further the girls can travel."

Crouching while slipping from shadow to shadow, the band at last scurried breathless behind a low, rock wall directly east of the main gate. To Alton's dismay, a crowd of six or seven armed soldiers peered from behind the windows of the gate's dual stone guard huts. He could see another score of cultists in the desert beyond the huts, kicking apart patches of dark scrub brush in an effort to locate the intruders.

"That's not an option. We could take out the huts, but by then, half the people in this place would be breathing down our necks. We need a less fortified spot."

Shouts and flashes of light caused Alton to swing his head in the direction from which they had just traveled. The Brotherhood members had apparently recognized the best potential escape route from the compound: the one they were on. Rounding the bend in the site's southern arc was a cultist search party, fifteen or so armed men sweeping the berm with flashlights. They would spot Alton and his friends within seconds.

Alton removed the A4 from his shoulder. "There's no gap in the guard huts, and that search party will see us any time now. This is where we make our last stand."

CHAPTER 71

"Wait. I know this place," said Mastana, casting her gaze around their surroundings. "I saw it from out there, when I almost escaped a few days ago. There is a spot near here where the ground is low, where the water used to flow. It is a little further along, the same direction we are going."

Alton shouldered his carbine. "Let's go. Hurry!"

As they stumbled forward, Alton turned to his young friend. "Show me the place as soon as you see it."

She nodded, too exhausted to vocalize an answer.

They crept past the compound's ten o'clock position. Hadn't she said the dried creek bed was nearby?

"There it is!" hissed Mastana. "See how the ground goes down?"

Patches of scrub brush concealed both sides of the culvert. But they'd have to cross an open field to reach it, and the crowds of cultists searching for them seemed to grow thicker every moment. They needed a way to travel to the escape route unseen. In the meantime, they moved a bit further into the compound, ducking under the shadows provided by a nearby building's crumbling eaves.

"We need a diversion," said Alton to David and Mallory. "How about the M two-oh-threes? The rounds travel about four hundred meters. That's gotta be more than halfway to the other side of the compound. And from here, they won't see us launch."

"Sounds good," said Mallory, glancing in the direction of the search party they had spotted moments ago. "We'd better make it quick."

Alton turned to the rest of his group. "Be ready to run. We're going to fire the grenade launchers. When the Brotherhood members run off to investigate, we'll head for the creek bed."

Fahima explained the strategy to the escapees in Pashto while the former soldiers pointed their rifles skyward.

"Fire!"

Stubby rounds streaked into the night sky. By the time the sound of distant explosions ripped through the compound, the group had already moved to the edge of the building, waiting for their chance to break for the culvert.

Explosions boomed, and the cultists' heads turned in unison. Nearly all of them dashed in the direction of the noise.

Two of them remained at the main gate, standing in the road between the guard shacks. They seemed mesmerized by the cacophony but unwilling to leave their assigned posts.

Alton lined up the closest one with his SIG Sauer. Doing his best to steady his frenetic breathing, he squeezed off a shot. The target fell to the ground.

The second cultist registered shock, then swiveled his head wildly. Unable to spot his adversaries, he bolted for the safety of the nearest stone guard hut.

Alton aimed again and fired—and missed. The guard continued running. Mallory and David had their Sauers out by now and fired as well. After errant shots ricocheted off the ground and hut, one finally found its mark, sending the guard collapsing forward in an unmoving heap.

"Let's go!" said Alton. "We'll only have a few minutes before they realize what's happened and return."

They dashed across the open space and tumbled into the culvert. Mastana looked incapable of rising from the spot in which she had fallen, but Kamaal pulled her up and murmured words of encouragement. She nodded and wrapped an arm around his back to steady herself.

The group moved along the creek bed, distancing themselves from the compound. By leaning over, their heads fell below the surrounding ground. They picked their way over dried channels, rocks, and scrub brush, attempting to strike a balance between speed and stealth.

"Alton," whispered Mastana, "I am worried about the

dogs."

"What dogs?"

"When I escaped a few days ago, they sent dogs after me. I could not run faster than them, and there is no water out here to keep them from smelling me—not any that I could find, at least."

"Last time, you weren't armed," said Alton. "This time we are. I hope we won't have to use a weapon against a dog, but we may have no choice."

After traveling twenty minutes along the culvert, Alton waved to the others to stop. Thankfully, no canines had appeared. Deprived of their leader, the cultists seemed incapable of rising to that level of independent thought.

Alton peered over the culvert's edge. Using the compass app on his cellphone, he located the mountain road on which his party's vehicles were hidden, then rejoined the others. "Let's head south, straight back to the tree line on the mountain. That will minimize our time and distance in the open. Then we can make our way east again, staying above the tree line, until we hit the mountain road. We'll follow the road up the slope, back to our SUVs."

Pulling themselves out of the culvert, the exhausted party staggered towards the safety of the mountain ridge. Their distance from the compound eliminated the risk of giving themselves away with sound, but in the dark desert night, any light would have been spotted immediately. They picked their way across the obscure landscape, often stumbling but always pressing forward.

Alton felt the drip of blood from his head wound reach the left side of his neck and trail down to his collar. He didn't bother to wipe it off.

The disheveled band reached the mountain at last. Plodding up its slope a hundred meters, they collapsed behind a clump of blackberry bushes.

"Alton, do you have any water?" asked Mastana.

"Not here, but we have plenty in our vehicles. And food, too. If you can make it just a little further, you'll have both."

"That is good."

"I know we're all tired, but we need to leave," said Alton, still breathing deeply from the exertion. "The Brotherhood will soon realize we didn't get to their compound by walking. They'll know we drove, and the mountain road is the first place they'll look for our vehicles. It's the only place to hide them. We need to get back to our SUVs before they find them."

The thought of escaping on foot without food or water spurred them to action. Thankfully, they hadn't arrived at the mountain too far west of its solitary road. They rose in unison and stumbled in a daze across the mountain slope, using trees and bushes to hide their movements. In the space of thirty minutes, the exhausted party reached the road and wound their way back to the two SUVs.

Alton climbed behind the wheel of the lead vehicle, while Mallory volunteered to drive the second one. The others fell inside. In Alton's SUV, David leaned over in the backseat, the bloody stain on his shirt growing larger and his chest expanding with deep breaths. Mastana and Fahima sprawled in the seat next to him, soiled, sweaty, and too exhausted for further movement. Alton felt sure a similar scene was playing out his wife's Cherokee.

"Ready?" asked Alton into his microphone.

"Yep," replied Mallory. "Let's roll."

The lumbering vehicles bounced over the rough terrain and turned onto the treacherous mountain road. Unwilling to reveal their position by turning on their headlights, Alton and Mallory instead trusted on the waxing moon's dim light to illuminate their way. David groaned a little as the SUV bounced over the uneven ground, jarring his wound.

Alton breathed a sigh of relief as they crested the mountain and began to nose down the other side.

The respite proved to be short-lived. Rounding a bend in the road, the glare of headlights coming up the road signaled a convoy of vehicles headed straight for them.

CHAPTER 72

"Off the trail!" said Alton into his mike. "Follow me."

Alton swung his wheel hard to the left, jostling downslope towards a heavy grove of evergreens mixed with scrub brush. He pulled behind the foliage and nosed into the plants, leaving room for Mallory to pull in beside him.

"Kill the engines!" hissed Alton. The two vehicles sat motionless in the night. He slipped on his night vision goggles to get a better look at the oncoming vehicles. He could scarcely believe his eyes as he identified them. The convoy reached their position and rolled past for five minutes. It left as suddenly as it came, leaving a cloud of dust behind.

Not wanting to break radio silence with the convoy so close, Alton exited his SUV. He limped over to Mallory's Cherokee and knocked on her window, causing her and the rest of the vehicle's occupants to jump.

"Sorry," he said as his wife cracked the door. "Can you come talk for a minute?"

She climbed out and met him in the darkness.

"What the hell are US troops doing here?" asked Mallory.

"Reinforcements?" suggested Alton.

"Wait—you think our guys are allied with those lunatics? How? Why?"

"I don't know, but don't you think it's weird that they showed up just as the Brotherhood started getting their asses kicked?"

"There must be another explanation."

"I hope so," said Alton. "In the meantime, let's get out of here. If they're looking for us, we don't want to give them too much time to figure out where we've gone."

Alton limped to his SUV's cargo area and retrieved a case of water bottles and a stack of *naan* bread they had purchased on their way out of Kabul. He divided the supplies between the occupants of the two vehicles, along with an admonition to the former prisoners. "Start with the water. And don't eat too quickly or you're liable to throw it back up."

Alton and Mallory mounted their SUVs and pulled back onto the mountain road. They rumbled down the winding passage, then pulled a hard left onto the dirt road at the foot of the mountain. Tires spun as they accelerated on the flat surface, which soon transformed to asphalt.

The Devil's Due

Alton used his rear-view mirror to peer into the back seat. "Fahima, we need to find a safe house. We can't go back to Kamaal's place, and I'd rather not return to his friend's inn, just in case anyone tracked us there. Is there another spot you'd recommend?"

"I think so. I have a friend, Ozra. She stayed with me for a few weeks after her husband died in an Al-Qaeda attack on his mosque. I will call her and see if we can come over."

"Perfect. Your shroud app is still on, right?"

"Yes." Fahima made the call and spoke for upwards of ten minutes. She ended the conversation and leaned forward to the front seat. "She says we can stay with her. I told her the troubles David and the girls are having, so she is going to buy medicine and food that is good for the stomach."

"Good. When we get there, we'll need to assess everyone medically. David's shrapnel wound is bleeding, and the girls look like they're on the verge of starving to death, especially Mastana."

Alton called Mallory and shared the plan.

"Thank goodness," said Mallory. "I was just getting ready to call you to ask where we were going to go."

"Yeah, Fahima saved the day. She's going to guide us in to her friend's house. Just follow me, and we'll be safe in a matter of minutes."

CHAPTER 73

The following morning, Alton awoke with a clarity of mind he hadn't enjoyed since arriving in Kabul. Was it a result of bringing Mastana to safety? Eliminating the cult leader? Knowing his combat in Afghanistan on this trip was over? Perhaps all three elements contributed to some degree.

He rolled over on the floor mat and gazed at his sleeping wife. She looked beautiful, resting or awake.

Glancing around the room, he saw that everyone else remained asleep as well. David and Fahima nestled on a futon. The former had needed his wound re-stitched but had sustained no worse injury. The three teenage girls shared a large comforter Ozra had spread in the den's open space. Alton wondered how long the former prisoners would require to recover from the ordeal of their captivity. Physically, they were already on the road to recovery, having enjoyed mild broth, rice, and *naan* bread the previous evening. The psychological healing, though, was bound to take more time.

Sitting up, Alton took a second to assess his head

wound and disabled leg. Mallory had expertly cleaned and dressed the cut on his scalp, which throbbed with a dull pain. It might need stitches later, but he would address that back in the States. As expected, his leg's usual aches were more acute, a result of the previous day's exertions. Yet the strange, niggling feeling he had felt upon arriving in Kabul had disappeared. He stood and took a few minutes to warm up his leg, knowing he'd feel more comfortable as a result.

Alton wandered into the kitchen, hoping to find some coffee to brew. Ozra was already there, boiling a kettle of water and laying out vegetables and hard-boiled eggs for their morning meal.

"Good morning," said Alton, who had been pleased the previous evening to learn his host spoke English, allowing him to thank her directly. "Can I help you with breakfast?"

"Alton, after you and your wife went to sleep last night, Fahima and I stayed up for a long time, talking. She told me about your rescue yesterday. You risked your life to save these girls."

"We all did," said Alton, "including Fahima."

"That is true. And if you can do these dangerous things, I can make a breakfast all by myself."

"Okay. Thank you. Can I keep you company while you work?"

Ozra smiled. "I would like that."

Alton listed to the sounds of bubbling water and

vegetables being cut on the chopping block. He inhaled deeply, detecting the scent of Ozra's green tea. He couldn't remember ever feeling so much gratitude for the tranquility such simple noises and aromas could evoke.

Soon, the others awoke, and they all enjoyed breakfast together. His leg still feeling sore, Alton retired to the futon after the meal.

Mastana took a seat next to him. "Alton…" Her eyes brimmed with tears.

"I know. I'm happy to see you, too. We have a habit of saving each other."

"But I have never—"

"You did," said Alton. "You just didn't know it."

"How?"

"When you know someone is counting on you, like a certain hospital patient recovering from marketplace bomb wounds, you're less inclined to do something to yourself you can't take back."

For a few seconds, Mastana's eyes narrowed in confusion, then widened in epiphany. "Alton, you don't mean you would hurt yourself?"

He studied her for a moment before answering. "I didn't. But that doesn't mean I didn't think about it."

"I am so sorry. I never knew."

The Devil's Due

"It's not your fault. I never told you. And I don't bring this up to seek out pity. I just want you to know...don't underestimate your importance in the lives of others. You're probably making more of a difference than you realize."

Mastana nodded. She laid her head on his shoulder and held his arm. "Thank you, Alton. I know you are aware of it, but you've made the biggest difference in my life a person can make. I am here because you saved me from Divband and his crazy people."

"As did David and Fahima. David was the very first person to suggest coming here to Kabul, in fact."

She sat up. "And here you all are. I do not feel worthy of putting so many lives in danger."

"It was our choice. You did the same thing to help rescue Fahima, and you were only twelve years old. At least we're ex-soldiers, trained for this sort of thing."

"I could see that last night. I would not want to fight you." She smiled and resumed her grasp on his arm.

Leaning his head back on the futon, Alton had almost dozed back to sleep when his cellphone rang.

As he reached into his pocket, Mallory called out. "We're all here, so who is that?"

"Colonel Rand from Camp Eggers' MI."

"That's the guy David said gave him a 'just-doesn't-feel-right' vibe. Are you sure you want to take the call?"

"Yeah. It could be interesting."

"You still have your shroud app turned on?"

"Yep. Let's see what he has to say." Alton answered the phone and switched it to speaker so all could hear.

"Alton Blackwell?"

"Yes."

"This is Colonel Rand. I spoke to your friend David Dunlow a few days ago."

"I remember, Colonel. How can I help you?"

"I'd like to talk with you about last night."

Alton shot a glance at Mallory. "What about it?"

"Mr. Blackwell, I'm going to be frank with you. We here at MI started getting rumors about a new cult, the Brotherhood of Stones, a couple of months ago. We opened up a covert investigation last month to discover more about them. We've been compiling facts, trying to build a solid foundation of evidence, when all of a sudden last night, all hell breaks loose at their compound. I remembered Mr. Dunlow asking me about the Brotherhood a few days ago, so I wondered if, as the leader of your group, you knew anything about last night."

David nodded, and Alton decided to trust the man.

"We didn't have time to compile facts," said Alton. "We knew this cult had murdered a string of teenage girls, and a good friend of ours was next on the list. If we hadn't acted, she would have died. It was as simple as that. If I may ask, Colonel Rand…why didn't you share your information with us when David called the first time? If would have made our lives—and yours—easier."

"I'm not in the habit of disclosing information about covert projects to some ex-soldier who calls me out of the blue. You and your friends could have been working for the Brotherhood, for all I knew."

"Fair enough."

"But last night, some of your fireworks at the Brotherhood's compound appeared on our satellite imagery. We figured someone beat us to the punch, maybe the ANP," he said, referring to the Afghan National Police. "We had no idea it was you and your friends. Why didn't you tell us before you moved in?"

"The same reason you didn't trust us. We discovered an Afghani cop was a cult member, so why not an US Army Officer?"

"You left off the part about my dual citizenship. I'm guessing that played a part in your silence, too."

"Yes," admitted Alton. "That fact implied you're familiar with the legends of the *jinnd* and might be swayed by the same logic. I'm sorry I doubted you."

"I suppose we each had a reason to be suspicious. On a better note, though, we have the laptops from the compound. We'll be searching them for information over the next few days. I'd like to have you debrief me in detail later, but I'm curious to know if you encountered any moles at the temple last night."

"Moles?" asked Kamaal.

"I think he means any more high-ranking Afghani officials who are members of the Brotherhood," said Mallory.

"That's right," said the colonel.

"Most of the cultists scattered like rats," said Alton, "but we did make an interesting discovery, one that explained the Brotherhood's success in recruiting from all walks of life."

"Do tell. Wait, before you say anything…was it Governor Bina? Is he a member?"

"No, although I wouldn't have been surprised."

The colonel seemed disappointed. "He was my primary suspect. Anti-US and anti-Taliban. He fit the profile perfectly, and his job gave him a vested interest in preserving the status quo, one of the advertising points of the Brotherhood, from what I could gather."

"Who knows?" said Mallory. "Maybe he really is a member, but we didn't see any trace of him last night."

"True," said Rand. "So who *did* you find? Some other official?"

"Yep," said Alton, "one whose identity may come as more of a surprise."

CHAPTER 74

"All right," said Colonel Rand. "You've piqued my interest. Who'd you find?"

"Let me explain. In retrospect, I shouldn't have been too surprised by the identity of the cult's Divband, the leader we saw overseeing a sacrificial ritual last night. We'd already seen a cop join the Brotherhood, which leads to a question. How was a policeman like Sergeant Gulzar Majid, 'Ghoyee' within the cult, convinced to join an organization like the Brotherhood of Stones?"

"I have a feeling you're getting ready to tell me."

"Yes, he was recruited by his boss, Captain Hadi Poya."

"The police captain?"

"Yes. It all makes sense, in a twisted sort of way. Hanif, a friend of ours, told us how the Taliban had killed Poya's father, so we know Poya had no love for the insurgents. Poya's career languished under Taliban rule and only picked up after their elimination. But he saw the

Taliban regaining power as coalition troops have been withdrawn. Mastana told us that she heard Poya brag to his followers about the power of Iblis to defeat the Taliban and 'all enemies of Afghanistan.' So ostensibly, Poya told his followers that he decided to resurrect the Brotherhood of Stones as a way of combatting the Taliban."

"But you don't think that's true?" asked Rand.

"Surely a man of Poya's intelligence had to know the chances of building a force that could actually threaten the Taliban and Al-Qaeda were small."

"You have to start somewhere."

"True," said Alton, "but Mastana, one of the girls we recovered last night, has told me about some of the things Poya said to her about women. He wasn't a big fan of the fair sex."

"So you're thinking Poya's whole Satanist shtick may have been a ruse for a more personal agenda?"

"Could be. Suppose you hate women—or at least teenage women. You're the chief of police, so you and your crony sergeant can suppress any investigation of crimes you commit against them. But you still need to collect your victims. If you also happen to be a power-craving, charismatic, self-appointed prophet of a revived power—Iblis—you can tap into your countrymen's need to regain control in their lives."

"I see," said Rand. "Leverage your leadership skills and position of power to rope others into helping with your serial-killing fantasies."

"Something like that. I guess we'll never know for sure."

"So was Poya the dead guy wearing the red sash?"

"Yeah, that's him," replied Alton.

"That's good to know. His face was pretty obliterated. I wasn't sure we were ever going to get an ID on that one. I've gotta say, Mr. Blackwell, that your friends must have been pretty well armed. It looked like a frikkin war zone in there."

"It felt like one, too. Say, Colonel, do you know the next steps for reuniting the kidnapped girls with their families? As you can imagine, I'm a little leery about going to the police."

"I'll work with the local social services department to take care of that. I'll give you specifics once my team contacts them."

"Great, although one of the girls is headed to the US, the one we specifically came here to rescue. Her visa was approved just before she was kidnapped."

"I see. Mastana, you said?"

"Yes." No one spoke for a few seconds. "Will that be all, Colonel Rand?"

"Yes. We'll be in touch about the other girls, and possibly after we've researched the contents of the cult's laptops."

"Okay. You have my number."

Alton switched off his phone and looked around at the weary and expectant faces surrounding him. "And so that's that. Time to put this chapter of our lives behind us. We'll get Sita and our other young friend back to their families, and we'll press forward with Mastana's immigration—finally."

For the first time since rescuing Mastana, Alton saw her break into a smile.

CHAPTER 75

Two days later, Alton and the others gathered in Kamaal's den, discussing in quiet tones their travel plans for the following day.

Alton sat apart in a wicker chair, a spot that afforded him a little more space to stretch out his damaged leg. He was glad to be going home. Recovering Mastana had eliminated the worst of his latent anxiety, but the sounds and aromas of Afghanistan continued to fill him with restless uncertainty.

An imam's call to prayer drifted in through the window. Alton felt himself slipping to another reality, a time of recovery while serving at Kabul's Camp Eggers. The faces of his dead soldiers appeared unbidden before him, stirring the horror and regret of the day his life had irrevocably changed with the explosion of the IED.

The chants of the imam ended, and Alton's vision refocused on those sitting before him: Mallory, David, Fahima, and the rest. The ex-officer reflected on the past week's rescue mission. Hanif had died, certainly a horrible outcome, but the rest had survived—perhaps not unscathed but at least alive. The thought gave rise to hope for the future. He doubted the psychological impact of his service in Afghanistan would ever fade completely, but the greater success of protecting the lives of those he had recently led into combat conferred a measure of comfort.

Alton gazed at his wife. The wound on her arm was convalescing nicely. Seeming to sense his gaze, she turned and smiled in his direction. Alton smiled back, lifting a silent prayer of gratitude for the tranquility to which the meandering, lonely path of his life had led him.

CHAPTER 76

A week later, Alton and Mallory held a bouquet of balloons as they waited with nervous anticipation at Washington's Dulles airport. A State Department employee, the matronly Mrs. Kemp, had accompanied the couple to the airport and chatted with them as they waited behind the security line.

Eventually, the delightful form of Mastana appeared. Spotting Alton, she ran into his arms, both laughing and crying, and embraced him for a full half-minute.

"Ha! We just saw you last week, remember?" said Alton with a smile, even as he returned the hug.

"Yes, but I am so happy to see you!" said Mastana, who turned to Mallory and expended her remaining strength on nearly squeezing the life from her. "And now I am really, truly in America. Last week, when I was with that evil man, I did not think I would see you ever again. And now here we are."

"Indeed," said Alton. "You know, Mallory and I have been talking about you all week, including how you and I first met and became friends."

"The bomb in the bazaar? That was a sad day, Alton."

"Yes, but it had a nice outcome. That's how you and I got to know each other."

"That is true," said Mastana, brightening. "Maybe is not such a sad day, after all."

"Mastana, I'm Emily Kemp," said their companion in a kindly manner. "I work for the US State Department here in Washington. We can all grab a meal together, then we'll need to come back to my office to fill out some paperwork."

Mastana looked to Alton with alarmed eyes.

"It's okay," he said. "This is the normal process. It's for your safety. They can't turn over a sixteen-year-old girl to just anyone until all the paperwork is complete and they've had a chance to make sure I'm not some crazy guy."

Mastana giggled. "Well, you are a little crazy, but in a good way."

Alton turned to Mrs. Kemp. "How long will we be at your office?"

"Well, there's more paperwork than usual, 'cause she's a minor. It should take about three hours. Then she'll be released into your custody."

"Thanks," said Alton. "It looks like everything is finally coming together."

Nearly five hours later, with the paperwork complete, Mastana accompanied Alton and Mallory out of the State Department building.

Alton turned to Mastana. "Are you hungry?"

"Yes, I am very hungry."

"How do you feel about hamburgers?"

"I have been thinking this is a food I would like to try in America."

"Good," said Mallory. "We have just the place."

Alton called David. "We just wrapped up. Ready to meet at Lindy's?"

"Yep. See you there."

They drove in the direction of Lindy's Red Lion, a local joint famous for hamburgers.

"You know I've never eaten at Lindy's before, right?" said Alton.

"Yes, I know," said Mallory, "which is a crime. It's one of my favorite hole-in-the-walls here in town."

Upon reaching the restaurant, Alton parked, and they piled out. They found David and Fahima waiting for them in the foyer, and Mastana greeted them with the same enthusiasm she had earlier bestowed on the Blackwells, both laughing and shedding a few tears.

David leaned over to Alton as a hostess led them through a maze of tables. "How have things fallen out in

Kabul?"

"Kamaal says the shit hit the fan in the police department—nothing publically announced, but the government is conducting a top-to-bottom review of everyone on the force. He also said that the Brotherhood seems to be breaking up. Without their main site and their leader, people are just drifting away."

"Good," said David. "One less lunatic fringe in the world."

"Exactly. And Colonel Rand said MI hasn't found hide nor hair of Dani. It looks like he's gone into hiding."

"Also good, I guess. Too bad they didn't catch him, though."

"True," said Alton, "Say, how's your shrapnel wound? Still getting better?"

"Yeah. The doc says the stitches can come out in a few more days."

"Fantastic."

"What about you?" asked David. "Had any more of those flashbacks since you've been home?"

"No, thankfully. They stopped once I got back state-side."

The hostess gestured to a booth. Fahima sat next to Mastana and walked through the menu with her. The teen's eyes opened wide as she scanned the restaurant's many options.

"So much food," she said. "I will have a difficult time choosing."

"Why don't you try a basic cheeseburger this time?" said David, "Then you can experiment later."

"You mean we will come back here again?"

"Sure, if you like it."

"But maybe there will not be time. I do not know how long I will be in your house before I go to the new place—my new home." She cast her eyes down while finishing the sentence.

"You okay, Mastana?" asked David. "You look kind of sad all of a sudden."

"Yes, I am fine…and very happy. I do not want you to think I am not grateful to you all for saving me. I am so, so happy. But I cannot help wondering what my new home will be like."

"I guess we can tell her now," said David, grinning.

"Tell me what?"

"How would you like to stay with us for good?" asked David.

"What do you mean, 'for good'?"

"Forever—or at least until you're grown up and tired of us."

Mastana's chin trembled, and she squeezed her lips together as she struggled to control her emotions. "I won't have to leave? I can live with you that long?"

Fahima placed her hand on the teen's. "Not just live with us. We would like you to be our family, our daughter."

Mastana lowered her head, her body wracked with silent sobs.

Fahima reached over and pulled the orphan into a hug. "You will be safe with us…and happy, I hope."

The teen wiped her eyes and nose. "I know I will be happy—so very, very happy. In all my dreams, I did not think of this. It was too much to hope for. I told myself to be content being here in America, maybe seeing my friends here from time to time. And now I will not have to leave you."

Fahima turned to her husband. "I think she likes our plan."

David laughed. "I don't know. Maybe she needs some time to think about it."

"No!" said Mastana, shaking David's shoulders and laughing herself. "I do not need time. I know I will love you, both of you, forever."

David's rough demeanor softened, and Alton could discern a little extra reflection of the restaurant's lights in his friend's eyes. Clearly, David was as eager as his wife to welcome Mastana to her new home. "Well, let's wrap up this meal so we can show you your room."

"I already have a room? Wait, do not wake me, please.

I want to enjoy this dream as long as I can." Mastana pulled both benefactors into another hug.

After the meal, they all traveled to David and Fahima's house so Mastana could see her new home. They wandered through it, giving her a tour that ended in Mastana's bedroom.

"It is not completely ready," said Fahima. "We wanted to let you decide how to decorate it."

The teen walked about the room in silence, running her hand atop the surface of a white, wooden dresser and bookshelf and taking in the matching queen bed. "My mother resides in the next life, but I know she is pleased, seeing your kindness to me. I do not know how to say thank you for all this. I will be happier than I deserve."

"Hey, none of that 'I don't deserve this' talk," said David. "We'll all be happier with you here. Let's just enjoy it."

Alton and Mallory lingered for a few more minutes. Wanting to give the Dunlows time to settle their ward into her new home, they soon rose to leave.

As they walked to the front door, Alton handed Mastana a temporary, "burner" phone. "I imagine David and Fahima will be getting you your own cellphone soon, but in the meantime, you can text or call us with this. I've already programmed my number and Mallory's into it."

"Thank you. And Alton…," she said with a catch in her voice, "thank you for saving me—again."

"You're welcome. We all have our turn to help someone. Yours will come again, too."

Mastana gave each of them a hug, then they left the teen to her new family.

Alton and Mallory traveled to their condo, where Buster, their Labrador, met them at the door with a boisterous greeting, a welcome they had missed until picking him up from a friend's house the previous day. They leashed the dog and took him for leisurely walk, a nightly ritual all three enjoyed.

As the last glow of sunlight faded from the sky, Mallory turned to Alton and grasped his hand. "Remember what I said back in Bora Bora? That I'm all about happy endings? I'd say this qualifies."

"Yeah, I guess so." He shared Mallory's overall enthusiasm but retained a bit of lingering sorrow. Like the experiences of many in this life, he and his friends had gained a victory, but at a cost. Certainly Mastana's outcome exceeded everyone's expectations. Fahima and David also seemed to have benefitted with the expansion of their family, albeit at the price of the latter's shrapnel wound. Both Alton and Mallory had sustained injuries as well; he held no regret about his own, but Mallory's continued to trouble him. And then there was Nur Hanif's death, which could only be regarded as the worst possible outcome, for him and his grieving family.

Alton contemplated the events of the last few weeks—a blissful, romantic honeymoon with his new bride, followed by a descent into a nightmare of sadism, betrayal, suffering, and death.

Thank God for Mallory, the stabilizing influence in his life. Alton hadn't expected so much of the wedding vows he had uttered three short weeks ago to be put to the test so soon. Beyond fear or despair or yes, even a little madness, his wife loved him, and he adored her with an immutable, unconquerable passion. Walking beside his wife, his life, his soul mate, he knew the bond of their union would forever hold fast, come what may.

ABOUT THE AUTHOR

Author Steve Freeman is a former member of the US Army's Signal Corps, a twenty-seven year employee of a large American technology company, and an avid traveler who has visited five continents. The novels of *The Blackwell Files* draw from his firsthand knowledge of military service, the tech industry, and the diverse cultures of our world.

He currently lives near Atlanta, Georgia with his wife, daughter, and three dogs.

Visit www.SteveFreemanWriter.com for a complete list of his titles.

Printed in Great Britain
by Amazon